BOUND TO THE SIREN

ROMANCING THE SEAS
BOOK TWO

❦

ATHENA ROSE

BURTON & BURCHELL

COPYRIGHT

This book is a work of fiction. Any similarities to real life events is purely coincidental. No part of this book may be distributed or shared without the written consent of the rights holder.

All rights reserved Burton & Burchell LLC 2023

Edited by Tochi Biko

Proof read by Vanda O'Niell

All rights reserved by Laura Burton

To discuss translation, Film/TV rights please contact Laura Burton at Laura@burtonburchell.co.uk

This book is written in U.S. English

❀ Created with Vellum

*In loving memory of
Leroy Burton
(2003-2023):*

*A radiant spark, forever aglow,
Your laughter lingers, hearts in tow.
Though distanced, your essence remains,
In treasured moments, love sustains.*

Laura Burton

A NOTE FROM THE AUTHOR

This fantasy romance is set in a fictional/alternate 18th Century England. Names and places may differ from actual historical figures and it is not designed to be factually accurate. Mythological characters from across the world are interwoven in this tale, and their names, personalities and backstory may differ from actual mythology.

Trigger Warnings:

This dark fantasy romance novel alludes to sexual violence, suicide and domineering/possessive attitudes, pregnancy loss, infertility, brutal violence.

This book is written in U.S. English

BOUND TO A SIREN

Serena and Prince Edward

PRINCE EDWARD

Prince Edward stood still and silent as his father surveyed the room of Naval officers waiting for instructions. After listening to his report of the siren attacks, King George looked grim. There was not a sign of compassion on his features for the way things turned out with Georgette.

Nor did he bother to ask about Prince Mannington and whether he would return. He supposed that though Mannington was firm and commanding like their father, Prince Edward possessed his ability to shut away emotions altogether.

Since Georgette and Captain Stone had chosen to sail away on the Duchess to whatever ungodly danger lay ahead, King George and his Queen had not uttered a single word on the matter.

A formal announcement was made that Prince Edward and Georgette's nuptials would not take place due to a conflict of interest, but nothing stopped the whispers around the palace. The staff looked upon Prince Edward with pity and he hated it.

His father's cold stare was a welcome change.

King George's lips formed a thin line as he hummed deeply for several long moments.

Prince Edward knew what orders were coming. He had numbed his emotions after losing Georgette, but his stomach tightened all the same when his father finally uttered the instructions.

"I, King George, command the British Royal Navy to hunt down and kill every siren in the Pacific Ocean. Edward, you shall work with the blacksmiths to create weapons made of steel—as I understand it is their weakness."

Prince Edward curled his fingers to make a tight fist. He did not want the sirens to attack innocent sailors, but he could not condone hunting them like prey and slaughtering them in cold blood.

There had to be a better way.

Arguing with his father, however, was a one-way ticket to the Tower of London, so he held his tongue and gave a curt nod.

When they were excused, his heart weighed heavily as he walked out of the palace with his men. He walked in silence, listening to the soft murmurs of the men around him and ignoring the stares from the city folk on the streets.

When he reached the docks, he took a left away from his men and found the water's edge. He walked along the sandy shores for what seemed like several miles until he found himself on a private beach surrounded by rocks. The sun had already begun to set.

He shut his eyes and uttered the one name on his mind. "Serena."

When he opened his eyes, a head of red hair was emerging from the waters.

To his surprise, the sight of the siren brought him comfort. He found himself smiling despite his low mood.

"Hello, my Prince," she said, her voice laced with sympathy. She tilted her head and seemed to look right into his soul. He was certain she could see past his regal mask and feel the pain he was forced to endure.

"What happened with your lady Georgette?" she asked, her voice soft and musical.

Prince Edward's chest tightened at the name of his lost love. When he spoke, he tried to keep his voice steady. "She is a siren."

Serena's lips curved upward in a lopsided smirk. Prince Edward inhaled deep and slow. "But you knew that already, didn't you?"

When Serena did not argue, he dragged a hand over his stubbled chin with frustration. "All this time you knew, and you did not tell me?" he asked.

Serena swam closer and raised her torso out of the water, her fin peeking several feet behind her. The burnt orange sunlight danced across the shimmering scales of her fin in the most unearthly way. It was oddly soothing to watch.

"It is not my truth to share," she said simply. "But that is not the reason she is not with you." Her eyes bore into his.

Prince Edward scratched the back of his neck, unsettled under the strength of her discerning gaze. "She fell in love with the pirate," he muttered under his breath. Serena nodded and he knew she heard his words. Then he frowned. "But you knew that too, didn't you?"

Serena swayed and began to play with her damp hair. It dazzled in the amber light like a waterfall of fire. "Then tell me something I do not know," she said. "Why did you call me?"

Prince Edward sat on the sandy beach to meet her eyes. "There is a war brewing between men and sirens.

King George has ordered my men to hunt and kill any that cross Pacific waters."

Serena's shoulders stiffened, but she kept her expression neutral. "You underestimate our powers if you think we are frightened by the whims of a few men."

"This is not a few men," he insisted. "The entire British Navy and their allies from abroad will be on the hunt." He clenched his fists. "I cannot stop it. Nor will I be a part of it," he said, removing his Naval jacket with a noise of frustration.

Serena blinked at him slowly. She seemed to remain unfazed by his words, so Prince Edward gave her a piercing stare. "They're making weapons of steel."

Those words hit Serena hard, and she jumped back as though he had thrown a dagger in her direction. Her pretty eyes widened with alarm. "Why are you telling me this?" she asked.

Prince Edward shrugged and started to trace lines in the sand with his finger. "You went above and beyond to help me in my endeavor. It is time I repay the favor." He finally met Serena's gaze again as a cool ocean breeze rippled through his hair. The wind picked up a sweet scent and he wondered if it was hers. "I cannot bear the thought of you being hunted," he confessed.

Serena's face brimmed with happiness as though he had recited the most romantic poem for her benefit.

He interlocked his fingers and sighed as he crossed his legs. "Can you get me a meeting with Isis? Perhaps I can talk to her, and we can arrange an alliance of sorts?" he thought aloud. Serena scoffed.

"That is entirely impossible," she said, giving him a frank look. "Isis is vengeful, and she is done talking with men. You want your heart ripped out? That is all that waits for you if you approach Isis."

Prince Edward chewed the inside of his cheek as he recalled the sight of his brother's lifeless body on Imerta. As friendly as she appeared, he did not think Serena would offer up a single tear for his benefit should the negotiations go wrong.

He thought again. "What about Poseidon? He is your father, no? Can you get me an audience with him?"

Serena hummed lightly and swayed from side to side in thought. "The god of the sea does not deal with land folk. Especially men."

She twirled her hair and her gaze trailed down the prince's body before meeting his eyes again. "Except…"

"What?" Prince Edward asked, leaning forward with rapt attention now. "If you think of a way I can speak with him, then whatever the price, I shall gladly pay it."

Serena's teeth glittered in a dazzling beam. "He will grant audience to a man who wishes to ask for the hand of one of his daughters," she explained, shimmying her shoulders now. "And you are right, Lord Poseidon is my father."

Prince Edward swallowed as he understood what she was suggesting. "Will you take me to him if I pretend to ask for your hand in marriage?" he asked, not entirely sure of the wisdom of this idea.

But he could not think of a better plan. This was his only chance to save innocent lives. Besides, another mission would keep his mind from dwelling on heartache.

Serena nodded. "I shall take you to him now, if you want."

Prince Edward agreed and walked back to the docks. He told Serena to hide herself while he got a small fishing boat, and he did not call out her name until he had sailed far out into the sea. Port Harbor had shrunk to a tiny strip of land in the distance.

The sun was almost entirely below the horizon now, and a deep red tinge flooded the sky when he whispered Serena's name.

Her head popped out of the water almost instantly. Prince Edward sucked in a deep breath as her slender hands gripped the edge of the boat and she lifted herself out of the water to look at him at eye level. "We must go to Atlantis," she said, her voice a purr. Prince Edward looked at the murky waters and raised his brows. "How will that work?" he wondered aloud. "I will surely drown before we get there."

Serena rose higher, her long tail flipping back and forth to keep her steady. Then she took his cheeks in her cool hands and leaned forward. Her face filled his vision.

"Do you trust me, Edward?" she whispered, looking deeply into his eyes.

Prince Edward could not honestly say that he did, but he was unable to think of a reason to back out of the plan. Besides, her touch sent a rush of delightful tingles through his senses. He nodded.

Suddenly, her bare breasts were pressed against his chest, and she was kissing him fully on the mouth.

The earth turned on its axis as Prince Edward tumbled out of the boat and Serena dragged him underwater, her lips still pressed against his.

Prince Edward felt his panic rising as he realized he was being dragged to his death. He wanted to scream, but it was futile with Serena's lips sealed over his. Yet, as they moved in harmony and the warmth of her embrace surrounded him, he was flooded with a sense of calm. Gradually, his fear receded, replaced by an indescribable peace until the weight of his distress was gone.

Prince Edward was no longer fearful as Serena's lips caressed his own. He was content to drift helplessly in her embrace, even to his demise.

Then, suddenly, Serena breathed into his mouth and a flood of cool air rushed into his lungs. By some unknown magic, she was breathing life into him.

They descended further into the darkness of the ocean until he could no longer tell which way was up or down. The water was pitch black and seemingly endless, yet still, he was content in Serena's arms. Now that his sense of urgency and danger had evaporated, he did not care if they stayed in the darkness for all of eternity.

As they moved further and further into the depths, Prince Edward embraced this new peace that had taken hold of him. The two of them swam together in accord, their movements growing more and more graceful—almost ethereal—as they glided along like two sea creatures made for each other.

A warmth spread throughout Prince Edward's body. He felt entwined in an embrace that seemed to transcend time and space. He could not say how long they had been sinking—it could have been moments or hours. Anything seemed possible.

A sponge-like substance gave way as his foot collided with it. Startled, he instinctively wrapped his arms around Serena for protection and was immediately reminded of the pertness of her breasts on his hard chest.

The sensation of her soft curves against him sent a zing through his body that he had never experienced before. Even through the fog of the moment, he was aware that their entanglement was scandalous by any moral measure. But a deeper part of him could not help but savor it in all its forbidden glory.

As they continued to drift through the darkness, Prince Edward found himself marveling at this newfound feeling of safety; as though nothing bad could ever happen as long as they stayed together.

She had become his lifeline. Something deep within him knew that if he were to let her go now, he would drown. Moving on instinct, his hands found her waist and clutched it, prompting her mouth to move. His eyes were closed, but an image of her smirking flashed through his mind.

His feet hit solid ground suddenly, and Serena's body ripped away from him so fast he reeled.

He staggered a few paces, dragged a hand over his clammy face, and blinked several times to make sense of his surroundings.

The sea flowed above his head in a foaming pattern

that looked equal parts sponge and bubble. It was as though an invisible wall divided the vastness of the waters around him from the space he was in.

The depths were as silent as a tomb.

It struck him that they were not standing in pitch darkness. The inky blackness that had accompanied them on their way down had given way to a soft, almost moonlit glow. The light seemed to emanate from clusters of glowing rocks on the sandy floor.

A flash of movement to his left caught his attention.

Serena now stood before him, her eyes twinkling in the dim light. Her long, glittering tail was gone. She stood on two legs, and she was entirely nude. Prince Edward took one involuntary step backward. He felt a mild heat radiating off her, warming not just the air around them, but also his heart. She looked like a Grecian statue, standing there so confidently, carrying so much grace — beautiful and strong all at once.

His eyes roamed over her body, taking in every inch of her with his eyes—from her slim yet shapely legs, up to her curves and full breasts, and finally, the long red hair that flowed past her shoulders like a river of lava.

His eyes met hers and he realized she had watched him take in her body. His face heated as he remembered his manners and averted his gaze. Her giggle surprised him, and he looked at her again. She flicked her wrist just as he looked her way, and a silver gown materialized from nothing—flowing over her body like molten mercury until it had fully covered her nakedness.

Serena spun and the dress glimmered in the reflection of the water. "What is your verdict, my Prince?" she demanded, her eyes heavy with anticipation. They sparkled, daring him to deny her. "Do I have your approval?" The question hung over him like a guillotine blade awaiting its inevitable descent.

Prince Edward swallowed and tried to make sense of what was happening. "Approval for what?" he asked, looking up again.

A school of fish swam by, their movements lazy and carefree, seemingly oblivious to them. They glowed with an ethereal light as they swam past, illuminating the area with their pale blue hue.

Prince Edward's attention was drawn away from the vibrant scene and back to Serena by the sound of her melodic laugh. It was like a siren's call, urging him closer to her. He hadn't taken a step before she moved to him, playing with her hair as she walked. She seemed to float, and the sight of her luminescent form approaching him with the deep darkness of the ocean surrounding them struck deep terror and delight in his heart.

She now stood before him, with eyes as deep and

dark as the ocean fixed on him. "We are to meet my father, remember?" she reminded him. "If you want his approval, we shall have to convince him that we are hopelessly—" She cupped a hand between his legs abruptly, causing Prince Edward to lurch back in surprise. Her hand remained firmly cupped, and he almost lost balance. Serena's mischievous smile only grew wider, adding a wicked glint to her gaze. "—and utterly in love," she finished. Prince Edward swallowed, standing as still as he could manage. "I am not sure what your customs are, but where I am from, it is most inappropriate to touch a man like that," he said, carefully extracting himself from her grip. "Even if we are in love."

Serena stepped back and her expression softened, as though she had just remembered something important.

"My apologies, my Prince," she said gently. "It seems our customs differ greatly in this matter. Where I am from, touch is the only language of love. To deny it would be to cut ourselves off from one another's souls. It is most unnatural. If you wish to be convincing in my father's presence, you will need to get comfortable touching me."

Prince Edward remained a few steps away from her, unsure of how to respond. Serena huffed a disappointed sigh.

"Very well," she said, flicking her hair back from her slender shoulders. Then she reached for his hand. He managed not to flinch and allowed her to take it in hers. Serena smiled again as she twined her fingers with his. "Perhaps, a compromise. May I touch you like this?" she asked.

Prince Edward remained still and stared at her. "I... suppose it would be acceptable," he replied carefully, his throat tight with hesitation.

Serena smiled in relief and brought his hand to her lips, pressing a gentle kiss to it before lacing their fingers together again. Prince Edward's pulse quickened as the warmth of her skin transferred to his own.

"There now," Serena said as she released him and stepped back. Her hands swept up to rearrange her hair again before settling on her hips as she regarded him with a satisfied smile. "Much better. Now we may just convince my father of our love."

Prince Edward nodded silently, part of him still skeptical of the situation he had found himself in. But as he watched Serena's gaze soften, he loosened in response. He knew that this plan was insane, and yet here he was, drawn inexplicably and willingly into something that could only lead to destruction.

Too late to turn back now. He had chosen his course and he was determined to follow it.

He looked around them again and glimpsed the mouths of caves. Sparkling stalactites and stalagmites glowed within them in various hues of purple and blue, casting an eerie light within and out toward them. The air was still and dense, his breathing—as unusual as it was to feel that he was breathing—faltered. He glanced at Serena who stood there expectantly, her gaze never leaving his face. "Is this Atlantis?" he asked her quietly.

She scoffed. "No. What a terrible disappointment that would be if it was," she said. "Come, my Prince."

The further they went, the more beautiful their surroundings became. The stalactites and stalagmites sparkled like stars beneath the gentle waves of blue light that surrounded them. The walls glistened with a rainbow of gemstones and crystals and awe rushed through Prince Edward as he beheld their magnificence.

Serena laughed. "Worry not, my Prince," she said with a smile. "Atlantis is but a four-mile walk from here. Trust me, you will know it when you see it. And consider yourself quite lucky. My home is at the bottom of the Atlantic you see, and no human has been there for more than two hundred years."

Prince Edward nodded, dazed by the information.

He glanced over at Serena, taking in the sight of her gleaming form. He found himself entranced by more than just her physical beauty. She captivated him, and he could not understand if it was her walk or her smile, or just the confidence of her mannerisms. She was like a fire he could not help but be drawn to, knowing full well that fire would burn.

A wave of conflicting emotions washed over him as he walked alongside her. On the one hand, he had an irresistible sense of peace and calm down here with her. Yet, he was filled with guilt, knowing that her sisters above were facing peril and she'd had no choice but to accompany him. He never wanted her to have to make this kind of sacrifice—especially when it meant she could be in danger too.

Despite the danger ahead, he could sense a contentment coming from Serena that he had never felt before. It made him question how she could remain so calm while their lives were on the line. He wondered if she knew something he did not. Most likely. He was struck then by a remembrance of the fact that the magnificent woman he was looking at was not human at all.

The thought made him swallow against a hard lump in his throat as he processed it anew.

If they were to succeed, and Poseidon agreed to grant him an audience, how could he negotiate with him? What did the prince have to offer, that the god of the sea might help him?

Before he had a chance to consider the weight of his

odds, bright beams of golden light flooded his vision. The brightness was so intense that it was like the noonday sun in the height of summer, and Prince Edward had to raise a hand in front of his face for protection.

Serena's hand squeezed his. "We are getting close, my Prince," she said with a squeal. Then she tugged on his hand, dragging his ear to her lips. "There are eyes and ears everywhere from now on. Follow my lead."

Prince Edward nodded, more than aware of the stakes. When he looked around, he noticed they were now on a path lined with small wooden houses. Massive golden gates stood tall in the distance.

As they approached the gates, Prince Edward began to notice animals he did not recognize. They crawled on their bellies like lizards, with spiked armored shells. But instead of reptilian heads, they looked like monkeys.

Other forms began to step up to the path. Prince Edward looked wildly around him. He was met with a sea of eyes. Eyes of men with broad arms, muscular bare chests, and thick legs dressed in subligaculum— a brown canvas of leather. Serena stopped walking.

Prince Edward slowly realized that these must be the Atlanteans of legends—a race of strong, proud warriors who dwelled in the depths of the sea.

Serena stepped forward with confidence, her hand still tucked into Prince Edward's. She stood tall and spoke in a foreign language, gesturing widely as she spoke. Before he could get over his alarm at the fact that he could understand her, he was struck by the fact that he knew what the language was—ancient Greek. The men understood her as well, their expressions quickly changing from animosity to respect. It seemed Serena had earned their trust in a matter of moments.

But then their eyes turned to Prince Edward once more and their faces hardened again.

"Kiss me," Serena ordered, her voice harsh for the first time.

"What?" Prince Edward asked in a daze. Before he could process what was happening, Serena's body was on his again.

She gripped his back, pulled him to her, and rose on tiptoes.

Prince Edward's eyes remained open in shock, and he read the suspicion the warriors wore as they looked on. He supposed they were not accustomed to strangers. If he could not persuade them he was with Serena, what would happen to him here at the gates of Atlantis?

Prince Edward turned his full attention to Serena, determined now to put on a show. Serena's hair floated against their faces. He brushed the soft strands away from her brow and cupped her face. The flame of her body heat flooded him with warmth. A tender smile played across his face, then he leaned in and captured her beautiful lips with his own.

A swell of whispers grew around them and died down into mutters as they broke apart. Prince Edward noticed that the men were no longer standing with their arms crossed, but now conversing with each other.

Serena beamed at him and put her mouth to his ear. Her breath tickled his neck. "You are quite a gifted kisser, my Prince. Even now I feel the warmth of your mouth."

Then she turned and waved to the men watching as they continued toward the gates.

"Let us proceed."

Most of the men nodded, but one Atlantean, particularly tall, stepped in their path just before they could move any further.

"What are you doing, Serena? Why have you brought a human here?" he demanded. His figure was an imposing form, and Prince Edward sensed an unmistakable sense of authority in his stance.

The surrounding Atlanteans fell silent. Serena's hand grew stiff in Prince Edward's, and he gave it a reassuring squeeze.

"Stand down, Ajax. He is here to see our father," she replied. Her shoulders trembled slightly, as though she had considered squaring up to the man but was not entirely committed to it. He had a long, black braid of hair resting on his shoulder. Battle scars were spread across his muscled torso. Prince Edward's jaw tightened at Serena's words. *Our father.* Did that mean that this beast of a man was a big brother?

He looked about at the sea of skeptical stares aimed in his direction and wondered just how many brothers Serena had.

"Poseidon is away on business," Ajax said. "Our orders remain unchanged. All humans who near here are to be slain."

He pulled out a dagger from his sheath and aimed it directly at Prince Edward's throat. Prince Edward was too stunned to react. The rapid thump of his own heartbeat filled his ears.

Serena bristled next to him. She was angry now. "You would dare kill my love?" Her words were a menacing hiss. "You know the law, Ajax. A human may enter Atlantis so long as their heart is pure. A human seeking marriage to one of us sirens has a right to be heard." She shook with restrained rage.

A murmur rose around them again. Ajax lowered his knife and cocked a brow at Prince Edward instead. "Who are you, human? And what do you want with our sister?" he asked. Prince Edward resisted the urge to cower and squeezed Serena's hand again. This time, he was not sure whether it was for her benefit or his own.

"My name is Prince Edward. I am here to seek Poseidon's approval to take his daughter as my wife," he declared confidently.

Ajax's dark eyes glinted like black diamonds, then turned into slits.

Prince Edward stood his ground and held Ajax's gaze. He knew he had to make a bold move if he was going to win the approval of the Atlanteans. So, remembering Serena's words, he slid a hand around Serena's waist and pulled her close until her hip bumped his. She reached around him as well and gripped his waist.

The Atlantean warriors standing in a circle around them seemed to go still at their public display of affection. A smile appeared on Ajax's face.

"Very well, then, Prince of the dry land. What say you prove your worth by winning a challenge? We cannot allow you to lay claim to our sister until we are sure you are able to protect her." Ajax gestured to the others to back away from him and Serena.

Prince Edward's stomach was in knots as he nodded his agreement. An Atlantean stepped forward and thrust a spear between him and Serena. The cold steel was inches away from his neck. Serena hissed.

Ajax raised his hand.

"We only need your human friend for a short time," he assured her. "We shall return him soon."

Serena and Prince Edward shared a long look full of emotion before they let go of each other. Ajax turned and walked down a narrow path away from the city gates. Prince Edward followed with a rock at the pit of his stomach.

SERENA

Serena ignored the stares of her brothers after Ajax and Prince Edward disappeared from view. Instead, she made a beeline for the gates to Atlantis City.

Many months had passed since she was home. She had spent so much of her time and energy exploring the seas and searching. Searching for a good man.

And then she found Prince Edward.

Or rather, he found her. Nay. *Rescued* her.

She remembered the burns of the steel net like they had happened yesterday. The scores of Naval Officers that had her surrounded, caught like a fish with their pointy weapons aimed at her.

If Prince Edward had not stepped in and shown her mercy, she would have ended up like one of her sisters.

Serena shut her eyes at the memory of finding the

siren floating in a pool of red. Her body limp and swollen. The huge gash in her stomach.

Isis was not entirely wrong, Serena thought. Men were cruel and heartless. But not all men.

Serena knew that Prince Edward was an important part of her plan. If she played her cards carefully, everyone would get what they wanted.

Everyone except Isis. Serena did not care for her mother's vengeful wishes. There were more important desires to consider.

She cleared her mind and put on a poised smile as she approached the glistening gates.

Two guards in suits of golden armor took one look at her and bowed, then pulled the gates open. She walked through with her head held high.

Of all the sirens, Serena was the only one who had dared dwell in Atlantis. Isis forbade her daughters from going anywhere near their father, Poseidon. But Serena was the baby of the family—the last siren to be born in over twenty years. Her birth status granted her favor with Father, but the downside of residing in the underwater kingdom was the constant attention of her nine hundred brothers. Each one trained in battle and fiercely protective of their baby sister.

She knew it was a risk to bring the Prince to Atlantis—a place where a long-standing custom of defense was to kill any human on sight. But she'd had to try.

Of course, Prince Edward was under the impression that it was for the good of the world—to stop the war between sirens and men.

A frown tugged at her lips as she walked through the golden streets. Tall buildings loomed over her, sparkling like jewels in the embers of light from the rocks that lined the streets.

She placed a hand over her flat stomach and sighed as the all-too-familiar ache throbbed. Not one of her brothers had married. Every one of them had chosen to give their lives to the protection of Atlantis. Even if they were to marry, they would not be able to produce heirs—thanks to a cruel curse Isis had put on them after she divorced Poseidon.

Her sisters loathed men—brainwashed by Isis who preached firmly that falling in love only brought suffering and death.

Despite that, there was one sister who had married.

Half-sister, she corrected herself as she reached the steps to the palace.

She hugged herself, a sudden chill taking over as she thought about Georgette. She was the precious treasure Prince Edward had scoured the seas to find. A sister born of Isis and a mere human man.

A man who had taken his own life, unable to live with the guilt of selling his only daughter to a pirate.

How could men be so bad, if one could possess such guilt over something so understandable in her mind?

Her own father, Poseidon, would gladly sell her to a pirate if the price was high enough.

She reached her small home and a flood of relief washed over her as she opened the front door. She rummaged through her drawers, looking for the perfect gown to wear for the evening.

The moment Poseidon returned; she would need to persuade him to keep Prince Edward alive long enough to negotiate.

She wanted to look alluring, vulnerable, and innocent all at the same time. Unable to find anything suitable, she stripped off her silver dress, threw it on the tiny bed, and walked into the bathroom.

Her home was one of the smallest in Atlantis, but every dwelling had the finest plumbing. Marble covered the floor and walls of her bathroom and jets of hot water flooded the space with menthol-smelling steam.

Serena gave her body a thorough scrub and rubbed shampooing oils in her long hair until it fell in soft, smooth waves.

She flicked her wrist, picturing a soft fluffy towel in her mind. It appeared in her hand in an instant.

She could materialize anything with her mind. A dress, a towel—even an entire city. Her only limitations were her imagination and energy.

With nothing satisfactory in her drawers, she conjured a long, yellow satin gown with a bow neckline and low back. Then she inspected herself in the mirror, twirling on her toes, making the skirt of the dress woosh. It rippled with her movements and flattered her curves.

The soft, sheer material clung to her upper body like a second skin, and her red hair fell like a waterfall to her waist.

She tucked a lock of hair behind her ear and wondered what Ajax was doing with Prince Edward.

Ajax was the lead of the second division in the Atlantean army. He would likely spend several hours sparring with Prince Edward to test his strength and endurance. Such qualities were the only things that mattered to her brothers.

Serena would have been concerned for the prince had she not seen him fight. He may very well be the best swordsman she had ever seen. She thought back to the time she had spied on him and watched him press on in battle with a pierced thigh, like the wound was nothing more than a bee sting to him.

But as hours passed by and there was no sign of Ajax or the prince, Serena grew uneasy. She strolled along the streets, watching her brothers at work. Some were fixing up houses. Others tended to the winged horses at the stables. Something kept Serena on edge, but she could not put her finger on what it was.

She closed her eyes and went inward, listening for the familiar rumble of Prince Edward's voice. She could hear grunts and was certain they were from him, so she shook the sense of foreboding away and climbed the marble steps to the palace.

The banquet hall was all set up for dinner. Fine plates and all manner of food had been laid out. It was customary for Serena and her brothers to join Poseidon in the banquet hall at the stroke of midnight for their main meal. Serena knew that soon, everyone would return from their duties and dig in.

She grew jittery, checking her reflection every two minutes in the floor-length mirrors, and busied herself in the kitchen with the cooks.

As midnight came and went, her brothers filled the hall. Serena did her best to swallow her nerves, looking out for Ajax and the prince.

Her insides writhed.

"Serena."

He called to her. Without hesitating, she dashed out

of the palace, running down the steps on bare feet, her dress billowing out behind her. She could hear him breathing hard and heavy. She followed the sound, cursing the frailty of moving on two legs. She could travel so much faster in the water.

Prince Edward's voice grew louder, and she knew she was close when she reached the training ground.

It was deserted but for two dark figures.

When she reached them, the silver glow from the surrounding rocks illuminated Prince Edward's clammy face. His dark brows were knitted together, and he was slumped over panting, while Ajax stood with his arms folded and a smug smile on his face.

"What did you do?" Serena demanded. The question was pointless. It was clear Ajax's intention had been to tire the prince out. They had clearly been fighting all evening. Ajax remained silent, and another figure stepped into the light. Serena shrank back in surprise.

"Father," she said through a gasp. Poseidon towered over the three of them, his arms thick and burly and a mop of long silver hair rested on his chest.

"Ajax said you were away, but I'm glad to see you," she said, trying to ignore her quickened heartbeat. Prince Edward cleared his throat and she glanced at him. He was standing upright again, trying to put on a regal show.

Nobody was fooled. His breaths were still coming out ragged and fast.

Serena's hands balled into fists. Was this part of Ajax's plan? To make him appear weak in front of Poseidon.

"I gather that you have not forgotten the rules of Atlantis, Serena," Poseidon said, his ice-blue eyes piercing as he gave her a discerning look. Serena lifted her chin, standing her ground. "This is an exceptional circumstance," she said.

When Lord Poseidon's white brows lifted, she took Prince Edward's hand. "I know humans are not welcome here, but Edward needed to speak with you."

Poseidon took in their joined hands, but his mouth remained a straight line. Ajax stood still and quiet.

Serena took the silence as an invitation to get straight to the point. She nudged Prince Edward with her hip, and he jerked like he'd just been kissed by an electric eel.

With gallant effort, he did his best to regulate his panting and cleared his throat again.

"Lord Poseidon, King of the seas. I, Prince Edward of England, wish to have your daughter's hand in marriage," he said. The steadiness of his voice surprised him just as much as it did Serena.

Lord Poseidon and Ajax exchanged looks and, for the

first time, Poseidon's face broke into a smile. For a glimmer of a moment, Serena thought he was glad.

After all, surely her father would wish for her to marry and continue the family bloodline?

But then Poseidon nodded to Ajax, who grabbed Prince Edward by the arms, yanking him out of Serena's clutches.

"Prince Edward of England, you are trespassing sacred ground and have committed blasphemy," Lord Poseidon announced.

"Blasphemy?" Edward repeated incredulously.

Lord Poseidon stepped forward and leaned down to give him a firm look. "I am God of the seas. Not just a king, you filthy little human. My daughter is a goddess. The very idea that you would assume to defile her is the highest offense." He stood tall and firm again. "I sentence you to death by hanging at sunrise. Ajax, take him to his cell."

"Yes, Father," Ajax muttered. Serena lunged forward, beating Ajax's iron-like arms and hissing. "You cannot kill him! I am in love with him! Father, how could you do this?"

Lord Poseidon was already walking away. Serena followed Ajax, cursing him with all the worst words she knew. It did not stop him. He did not stop until they reached the palace dungeon. Prince Edward, paralyzed in a surreal state of disbelief, gave her a hollow look. He saw the despair on her face and managed to muster a weak smile, as though to comfort her.

"It is all right, I do not think I have ever been afraid of death," he said to her as Ajax opened the steel door of the entrance. The hinges squealed as the door swung open, and Prince Edward staggered in, Ajax behind him. The door slammed in Serena's face.

She dug her nails into her palms and tried to calm the racing of her heart. Her breaths were short and wild.

She wasn't sure if it had been his exhaustion or a broken spirit talking, but she could not help being disappointed at Prince Edward's docility. She was not going to let him be executed. Her plan could not fail that fast.

She turned on her heels and made a dash for the library, concocting a plan.

GEORGETTE

Georgette gripped her sword with two hands while she sliced the air, sparring with a pirate.

He blocked her attack and stomped on her boot, crushing her toes. She bit back the pain, elbowed him in the ribs, and kicked him in the shin.

The pirate howled and dropped his sword. It fell to the deck with a clatter, and he followed, dropping to his knees.

Georgette poised her blade to his scrawny throat, and his Adam's apple bobbed. Beady eyes darted to the left.

"Please do not harm me. I know nothing. I swear on my mother's life!" he begged. He clasped his hands together as though about to launch into prayer.

Georgette remained very still, ready to slit the man's

throat, while she listened to the approaching footsteps from her side.

The man trembled from head to toe and watched as her husband, Captain Stone, emerged from the darkness and into the moonlight.

He towered over them, wearing a long, black leather jacket with fine golden buttons. His tanned face was framed with long, dark hair and a short, stubbled beard. He had such presence about him that all of the men on the ship stopped their work and looked on in fear. Georgette reasoned that they might have expected the captain to take his knife and gut the boy from navel to throat.

The pirate must have believed the same fate was upon him, for the whites of his eyes grew large when he looked up at the pirate captain towering over him.

"Your Highness, my sincere apologies, I did not see you standing there," the pirate said, bowing his head.

Captain Stone growled and picked him up with one hand on his neck.

Ever since the news broke out that the lost Prince of England was now going by the name of Captain Stone, the pirates had been unable to treat him as anything other than a nobleman.

It was something Georgette knew irritated her husband to no end. He had worked hard to stay under the guise of a ruthless pirate captain. Now the others knew of his nobility, some of the respect for him had gone. The result? He was no longer included in their correspondence, their mutineering, or their diplomatic meetings.

It was a fate worse than death for any pirate. Now he was truly an outsider, belonging nowhere.

Georgette sheathed her sword and rested her hands on her hips while Captain Stone continued the interrogation.

"Where are the pirate lords meeting?"

"I swear, sir, I do not know. I am new, you see; they tell me nothing."

Captain Stone fisted the pirate's shirt and lifted him in the air with one hand.

"Nothing? Are you telling me you know nothing?"

The pirate's legs scrambled like a bug on its back.

"Aye, sir. Nothing."

Captain Stone marched him to the edge of the ship and dangled him over the side. "Now, let us see. Does anything suddenly spring to mind?" he asked, holding the man by the scruff of the neck. The pirate squirmed, legs and arms flailing.

"Aye, sir. While I was on watch, sir. The captain was talking to the quartermaster, sir."

Miraculously, the pirate was able to come up with the exact coordinates of a small island in the Atlantic Ocean and a date.

Captain Stone hummed low and deep, and he looked like he was about to drop the pirate into a watery grave. They were far from shore and Georgette could sense sirens were not far from them. She was the only reason they had not come to rip apart the ship. If the man were to fall into the ocean, he would be considered fair game and the sirens would tear him to pieces before he could take his first breath.

Now that he was in the lamplight, Georgette could see that he was just a boy. Barely fifteen, at most. He had hollow eyes and sunken cheeks, and the terror on his face was most disturbing. Captain Stone shook him like a rag doll, demanding more information about the meeting, but the young pirate swore he knew nothing more. Captain Stone continued to growl.

Georgette grabbed his arm. "He has told you everything he knows. Let the boy go," she said, giving him a hard look.

Captain Stone stiffened under her touch. She knew that he hated to be interrupted, and he especially loathed to be undermined in front of other pirates.

But Georgette did not fear the captain. After all, she was his wife, carrying his unborn child. His punishments for her were carried out in private, often leading to Georgette's bloodcurdling screams. She resisted a smile at the thought. If anything, she enjoyed searching for opportunities to vex him.

The boy dropped to the deck and scrambled to his feet while Captain Stone looked on. "Go, take a dinghy, and tell your captain that I am coming for him. I demand answers as to the whereabouts of my treasure."

The boy stuttered his thanks and scurried off the ship into one of the lifeboats while the rest of the crew looked on, their faces grim.

Captain Stone pointed at Georgette with a scowl. "In my cabin. Now."

A nervous wave of chatter crossed the deck, but they fell silent under one look from Captain Stone. Georgette walked with her head held high.

She knew she had stepped out of line and her punishment was coming.

The men watched her go like she was walking the plank, but she knew better.

When they entered the captain's quarters, Captain Stone locked the door. Then he grabbed Georgette by her arms and pushed her against the wall with a rough kiss on the mouth. His beard grazed her cheeks and neck. Before long, she was putty in his hands.

She melted against his body while he ravished her

with fierce kisses all over her face and décolletage. Her eyes rolled to the back of her head and a delightful sweat broke out on her body.

He was feral, with an aim to devour her. She was his willing prey.

He tugged on the neckline of her shirt and her breasts spilled out. The sight of them made him groan in delight. He cupped both in his calloused hands. Georgette shuddered with pleasure while he worked his mouth over them, then back up her neck. "You dare speak against me in front of my crew?" he growled into her ear.

Georgette fought a giggle. A rush of heat flooded her core.

"Have I embarrassed you, Captain?" she asked, batting her lashes at him. "Must I be punished?"

Captain Stone matched her grin, then ripped her stays with one forceful tug. Georgette almost protested. It was the third bodice he had ripped that week. She was quickly running out of attire.

But just then, he dropped to his knees and began to lick her exposed skin. She lost her train of thought, placed her hands on his shoulders, and threw her head back with a deep breath. With each wave of pleasure, she stifled a groan, holding onto his shoulders for support.

Captain Stone nipped and sucked on her heated flesh

while he caressed her curves. Then he paused at the small baby bump and planted a tender kiss right on her navel.

"You shall be punished, my lady," he said, rising to his feet.

He pressed his hips against hers, and her core tensed at the delightful pressure of his arousal between her legs.

The earnest need to be connected to him again drove her hands to move of their own accord.

She fumbled with his breeches to release him, but he caught her wrists in his strong hands and shook his head. "Nay, my lady. Not yet."

Georgette frowned.

It had been three days since their reunion, after she'd thought him dead. He had not bedded her once since then.

The last two punishments consisted of pinning her down while he feasted on her and refusing to stop even when an explosion of euphoria ripped through her body and erupted from her mouth in the form of a scream. But when he finished with that, he would simply go back to work, denying himself the same release.

Captain Stone had the self-control of a saint. While any other man would readily take his wife at the first given opportunity, Captain Stone enjoyed taking things slow. He promised he would only bed her when she was ripe, ready, and had released at least thrice. But with the war in full swing, and the crew anxious for answers, there was never enough time.

The captain pushed her hands back over her head, forcing her breasts to lift. They moved with Georgette's heaving breaths, and his eyes glowed orange in the candlelight as he spent one long moment just taking in the sight of her. "I need to show my crew that no one will get away with talking back to me —not even my wife."

Georgette held her breath as Captain Stone walked her back to the bed. She fell onto it, and he climbed atop her, pinning her wrists to rest on either side of her head.

"He was only a boy. I am not sorry for what I did," Georgette said, defiant.

Even if she did not expect joyous punishment from the captain, she would have spoken up. Amid the atrocities they had been through, Captain Stone became even harsher in his dealings with other pirates. She needed to keep him in line so as not to lose the last shred of humanity left in him.

With Captain Stone's hands pinning her wrists, Georgette used her legs to wrap him up and pull his hips to her again.

She needed to feel him inside of her. Not a finger, or the tip of his tongue. Him. All of him.

Captain Stone let go of her wrists to trace his fingertips all the way down her arms. Georgette writhed in bliss while the captain explored all the contours of her body. He pinched a nipple, then he slid his hands under the waistband of her trousers and roughly pulled them down over the swell of her hips.

Georgette lifted herself off the bed to let the cotton pants and her undergarments roll down her legs, then she kicked them off.

Now she was entirely naked, and he was fully clothed. It was not a fair fight.

Georgette frowned and picked up the hem of his shirt, but Captain Stone growled and started to kiss her neck instead.

"Enough," Georgette snapped, taking back control. Captain Stone tore away from her skin to give her an incredulous look. "Do you enjoy vexing me, my lady?" he asked. "Do you have any idea what that does to me?"

Georgette ignored him and reached down to grasp what was her marital right to have, her fingers curling around his girth. When the Captain let out a deep groan, she could not stop a triumphant grin from taking over her face.

"Do not fear, my Captain," she murmured against his mouth, fondling his length. "So long as you do as I say, I promise to scream very loud, so your crew knows not to cross you."

Captain Stone panted like a wounded wolf as she flexed her grip and stroked the length of him. They both knew he was utterly powerless now.

She sat up and pulled him to the bed. Then she mounted his hips and aligned him with her aching core. When she lowered herself and guided him inside her, the two of them let out a moan of relief. An overwhelming sense of homecoming flooded Georgette. She shut her eyes and let out a shuddering breath.

While Georgette adjusted to the new sensation, Captain Stone gripped her hips, squeezed her bottom, then reached up and cupped her breasts. It was as though he was trying to memorize her body while they were connected.

Then they moved in sync, like two lovers in a dance that was just for them.

As their climax drew near, her hands found his and they interlocked their fingers. They held on to each other for dear life and tumbled together over the edge.

As promised, Georgette let out an earth-shattering scream that lasted so long, it made the glass mirror rattle on the wall. There was no question of if the crew would hear it.

Panting and clammy with sweat, she collapsed on the bed beside her husband, who grabbed a fistful of her golden hair and gave her a devilish grin.

Then he leaned forward, kissed her on the cheek, and growled two words in her ear. "Good girl."

CAPTAIN STONE

CAPTAIN STONE LAY WITH HIS ARM AROUND HIS SLEEPING wife, her naked body pressed against his chest. He closed his eyes, reveling in the afterglow of their lovemaking. The contrast between her silky-smooth skin and his calloused fingertips was a marvel to him. He drew circles over her skin with his thumbs, sliding his hands down her spine. The small of her back was so smooth, he could imagine running his palm over it for all eternity. Then he couldn't resist giving her pert bottom another squeeze. She stirred, lifting her knee to rest over his hip. Her inner thigh grazed his length, and her core bathed it in heat. He throbbed, his body already pent up and yearning to be connected to her again.

He would gladly mount the woman and take her five more times that night, and she would have gladly allowed it. But he placed a hand over her swollen stomach and summoned restraint.

She was his most precious treasure in all of the seas. Silently, he swore to protect her for the rest of his days.

His heart pounded at the thought. He longed to possess the immortality ring once again. It was the only thing that could protect him from the wave of enemies growing ever closer. Without it, he was powerless, and all he could rely on was the terror his reputation had forged amongst his foes.

After Isis railed at him, a frenzied banshee from his darkest nightmares, he fell into Georgette's arms. Her body trembled beneath him. He would never forget the way she clutched him to her chest, her tears dripping onto his shirt.

Georgette's skin was warm, like the flames of a bonfire. Until darkness took hold and Georgette was gone, leaving him to drown in the cold clutches of death.

But then his cold body became wrapped up in a tingling fire. The warmth lapped over him, seeping into his heart, and bringing it back to life. Fingers of heat and vitality clawed at his chest, flooding him with excitement. Like a Phoenix, he rose from the ashes, renewed and whole once more.

He looked down at his chest, which had once been ripped open and oozing with thick blood. The skin had been sewn back together, but the scars were there—a reminder of the terrible attack.

Captain Stone pulled Georgette's sleeping frame closer and wrapped his other arm around her. Then he studied her face. Her thick black lashes rested on the top of her rosy cheeks and her golden hair fell in waves over her shoulders.

She was beautiful, yes. But that was not what made his heart swell.

It was the knowledge that while she was in his arms, she was safe. And she was carrying their babe. He would do anything and sacrifice everything to keep them both from harm.

But he could not rest.

He pressed his lips to her temple and slipped out of bed, tucking the white sheets around her. He stared at her sleeping form, cherishing the sight of her in his bed.

The cabin was dark, aside from the moonlight pouring in through the open windows. She looked so sweet and innocent, but beneath the tender surface beat the heart of a warrior queen. He'd given her a new life, one that would end the tyranny of her father once and for all. She was free to forge her own path. But that freedom was in jeopardy so long as men hunted sirens.

On the deck, the crew stood in a circle, jittering tensely. Their faces were pale and ghostly in the light of the full moon. "Smythe, report," the captain commanded. The second mate, who was steadfastly gripping the helm, snapped his head around to answer. The full moon illuminated the fearful faces of his crew as they looked at him. "Smythe, report," he barked again to the second mate, who stood at the helm.

The man was rich in years and poor in his remaining time on Earth. He sported a long, wiry gray beard that he tucked into his belt, and a wheeze audible from across the deck. But his eyes were sharp as ever and he had a stronger backbone than any of the other men. Captain Stone would know, for the man used to work as a blacksmith for the royal family. He crafted the finest swords and would not so much as blink before he cut a man from neck to groin for insulting his work.

The old man took to piracy like a moth to a flame. Captain Stone supposed the smith was drawn to the open waters and the untouched lands waiting to be discovered. Or perhaps, the freedom to sink his knife into the belly of any man who betrayed him, without being sent to the gallows.

Either way, Captain Stone was certain that Mr. Smythe did not sign up for a violent war with sirens.

"Another marker ahead, do you want to go around it?" he asked, his voice gruff and deep.

Captain Stone climbed to the helm and took the

spyglass from him. Then he pointed it in the direction of Mr. Smythe's outstretched finger.

A small wooden boat bobbed in the distance. The ship's mast had a dead siren pinned to it with a broad steel spear embedded in her abdomen. Her arms were tied above her head, and a curtain of dark, wavy hair obscured her face and breasts. Not that it mattered. The only face Captain Stone could ever see on the faces of those dead sirens was that of Georgette. And every time he laid eyes on a marker—as they called them—his blood turned cold.

His men took readily to fighting the sirens, seeing them as the deadliest enemy of all, but little did they know it was the sirens who protected them. Because of Georgette.

Captain Stone clenched his jaw as the ship approached. Thick, crimson drops of blood drenched the siren's shimmering tail. It was a most ugly sight, one that Captain Stone was glad to hide from his sleeping wife.

He lowered the spyglass and turned back to his second mate. "No. Stay true to the course."

"Aye, Captain."

Mr. Jones, the quartermaster, looked up from the piece of parchment in his hands and gave Captain Stone a disapproving look, but he did not say a word. He was not foolish enough to cross the captain under the eyes of others.

"If I may," he muttered into his ear.

The captain raised a brow but nodded. The two huddled at the very end of the ship.

"I believe the British Royal Navy is not far from here. If they were to discover us and learn of your wife…"

Captain Stone clenched his jaw. "What do you know of my wife?" he growled.

Mr. Jones scrubbed his jaw and shrank under the intensity of Captain Stone's stare. His eyes grew shifty.

"You know as well as I do, Captain, that pirates talk."

"And what, pray tell, are pirates daring to speak of concerning my wife?" Captain Stone said, gripping the side of the ship until the whites of his knuckles were on show.

The quartermaster swallowed so loud Captain Stone could hear it. "Men speak of her unnatural beauty. And her screams in the night…"

"Is it so shocking for a woman to scream in bed with her husband?" the captain shot back. He tried to summon a look of amusement, but a frown took hold of him again.

Mr. Jones cleared his throat and offered a false laugh. "Of course, Captain. It was only a rumor."

"What is?"

Mr. Jones looked out at the dead siren as the ship sailed by. "That your wife left the Isle of Imerta unscathed. She survived a siren attack as well. The men are dimwitted, for sure. No doubts about that. But they are not fools."

Finally, Mr. Jones met Captain Stone's burning stare. This time, he did not shrink back. "There are whispers that Georgette is a siren, Captain."

Captain Stone blinked, taking in the news. When he did not speak, it seemed to offer Mr. Jones enough courage to finish his thought. He leaned forward to whisper in the captain's ear.

"And if the Royal British Navy were to discover that the woman who jilted their future King is a siren, there is no telling what they will do to her."

Captain Stone slammed a fist on the edge of the ship, then pulled out his knife, a blade etched with intricate lines and symbols of the royal crest. He lurched forward and pressed the sharp blade against the neck of the pirate. "How dare you speak of such things?"

Mr. Jones's Adam's apple bobbed against the blade as he swallowed. "My apologies, Captain. I meant no offense, sir. I just thought you ought to know."

"Know what?" Captain Stone hissed.

"That it is bleedin' obvious, sir." Mr. Jones explained

carefully. "And if it's obvious to us, then maybe it will be to them."

Captain Stone shut his eyes and let out a breath. "Now you know why I am not concerned about siren attacks," he said. Then he glared at the man. "But if you tell a soul, I will take this knife and cut open your belly, letting your guts spill out before you die."

Mr. Jones nodded. "And what are we going to do about the British Royal Navy, sir?"

Captain Stone looked out at the dead siren again, deep in thought. Then he finally turned back and nodded to his quartermaster. "Tell the crew that if anyone so much as looks at my wife, they are to be killed. We are at war, but the child she carries might be the key to ending it. She must be protected at all costs."

Mr. Jones's eyes grew wide as he took in the news. Then he nodded his understanding. "Aye, Captain," he said. Then he walked away.

Now alone, Captain Stone leaned against the railing and looked out at the dark blue horizon. The silver glow of moonlight scattered itself into a million points of light on the surface of the sea, like stars in a dark sky. The air was crisp and cool, and the gentle sounds of water lapping the sides of the ship would at one time have soothed his troubled mind. But not even the sweetness of the open sea could calm him now.

His mind turned to his brother, Prince Edward—the ferocity in his eyes as he uttered the last words he had said to them: "You are both dead to me."

If the prince were to discover Georgette's true form, there was no telling how he would react. But if Mr. Jones was correct and Georgette's secret was obvious, then she was in more danger than ever.

He only hoped he could forge an alliance with the Pirate Lords. They needed money, supplies, and strong allies if they hoped to have any chance of making it out of this war alive.

But persuading the very men who so gladly stabbed him in the back and left him for dead would be no small feat.

He turned and headed for his cabin, his heart burning with the blazing need to protect Georgette. When he found her sitting up in bed, her eyes shining like moons as she looked up at him, his heart soared.

Her hair covered her nipples—those succulent peaks of her breasts that only he was permitted to enjoy.

"What is wrong, my Captain?" Georgette asked, her brows knitting together as her face settled into a frown. Clearly, she could read her man like a book.

He did not want to burden her with his concerns. Nor did he wish to discuss the nightmares that plagued his mind.

Her pouty lips called out to him like an oasis in the desert. He reached for her and kissed her roughly on the mouth.

"Nothing is wrong, my lady," he murmured into her neck when they broke apart. She wrapped her arms around his middle while he unsheathed his aching length and nudged it between her thighs. A welcome heat flooded him, sending all of the blood in his racing mind south and quieting his thoughts.

He picked her up, clutching her milky thighs as lined the tip of his erection to her core. "I was merely thinking that it has been too long since I felt this." He pushed himself inside and Georgette threw her head back with a shudder.

Once again, they were one. For that moment, all of Captain Stone's fears dissipated.

They flooded the cabin with the sounds of their love-making, and the air was sweeter than before. Then they collapsed in a tangled heap of sweaty limbs, not knowing where one person began and the other ended.

Captain Stone lost himself in Georgette's arms, content. He only wished that the sweet bliss of her body enveloping him could last forever.

PRINCE EDWARD

Prince Edward sank to his knees in the dirty prison cell and rested his clammy forehead against the cool iron bars. He did not know how many hours had passed since he had been locked up. Atlantis did not have sunlight to decipher the difference between night and day. But he supposed it had been many hours because his body was cold and rigid, every muscle throbbing with his movements. Even breathing had become cumbersome.

It was a most clever plan, he thought.

Poseidon must have ordered his warriors to spar with him for hours, not to test his strength or loyalty to Serena. But rather, to weaken him. So that when the time came to execute him, there would be no fight.

Not that it mattered. His heart had already been

brutally torn from his chest and sliced in two when Georgette left him at the altar.

Georgette Harrington, the sweet, innocent maiden he had been betrothed to for a decade. He had seen her grow into a fine young woman. Her voice, a gentle purr, rang in his ears.

"I am with child."

His jaw ached as he gritted his teeth, replaying the events that led him to his impending demise.

All the time and energy wasted. All the resources spent to rescue her from the ruthless pirates who had captured her. All of it spent in vain while Georgette fell for his brother's charms. He had happily defiled her innocence.

Prince Edward's hands balled into tight fists.

His brother could have had any woman in all of the lands. Why did he choose Georgette?

And how could Georgette fall for such a monster?

A Prince who had turned away from his royal duties, even from his own family, in favor of living a life as an outlaw. Plundering, pillaging, treating ladies like whores, and slaughtering gentlemen like pigs.

To be betrayed by his own brother cut deep.

Georgette was to be his queen.

Now she belonged to his pirate brother, and they expected a child.

It was unthinkable… Nay, unforgivable.

He found purpose in Serena's plan—if he could put an end to the brutal war, then perhaps all of his suffering was not in vain.

But alas, he would be executed.

The door to the cell opened and Prince Edward looked up with a squint. A woman stood in the doorway, framed like an angel in brilliant white light from the hall.

Then she dashed forward, and the door swung shut again. Serena's seafoam blue eyes sparkled at him as she fell to her knees.

"Forgive me for taking so long," she said in a breathy voice. Her slender arms reached through the gaps between the bars to gently squeeze his shoulders.

As she spoke, her sweet fragrance filled the air, and for a brief moment, Prince Edward was transported to another place. Yet, his grim destiny came crashing back into his consciousness and he was plunged back into despair.

"No matter. There is nothing to be done, you should not have come here," he muttered, looking darkly at the floor.

Serena's hands were soft as they cupped his cheeks, and she gently turned his head so he could not look away.

"All hope is not lost, my Prince." She looked him

straight in the eyes and her gaze was unwavering. "There is a way to set you free and proceed with our plan."

Prince Edward frowned, searching her eyes, and wondering how the siren could still possess any hope. Then he raised his shackled hands. "Do you have the key to release me?"

Serena bit her lip. "No." She glanced over her shoulder at the door to the hall. "Even if I did, there are too many guards with orders to kill you on sight if you try to escape."

Prince Edward's shoulders sank with disappointment. "Then what can be done?"

Serena's eyes blazed with intensity as she reached deep into her dress, her delicate fingers pulling out a sleek silver knife that glinted in the blue light. Prince Edward swallowed as he watched her hold the blade in her steady hand.

"You wish to kill me yourself?" he asked.

Serena gave him a look of disgust, as though he had insulted her. But the prince could not imagine what other plans she had involving a knife.

She studied it in her hands, running her thumbs along the markings etched into the handle. "There is an ancient ritual... I had to sneak into the restricted section of the library to read about it." Her eyes shone like orbs as she looked at him again. "It is an unbreakable oath. No one, not even my father, can hurt you afterward."

Prince Edward shifted his weight and frowned deeper as he thought about it. "An oath, you say. What kind of oath?"

Serena's lips curved upward but the smile did not reach her eyes. "It is more than an oath. A binding, if you will."

She dipped her head and leaned in close. Her breaths misted his cheeks, and the sweet floral scent flooded the prince again. His defenses lowered with every breath she exhaled.

"If you bind yourself to me, you will become one of us. Siren blood shall run through your veins."

Prince Edward's heart began to race. He was not certain if it was due to anticipation or anxiety. Perhaps both.

"You mean to...?"

Serena flinched and looked at the door again, though Prince Edward heard nothing to raise suspicion. Then he remembered that Serena was able to hear even a whisper from a great distance. She turned back to him and grasped his hand.

"We must hurry. They are coming."

Breathless, she shuffled closer and turned Prince

Edward's hand over to reveal his palm. "This shall hurt a little," she warned.

Prince Edward flinched. "Wait."

Serena gave him a hard look. "Do you want to get out of this alive or not? And if you die, what will happen then? How many sirens and humans must perish until this war comes to an end?"

Her words struck Prince Edward like a thunderbolt. No, he was not certain he had much desire to live. But the thought that he and Serena could put a stop to all of the brutality changed his mind.

Even if their plan was fated to fail, he could not roll over and die until he knew that he had tried everything in his power to stop the war.

He nodded, resolute. "Do what you must."

Serena cut a line in his palm and the sting of the blade smarted, making his eyes prickle. Then she cut her own palm and clasped his wounded one in hers.

"Now repeat after me," she commanded in a slight whisper. "I, Edward, swear to remain loyal to Serena and all of my siren kin, by blood and oath, until death do us part."

Prince Edward repeated her words, feeling the pulsing of her blood with each syllable he spoke. Finishing the vow, they both began to chant an ancient song which seemed to emerge from deep within them both.

Prince Edward melted into the melody. A renewed sense of purpose soared through his veins and a zest for life took hold. The ache in his tight muscles dissipated and his limbs grew warm and strong once more.

The final vow was sealed with a kiss, a final connection made between a jilted Prince and a siren who wished for something better than this world could offer them.

The door suddenly flew open, and Prince Edward jumped away from Serena, barely having the time to compose himself before Poseidon burst through the doorway with a group of Atlantean warriors. His heart slammed against his chest like a hammer as he faced them all at once.

Before anyone could speak or even make sense of what was going on, Serena jumped up and stepped forward. She lifted her bloodied hand and declared:

"I am bound by an unbreakable oath to this human! You cannot harm him."

Everyone froze in shock as they looked between her and Prince Edward, who lifted his palm to show them the identical cut.

Poseidon's face twisted with rage. Serena continued quickly; "To break this oath would bring shame upon us all! I will not dishonor my word, nor will I risk bringing more bloodshed onto our people!"

Poseidon's face looked like thunder. His eyes bore into hers. Serena looked back at him, defiant, with her shoulders squared. Prince Edward was impressed by her strength.

"Do you accept my claim?" she asked, holding out her hand.

Poseidon's eyes locked onto her outstretched palm and his face darkened.

"It would be a terrible waste to spare this vile human at the last moment."

The cell filled with the murmurs of Poseidon's warriors while they readied their weapons.

Serena took another bold step forward. "My prince shall not be hanged! Nor will I allow him to sit in squalor like a thief."

"But he is a thief! A heartless, foolish, blood-thirsty thief!" Poseidon's rage poured from him like a deep-seated storm. He glowered at her with a mixture of fury and heartache that Prince Edward could not decipher.

The intensity of his anger reverberated throughout the room and sent a chill down Prince Edward's spine.

Still, Serena did not so much as flinch under the icy stare of her father. She squared up to him instead, crossing her arms in defiance.

You could have cut through the tension with a knife. Poseidon scanned the faces of his men. Then he snapped his fingers, and they bowed and filed out of the room, closing the door behind them. Poseidon's words rumbled. "Serena, let us speak privately."

"But Father–"

"Do not test me, daughter." he hissed. "I am not entirely against the idea of killing you both for what you have done. Now come."

He spun around and strode out into the hall. Serena cast one last glance at Prince Edward. "Do not fret, my Prince. I shall be back soon enough." She then scurried out after her father.

Prince Edward staggered back until he hit the cell bed and fell onto it, his mind spinning. He raised his palms to eye level and marveled at the wound healing before him until only a faint scar remained. His blood ran hot in his veins, pumping him with a strength he had never known before.

He was unsure of what would happen next, or what sort of binding ritual Serena had performed. But one thing was certain, it was magic, and she had changed him.

SERENA

Poseidon marched down the corridor to a small room. Serena followed, determined not to show any sign of weakness.

Her father valued two things: honesty and strength. She knew that it would require both qualities to make it out of this conversation with what she wanted.

He turned on his heel and faced her, motioning for one of his guards to shut the door. When they were alone, he perched on the edge of a plush chair beside a desk and gave Serena a hard look.

She met his stare and refused to blink until he broke eye contact with a heavy sigh.

"My dear girl, do you have any idea what foolish thing you have done?"

The softness in his voice threw Serena for a moment.

She blinked several times and gathered her thoughts. "I did what I had to. You were going to kill the love of my life."

Poseidon let out a snort of derision. "Love. What do you know about love?"

"More than you," Serena shot back, folding her arms. "You get your heart broken and spend the rest of your days hiding in this god-forsaken city at the bottom of the sea."

Poseidon rose to his feet, towering over her, and roared with fury. The ground trembled until he stopped.

"You know nothing about my affairs," he said in an acidic whisper. Serena dug her nails into her arms to stop her limbs from shaking. She needed to hold her nerve and show him no fear.

"Oh, I know plenty about the affairs, Father. I believe your lover's tiff is the reason Isis banished you here in the first place," she said.

Poseidon's eyes flashed dangerously but he remained silent. Serena could almost see his brain spinning, replaying the events of the past before him.

It was dangerous to trigger Poseidon this way. But Serena needed to weaken his defenses before she could land him with the truth. Otherwise, he would put his foot down and come up with some despicable notion that would end up getting her and Edward killed. Or worse…

Banished. Serena already exiled herself from her mother and sisters. To be banished from Atlantis too would leave her to the humans.

And now that the humans had discovered a way to harm sirens, she would be in more danger walking amongst them than ever. Finally, Poseidon spoke, snapping Serena out of her thoughts.

"Your mother is a jealous wench, to be sure, but there was no love there. How could there have been? She had already given her heart to someone else. Or has she not told you that?"

Serena dropped her arms while her face twisted in confusion. "What are you talking about?"

Her question prompted one of his thick, silver brows to rise. "It seems, my child, you do not know as much as you think."

Serena's brain started to spin as she tried to piece together her father's cryptic words, but there were far more pressing matters on her mind, and the old tales of her parents' tragic love life did not matter to her.

She rolled her shoulders back. "You must free Edward at once and give him your blessing. Only then can we approach Isis and demand a truce."

Poseidon folded his broad arms across his chest. His long, silver hair fanned over his muscled shoulders and shimmered in the slivers of dull blue light peeking in through the slit in the wall. He hummed low and deep.

"A binding ritual requires blood magic, Serena. A magic that is both dangerous and unpredictable. It is why I banned the study of it centuries ago. How did you come upon this knowledge?"

Serena tucked a strand of hair behind her ear, glancing away from her father's penetrating stare. "You know that I was born with a curious mind. The ocean whispers secrets, and if you did not want anyone to find out about it, Father, you should have removed all records of it in the library."

Poseidon lowered to his seat again. "The only records of such magic are written in hieroglyphs. No one has been taught to read the ancient writings since long before you or your brothers were created. How can you read them?"

Serena matched her father's stare with a smile. "It appears you do not know everything, after all."

Serena's triumphant smile faded when her father gave her a look of pure devastation. "Tell me, my child. Did you take the time to carefully study what the binding ritual will do?"

Serena stiffened. She had been in too much of a hurry to pore over all of the texts. Her knowledge of ancient Egyptian writings was limited, and she only had one evening to come up with a way to stop the prince from being hanged.

"I know that the binding ceremony is final. Two lovers are forever bound by blood and soul. They become one. If you were to follow through and execute him, then you would be condemning me to death as well."

Poseidon sighed. "Indeed." He dragged a hand over his face. "But the ceremony is not meant for mortals, like your prince. Now, you truly are one soul. Your fate is entwined with his. His mortal life will be extended because of your immortality. But the price you've paid is greater than you can imagine."

Serena frowned. She had not stopped to consider the consequences of her actions until her father spelled them out. A sense of foreboding crept into her chest. He leaned forward to give her a piercing look. "My dear Serena. I do hope your love is true, because when the prince is taken to the Underworld, Hades will come for you too."

Serena swallowed. This was news to her, but the concept of death was not something she was a stranger to. After all, if the war continued, it would only be a matter of time before she found herself pinned to a sailboat by a steel spear.

"The Prince and I are aligned in our motivations to end the war. We both yearn for peace on the waters, so humans and sirens can stop these savage attacks and no one else needs to die," Serena said, finally taking a seat.

Poseidon pinched the bridge of his nose with a sigh. "So. This is not about two star-crossed lovers paying the ultimate price to be together," he said. "It is a feeble attempt to stop a war much bigger than you two could ever comprehend."

The words stung, and Serena blinked several times as she took them in.

"I—" For the first time, words failed her.

But then she shook her head. "There is another reason I need him."

Poseidon stayed silent, looking at her with an expression she could not read.

Slowly, Serena rose to a stand again and clasped her hands. "My one and only wish is to become a mother, and I shall sacrifice anything, even my own immortality, to become one."

Poseidon blinked, his expression blank, while Serena's heart rate quickened. It was the first time she had shared her deepest, most secret wish with anyone. Saying it aloud had sent a rush of exhilaration through her senses.

Finally, Poseidon reached out and took her hands in his. Warmth flooded her veins and the corners of his eyes creased as he smiled at her. "I wish you had come to me about this," he said, his soft voice raising the hairs on the back of Serena's neck. "Then perhaps you might not have thrown your life away. If you had known… I should have told you. I take full responsibility…"

Serena tried to pull her hands away, but she was trapped in her father's vice-like grip. "Told me what?"

Poseidon's ice-blue eyes grew big and watery as he leaned in closer.

"You can never be a mother."

The words landed like roaring thunder on her ears. Serena frowned. "I have no idea what you speak of."

Poseidon's sad smile prickled Serena's heart as confusion took over her excitement. "My dear Serena. You are not the first to practice blood magic."

Serena yanked her hands from her father's grip like she had been struck by one of Zeus's lightning bolts. "You're *lying*. I can become a mother. I've seen it with my own eyes. Georgette is with child. If she can have a baby with a human, then so can I."

Poseidon remained eerily calm as he watched her pace the room. Finally, he clapped his hands. "I shall release the prince. But you will stay here a while so that I might get to know him. If I find him worthy of your hand, I shall consider offering my blessing."

Serena stopped pacing and took a deep breath. It was all that she needed. But her father had filled her head with concern. She knew that Poseidon was many things… He could not commit to one woman. He battled like a savage beast, not adhering to any rules. And he was considered a tyrant by most of the gods. But he was not dishonest.

Which meant that he truly believed Serena could not bear a child. She turned to him. "Tell me about this curse. Who is it on?"

Poseidon stood. "All Sirens and Tritons are affected."

"Who cursed us?" Serena demanded, grabbing her father's arms. "Tell me."

Poseidon cupped his daughter's face in his huge hands and gave her a look of sadness. "Who do you think?"

He did not say it, but deep down Serena knew the answer and her heart sank like rocks to the bottom of the ocean as she stared into her father's sorrowful eyes.

Isis.

Without another word, her father pulled her in for a comforting hug. Hot tears stung Serena's eyes. She clamped them shut. But her mind could not stop holding onto hope. Hope that he was wrong. Isis did not curse them. After all, there was one siren out there defying the odds. She had to believe that she could find her happy ending too.

GEORGETTE

Georgette woke with a start. Cold, sticky sweat clung to her temples. Her heart beat wildly and all of her senses told her something was wrong.

The hairs on her arms rose and she shivered, pulling the covers up to her nose. But then the metallic scent of blood flooded her senses, and she lurched back, throwing them off her again.

She patted herself down while staring at the blood-soaked blanket and frowned as she seemed to be unharmed.

With a sense of dread, she turned to wake Captain Stone but shrieked at the sight of his immobile body lying next to her. His lifeless eyes were glassy and dull, staring past her as she looked into them. His shredded chest leaked congealed blood, it was as though it had been ripped open in the night and he had been left to bleed to death.

Fresh sobs of grief and horror took hold and choked Georgette as she bit her fist.

"No, no, no, no," she moaned, shaking uncontrollably.

"Georgette!"

The sound of Captain Stone's harsh voice startled her, and the vision faded as she lurched awake—for real this time. Her heart hammered in her chest, and she clutched Captain Stone's shirt with trembling hands as his face came into view.

"You were dead," she moaned, letting her tears fall freely now. "You were dead."

Captain Stone pulled her close and wrapped her up in his arms. "It was just a nightmare, my love. Do not be alarmed."

But Georgette continued to sob anyway, her body wracked with a pain she had never known before. It was as if her soul could not bear the sorrows of mortality and was tearing itself from her.

After a few minutes of Captain Stone soothing Georgette and stroking her hair, he stiffened and stopped rocking her. "My love…"

The concern in his voice sent Georgette's senses running wild with fear once more. A chill crawled up her spine. She broke from the safety of his embrace and met his worried look. "What is it?"

He nodded and looked down. She followed his line of sight and looked down at her white cotton nightgown. White, except for the blood stains.

Georgette's heart jolted and she yanked the covers away. She was sitting in a thick pool of blood. "It's me, I am bleeding," she said in shock. She had guessed at the source of the blood and was not sure she could bear the truth. She placed a trembling hand between her legs. When she pulled it away, fresh blood glinted in the streaks of morning sunshine.

Her body began to tremble as another wave of pain shot through her core. With a groan, she bent over.

Without another word, Captain Stone got up and yanked on his boots.

"Where are you going?" Georgette moaned, panicked that he might leave and never return. Captain Stone did not look back. She supposed he was too disgusted at the sight of her sitting in such a state. "I shall return with the doctor," he muttered. Then he was gone. The door slammed hard behind him.

A few tense moments passed by. Georgette took a bundle of cloth and stuffed it between her legs. Then she stripped the bed, her arms shaking.

The door opened again, and Mr. Rogers, the doctor, came inside. Captain Stone was right behind him.

Rogers glanced at the discarded bundle of sheets in the corner. He turned to Georgette and surveyed her over his glass spectacles. "When did the bleeding start?" he asked.

Georgette tried to compose herself and stare back with a hardened look on her face, but she suspected the doctor could see the scared young woman behind the mask.

"I awoke from a nightmare just a few minutes ago, and there was all this blood," Georgette said, her voice wavering.

Captain Stone remained by the door, his face hard and unreadable. His shoulders were too high, and his jaw bulged. Georgette thought he almost looked like he didn't want to be there. She didn't blame him. She didn't want to be there either. If she had a choice, she would float out of her body and get as far away from the situation as possible.

Mr. Rogers opened his bag and pulled out a small pile of cotton padding. "How far along is the pregnancy?" he asked.

Georgette opened her mouth, but no sound came out because she was not entirely sure how to answer the question. She had not breathed a word to anyone of her pregnancy, let alone seen a doctor. Captain Stone cleared his throat and she looked blankly at him. Then she turned back to look at the doctor and panicked, for she did not know how to calculate how far along she was.

When did she fall pregnant? Was it during those blissful days on the island? Or during the weeks on the merchant ship after their rescue?

The Doctor seemed to read her thoughts. He coughed. "When was your last bleed?" he asked.

Georgette blushed under the frankness of his question and chewed her lip in thought. It had been before her capture... When she was still engaged to Prince Edward and excited to marry him. She thought about the dates.

"A little over two months ago," she said, marveling at how much had changed in such a short span of time.

The doctor hummed long and deep. "I will need to examine you. Lay down."

As Georgette lay back, she found herself sinking into a pit of despair. Rogers approached and she numbly let the doctor do his work.

She kept her gaze fixed on the wood beams along the ceiling, tracing the grain with her sight. She was drowning in the Arctic Ocean. Her heartbeat was slowing to that of a crocodile. She took long, deep breaths—slow and steady—and pictured herself far away.

She wished they had never left the island. They could have thrived in that treehouse with the villagers who believed them to be a god and goddess.

Their days would have been filled with laughter and hard work as they integrated themselves into the community. Georgette would never have discovered that she was a siren, and Captain Stone would never have been attacked by Isis.

Her swollen stomach would have formed into a nice round bump and grown until the pains came along and she had their baby.

The scene brought a tear to her eye. It leaked down her cheek as a sense of knowing took over the numbness.

Rogers straightened. "I am afraid you are in the process of a miscarriage. There is nothing that can be done but to wait for it to pass."

The doctor's words hit Georgette like a thunderclap. She could not move. She lay still, staring at the wood beams. She followed a small crack that ran along the timber. How long had that crack been there? All this time, it had been weakening the beam inch by inch. At what point would the crack deepen until the beam broke entirely?

Georgette chewed her lip, willing the tears to stay in

her eyes as she wondered what she did wrong. Had their lovemaking been too rough? Or had the damage already been done during one of their battles?

She replayed every twinge of discomfort she had. Were they early warning signs? If she picked up on them earlier, was there anything she could have done to stop this from happening?

She closed her eyes and tried to listen for the familiar heartbeat that she had tuned into before. She could only hear her own. A hot tear trailed a burn down her cheek as she wondered if it had all been her imagination.

Perhaps she was never with child. Perhaps the stress on her body simply made her late. She opened her eyes at the sound of a small scuffle.

Captain Stone had picked the doctor up by the scruff of the neck. "Do something!" he growled at the man. "For heaven's sake!"

Georgette watched the doctor and Captain Stone argue, as though she was not even in the room.

The old man remained calm as a summer's day. Deep lines formed around his eyes as he looked up at Captain Stone with sympathy. He placed a hand over the fist on his collar.

"There is nothing anyone can do. It is terribly common this early, and Georgette is weak and malnourished. If you want to do something, get her supplies. She needs red meat to recover her strength."

Captain Stone let the doctor go and began to pace the room, a flush of red rose from his neck to his temples and he began to pant like a dragon. "There must be something. She's a siren, for crying out loud. She—" He ripped open his shirt to reveal the jagged scar on his chest. Then he moved quickly to Georgette and sank to his knees beside her, clutching her hands. "Perhaps you can… Maybe your tears…"

Fresh, hot tears welled in Georgette's eyes at the sight of her husband's devastation.

Captain Stone grunted at the doctor. "Give me a vial."

The doctor rummaged in his bag and pulled out a small glass bottle with a cork. Captain Stone unstopped it and pressed the cool glass to Georgette's cheeks, capturing her tears.

"I'm afraid it is too late," Mr. Rogers said.

His words fell on deaf ears. Captain Stone took the vial and looked up and down Georgette's body. She could see the cogs in his brain spinning as he frantically thought of ways to fix her. She sniffed. "Captain—" she whispered. She choked on another rush of emotion. "Manny," she tried again. His dark eyes glistened as he met her gaze. "This is not the same. It's gone, I can feel it. Not even my tears can bring our baby back."

The seas grew violent and choppy as the ship sailed toward its destination. It was as though the waters were in mourning too, as Georgette and Captain Stone grieved. Two weeks passed by in a state of constant pain and suffering. The pirates wretched over the sides of the ship, their stomachs weakened by the vicious waves endlessly rocking the boat.

Georgette fell into a black state of despair. This new loss had unraveled a grief she buried deep inside. Instead of processing the horrors of what they had found back at Harrington Manor, she took solace in looking forward to their new lives together... Raising their child. But now her baby and that rosy future were gone, her wound was open and raw. The constant sound of her wails and sobs struck deep terror in the hearts of the crew. Vivid imaginations of the darkest depths of the Underworld accosted them at night.

After fourteen nights spent comforting his wife, Captain Stone's patience had worn thin. He was ready to see Georgette's fight again. He caressed her tear-stained face in his rough hands.

"Georgette, my love. The doctor says you are healed now. And we have a lot of work to do if we wish to find a place among the Pirate Lords. I need you to be strong." He pulled her in for a hug, but she pushed him away, her sadness giving way to anger.

"You do not understand, do you?" she spat. Tears leaking from her sore eyes once more.

Captain Stone gave her an incredulous look. "No, I am afraid I do not understand how you can be so consumed with sadness when we are at war. If you do not pull yourself together soon, I fear that the Pirate Lords will never agree to a—"

"I do not care for your pirate politics, or whatever other lawless plans you have in mind!" Georgette snapped. It felt good to allow this new emotion to seep through her body. It was a blessed relief, at least, from the despair that claimed her heart.

"I have so many unanswered questions for my father. I never even got to say goodbye to him. If I could have just seen him one last time…"

She broke off. But her words seemed to have riled Captain Stone up. He dropped his arms and stood, eyes blazing. "You blame me for your father's fate?" he asked.

Georgette wiped her face and sniffed, a bubble of indignation rising to her chest. "If you had not taken me, my father would not be dead!"

Captain Stone held Georgette's gaze for several long moments, his mouth opening and closing soundlessly. Finally, he balled his hands into tight fists.

"Right. Well, I…" It was all he could say before his face darkened and he stormed out of the cabin. The door slammed so hard the portraits on the walls rattled.

CAPTAIN STONE

CAPTAIN STONE CHARGED ACROSS THE DECK OF THE SHIP, ignoring the groans of his crew as they labored with seasickness. He clutched the side of the ship in a white-knuckled grip and roared into the winds like a lion. It did nothing to relieve him. His body was wracked with grief and frustration.

He could not make sense of a problem that could not be solved by the brutal killing of evil men. Nor could he heal his wife's wounds by means of pleasure. Ever since the miscarriage, she had pushed him away, growing cold and distant.

Now he knew why. She blamed him for her suffering. For the death of her wretched father. A father who gambled away her dowry and sold her to a pirate. The same father who proceeded to arrange for her capture and sent her to the engagement ball without so much as a word.

She blamed him for the miscarriage too, no doubt.

He shook his fists at the weak sunlight breaking through the storm clouds and cursed every single god he knew by name. His muscles trembled with the need to break something. No man dared to so much as look in his direction, for fear that he might break them in two with his bare hands. Fury mingled with sorrow flooded his body. He filled with pure rage and had no way of expelling it.

The conflict in his mind reminded him that there was a grain of truth in Georgette's sentiments.

If he had let her father off instead of tricking him into gambling his daughter, she would be a princess by now. Married to his younger brother, no less.

Prince Edward was devoted to Georgette. So much so that he followed her across the seas in a valiant attempt to rescue her when she was taken.

And even after she had married Captain Stone, he let her return to him.

Captain Stone shut his eyes and banged a fist on the wooden edge of the ship. The force sent a jarring pain up his arm, right to his shoulder. He paid it no attention. He deserved to suffer.

He thought perhaps Isis was right to kill him.

If he had stayed dead, Georgette might not have lost the baby, and the prince could have been fooled to believe the child was his.

The thought curled around his heart like two clawed hands and squeezed until he could not draw breath. He clamped a hand over his chest, checking that he was still alive.

He implored the heavens to tell him what to do. For a splinter of a second, the thought crossed his mind to walk the plank and let the sharks or sirens take him.

He cared not which.

Just then, he heard a strange sound. His ears pricked up to separate it from the howling winds. He squinted through the pouring rain as it lashed against the ship. In the far distance, he could just make out an outline.

He pulled out his spyglass and extended it to take a closer look. Then he caught sight of familiar white sails and a ship painted yellow and black.

He turned and climbed the ladder to reach the helm, where his second mate stood at the wheel.

"Don't worry, Captain. I see her," he said, his voice gruff as he turned the wheel. "We'll steer clear and go around."

"No," Captain Stone barked, taking over the wheel and readjusting the ship's direction. "We're not going around. Not this time."

Mr. Smythe's face contorted as giant drops of rain splattered over it. "I'm sorry, Captain. My ears must be failing me. You do not surely mean to steer into the carnage? There are sirens attacking, sir."

Captain Stone growled. "Exactly."

For the first time in weeks, the seas calmed as the ship sliced through the water, heading straight for its doom.

The men watched in terror as the naval vessel drew larger, towering over them as they grew closer. But it was not the magnitude of the naval frigate that had them cowering with fear. It was the cold stink of death that hung in the air.

The rain slowed to a pitter-patter, and soft peaks of sunlight broke through like spotlights. The wailing winds calmed down, only to be replaced by the sounds of grown men shrieking and crying for their lives.

Captain Stone kept his eyes fixed on the ship, his jaw clenched, and mind set on what he was going to do.

"Captain, with all due respect, you are leading us all to a watery grave,"

Mr. Smythe's voice was hollow.

Captain Stone ignored him and paid no attention to the pleading cries from his crew. He squared his shoulders, scowling at the ugly sight ahead. "Prepare for battle, gents," he barked.

The scrape of metal sliced the air as the men withdrew their swords and handled their flintlock pistols. But none of them were in any state to fight.

In an ordinary battle, they would not last five minutes. And what they were sailing into was no ordinary battle. They entered crimson waters, the shrieks growing louder on their approach. Captain Stone knew it was not going to be an ordinary battle.

He turned to Mr. Smythe. "Ensure my wife is secured in the captain's quarters and guard the door."

His first mate nodded, supposedly relieved that he would not be involved in whatever dastardly plan Captain Stone had in store for the rest of the crew.

When the ship drew level with the frigate, Captain Stone ordered the anchor dropped and his men aboard the enemy ship.

As they climbed the ropes along the sides of the vessel, Captain Stone muttered orders to kill any and every Naval Officer they came into contact with.

"All except the Admiral. Leave him to me," he ordered.

Captain Stone did not know exactly what he would say to Prince Edward should they meet face to face. The last time they were in the same room, he had stolen his bride—for the second time—and his brother declared he was dead to him. For all Captain Stone knew, his brother would try to smite him again.

And perhaps this time, Captain Stone might not fight. Perhaps Prince Edward should put him down like a rabid dog and claim Georgette for his own. But just as quickly as the thought crossed his mind, he shook it away.

Georgette was his wife. He had vowed to protect her. And she already had one cowardly man take his own life. He would not make the same mistake. He would fight until his dying breath to make it up to Georgette.

They met the aftermath of a blood bath. Dismembered bodies lay strewn across the blood-soaked deck of the frigate, and water was gushing into the ship through holes in the lower deck. The ship was sinking.

As expected, the sirens had scattered at the sight of Captain Stone and his crew. They knew who he was, and who Georgette was. They still honored their values.

With no naval officers left to fight, the pirates put the dying men out of their misery. They went about slashing throats or sticking the tips of their swords into chests with a crunch, while Captain Stone searched for his brother.

When he caught sight of a decapitated body slumped against the main steps in admiral uniform, his heart began to hammer in his chest.

Captain Stone looked wildly around him, dreading the moment he would lay eyes on his brother's face. But the moment never came. When he had finally found the head, he sank to his knees and picked it up. The soulless eyes of a stranger stared back at him.

Captain Stone dropped the head and wiped his hands on his jacket with a grimace. He was certain his brother had been promoted to Admiral. He would never have abandoned his men.

That meant his brother was not on this ship. But if that were the case, where was he? Had he already died in combat? Sunk to the bottom of the ocean by some murderous siren?

He looked up at the sound of a quiet whimper. A steel net swung from side to side on the edge of the frigate. Trapped within was a siren with long, mousy blonde hair that fell in waves over her narrow shoulders.

She hissed as her bare skin repeatedly touched the steel, and the sound of sizzling flesh crackled in the air. Captain Stone rose to his feet and approached.

"You," he barked when he reached the siren. "What is your name?"

The siren's cold stare landed on him as she crossed her arms across her chest and tried to keep away from the sides of the net. "Why would you want to know that?" she asked, her face filled with a look of derision as she took him in. "Pirate." She spat the last word like she had uttered a profanity.

Captain Stone unsheathed his sword and pointed it at the net. "If you play nice, I may let you free."

"You will not. You are one of them."

Captain Stone looked around him with his brows raised. Then he laughed. "I assure you; I am nothing like these foolhardy men. Believe me, I mean you no harm. I bear you no ill will for slaughtering them."

The siren stiffened but remained silent. Sensing that he was not going to get anywhere with small talk, Captain Stone cleared his throat and got straight to the point.

"Allow me to introduce myself. I am Captain Stone. My wife is Georgette—"

The siren hissed and her eyes flashed with recognition. Her look of derision had turned into one of curiosity. Good, thought Captain Stone. She had heard of him and Georgette.

"You know what Georgette is, therefore, you know that I am family."

The siren blinked. "I know that Prince Edward is your family. And he is a traitor."

Captain Stone frowned. "Traitor? What have you…" He shook his head. "Do not play games with me, siren."

"Ava," the siren corrected him.

He smiled. It was the first sign that she was beginning to trust him. "You see this brutality? I want nothing of this. My wife and I wish to form an alliance. We are meeting with the Pirate Lords—"

The siren hissed again, and her eyes turned red, like two garnets. "Pirates have been hunting sirens for decades. What makes you think we can form an alliance?"

"Because I am a pirate. And I shall be their king."

Captain Stone held Ava's stare, refusing to back down under her look of disbelief. She scoffed. "You, pirate king? I have heard the whispers. They betray you. They leave you for dead. They steal your treasure and plan to steal your wife."

Captain Stone's hands clenched, and his nails dug deep into his palms as he bit against a retort. He took a breath instead to keep calm.

"I will become Pirate King, and when I do, I wish to have an audience with Isis. To form an alliance. Can you arrange this for me, Ava?" He took great care to soften his tone, and for a moment he thought it worked. The siren's shoulders dropped, and a smile flashed across her face.

"Isis does not make alliances with men."

Captain Stone scowled in disappointment. "She will," he countered. "But you must help me. Tell me what it is she desires most…"

The siren inhaled long and sharp and shut her eyes.

Then a wicked smile crossed her lips. "Bring me the head of the pirate responsible for the most siren deaths."

Captain Stone frowned at that and scrubbed his face with his hand in thought. "How can I possibly know who—"

"They say he is mad. A wild man who will cut off a man's lips and send them to his mother. A man who will plunder an orphanage and even cut the throat of a unicorn if given the chance."

Captain Stone hummed in thought. "There is only one pirate with such a beastly reputation," he murmured to himself. Ava agreed.

"His eyes are black as coal, his skin as white as snow. And his beard smolders with a poisonous smoke, dragging anyone who draws near to Hades in the Underworld."

Captain Stone stopped pacing and locked eyes with the siren. They both uttered his name in unison.

"Blackbeard."

When his men were done ensuring that every man on the frigate was dead, Captain Stone cut the net, freeing Ava from her prison. She rubbed the red burns on her body and wriggled to the edge of the ship.

"Bring me the head of Blackbeard, and you shall have your meeting with Isis."

"Does it have to be the head?" he asked, thinking he'd rather not drag something so heavy across the seas.

"Isis wants to look into the dead eyes of the pirate responsible for so many of her daughter's deaths."

Captain Stone raised a finger. "Then I shall cut out his eyes," he suggested. "I'll even put them in a nice box for you."

Killing Blackbeard was going to be as easy as wrestling a lion with bare hands. If he could fool Isis with a pair of eyes, then he could—

The siren's glare stopped his thoughts in their tracks. "The head, or there is no alliance."

Captain Stone sighed, then he nodded. "Fine."

"Until we meet again, Captain Stone," she said, lifting herself up on the edge of the ship. Captain Stone saluted her before she thrust herself over and into the sea.

He turned smiling, but his smile dropped when he came face to face with Georgette. She stood strong and resolute with her hands on her hips—a stance he knew meant he was in for a tongue-lashing.

"What in the *blazes* have you agreed to?" she asked, staring him down with fury. Captain Stone could not suppress the glimmer of joy he felt, seeing the spark back in her eyes. She needed to be hard if she was to survive this world. He resisted the urge to grab and kiss her right there on the deck and walked past her instead.

"We are going to the Pirate Lord meeting, as planned. I shall kill Blackbeard, become Pirate King, and we will form an alliance with Isis. Then, this brutal war will be over."

"How can you be so foolish?" Georgette asked, following him as he walked amongst the dead bodies. "Blackbeard? You *know* what he is capable of, you know what he will do to you."

Captain Stone patted his jacket, over the place where he'd kept the vial of Georgette's tears. "I have protection, thanks to you."

Georgette looked at his jacket and her eyes stretched wide with understanding. Then she frowned again. "It won't work if you've lost your head, and he will surely cut it off—"

"Not unless I cut his off first!" Captain Stone interrupted her, forcing a smile. Her mouth did not so much as twitch.

"Don't do this." She was almost pleading now. "I will not stand by and watch you put yourself on a suicide mission. There must be another way."

Captain Stone ignored the sea of stares from his crew and glared at Georgette. He wished she could understand.

"Don't you see? I'm doing this for *you*. For *us*. I will do anything to keep you from harm."

He tried to take her arm, but she shrugged it away. "No. You're doing this for your own pride! We could run away. Let's take the ship and just go. Go to the Grecian islands… or East! As far as the horizon will take us!"

She reached for Captain Stone's hand and squeezed, but he gritted his teeth. "I cannot run from this war. Neither can you. Whether we like it or not, our fates are entwined in this. Would you let your sisters be picked off one by one until there is not one left?"

He pulled on her hand and led her to the edge of the ship, then pointed out at one of the markers in the distance. "Do you really want this to continue?"

Georgette looked out at the dead siren pinned to the small boat bobbing in the distance. Then she turned and looked into his eyes. "I cannot bear to see you die. Not again. Do not do this," she begged, her voice soft and eyes misty.

Captain Stone gripped her waist and pulled her to him, enveloping her body with his arms.

Then he kissed her. He allowed all of his stifled emotions to flow free in the form of tears as he held her body firm against him. Her lips were buttery and smooth, and the familiar taste of her soothed his inner demons.

But she put her hands between them and pushed back against his chest, ripping their mouths apart. "I cannot stop you, I know that," she whispered. "And there is something I must do. So, for now, we must part ways."

Captain Stone grabbed her by the arm as her words registered. A sudden panic descended on him. "What do you mean? I am not leaving you."

"I cannot bear the pain, Manny," she said, her voice cracking as she caressed his stubbled cheek. "I must speak to Isis. There are too many questions. Perhaps if I could find some closure, I shall be at peace."

Captain Stone clutched her tight. "Then I shall go with you. You know that I wish to speak to Isis. Perhaps you can—"

Georgette had turned to the ocean. A soft wind blew back the flyaway hairs from her face. "I can hear my sisters. For so long I blocked them out, but now it's a constant chatter. They say if you do not bring Blackbeard's head, she will give you the same hospitality as the last time you walked on her island unannounced."

Captain Stone rubbed his chest at the memory of Isis's claws ripping through his chest.

Defeated by her revelation, he kissed Georgette again. "Isis will not harm you. Perhaps this is best after all," he conceded. Georgette nodded, and they pressed their foreheads together with two heavy sighs.

"I am sorry, my love," Captain whispered, his eyes prickling. "For my part in all of your suffering."

Georgette lifted her chin to place a tender kiss on his lips, then she pressed his jacket where her vial of tears sat nestled in his pocket. "You will make it up to me by staying alive and coming back."

A single tear slid down Captain Stone's face as they broke apart. "I promise. Please be careful. I will tear the four corners of this world down if you are brought to harm."

Georgette smirked and the surrounding men gasped as she climbed over the edge of the ship. "For what it's worth… You would have made a wonderful father."

The words struck Captain Stone right through the heart. In spite of what he knew she was, he watched in horror as his wife jumped into the water with a splash. Every man on the ship, including him, ran to the edge of the ship. There were mutters of confusion until a long silver fin emerged from the waters. Georgette's face soon followed, beaming a smile that shone up at them like the noonday sun.

It was her first proper smile in weeks, but Captain Stone could not summon one in return. He watched her go with dread, praying feverishly to the same gods he had cursed that he would find her again. By that time, he hoped, this wretched war would be over.

PRINCE EDWARD

A door creaked open, and Prince Edward shot up from the bed, his heart racing. He hurried to the bars of his cell, eager to catch a glimpse of the person entering his cell block. Praying it was Serena.

To his relief, it was. She came toward his cell, followed by two Triton guards. One of them had a ring of keys tied to his belt, and they jingled as he strode forward.

"Edward, Prince of England, we hereby drop the charges against you. On order of Poseidon, God and King of the Sea, you will reside within Atlantis with Princess Serena for two weeks. During this time, you will be scrutinized. If at any point we deem this relationship to be inauthentic, you will both be executed."

Prince Edward swallowed as the guard without keys read out from a scroll.

Meanwhile, the guard with the keys slotted one into the lock and opened the door with a squeal.

Serena wasted no time. She ran to him, threw her arms around his neck, and pressed her body to his chest. "Come, my love. Let us not tarry a moment longer in this dreadful place."

She grabbed his hand and ran, dragging Prince Edward along. They raced down the halls of the palace and down the marble steps outside. Prince Edward's heartbeat thundered like the hooves of a thousand horses on a stampede. When they finally made it to a modest home, Serena pushed him inside and shut the door.

"What did they mean back there?" he asked, out of breath. Serena turned to him with a strange look that she masked quickly under a devilish grin.

"I am so happy. We are alone at last. I haven't stopped thinking about what I would do to you as soon as I got you out of that cell…" she said, her voice dripping with lust.

Prince Edward stiffened as he watched her slink over to the large porcelain bath in the corner. Two silver faucets stuck out from the wall. She turned one and a gush of steaming water poured out.

Prince Edward watched the water fill the tub.

Then his eyes nearly shot out of their sockets as Serena began to undress right before him.

"Do not pay any attention to my father's warnings. He knows we are devoted to each other. Not that we could possibly hide it if we were pretending." Her silky gown dropped and pooled at her feet. Prince Edward licked his lips as he drank in the sight of her.

His gaze followed the outline of her long slender legs and every curve of her body. Dimpled hips, a tiny waist, and a pair of petite, round breasts covered by waves of fiery red hair. She was like a living piece of art. A Grecian goddess. He had to be the luckiest man in the four corners of the globe to behold such beauty.

His mouth went dry as he took in her exquisite naked form.

He forcefully reminded himself that Serena was a siren, with the ability to turn into a vicious monster with claws and pointed teeth. He had almost forgotten that she possessed the strength to tear him limb from limb. Almost.

He swallowed hard.

"What did they mean by scrutinized?"

Serena's smile faded for a moment but then she giggled as she twirled her hair. "There are eyes and ears in every square inch of Atlantis. We are being watched right now…" She strutted up to him, prompting her squeezable breasts to bounce. He glanced at them before he forced his gaze to meet her shining eyes. Her hand found his chest and her breath tickled his neck as she leaned in to whisper in his ear.

"You must play along if you wish to live."

The next moment, her other hand slid roughly into his pants. His brain grew foggy as a rush of pleasure flooded his body and all of his blood traveled south.

"You are bound to me, my Prince," she moaned into his ear as she stroked his growing length. He began to pant, utterly under her control. He shut his eyes and let out a shuddering breath. "In our world, a binding ritual is a marriage. Ours is a union that cannot be broken, even by death."

Serena started to talk about the history of her people, but the words did not reach Prince Edward's mind. He moaned in a mixture of horror and delight as she removed his shirt and slid her hand down his torso. His muscles contracted under her touch, and he grew stiff and uncomfortably tense in his nether regions.

Soon, they were both naked. He opened his eyes and greedily took in the sight of Serena's beautiful form once more. Her hand remained on his manhood, and it throbbed under her advances. She knew what she was doing, and each movement was unabashed and heady. She pressed her hot lips to his pectorals and swirled her tongue over his abs. He fisted her long hair and found great delight in the feel of her silken strands in his clutches.

Serena kissed her way back up to his neck and lifted her knee to rest on his hip bone. The heat of her core warmed him, but a horrible thought took hold.

He grabbed her gently by the upper arms. "Stop," he urged, forcing her to meet his hard stare. Her lashes fluttered like the wings of a butterfly, and she pouted. Her lips were glistening and plump, begging to be claimed.

There was no way he could hide his desire for her. The proof was still nestled in her hand.

"Where I am from, sex is a sacred act. Something not to be witnessed. I cannot do this knowing that we are being watched."

Serena looked at him like he had sprouted two more heads and turned into a Hydra. "You cannot be serious," she whispered, releasing him, and backing away. "You will reject me because you are... Shy?"

Prince Edward ached for release as he stood, erect and throbbing. In the absence of Serena's warmth, he was cold. It would have been so easy to pick her up and claim the beautiful siren.

But it would be wrong. It would be a carnal, base act, and a prince was raised to respect a woman and her purity. "I will not defile you. Not like this. Not here," he said, covering himself up with his hands.

To his surprise, Serena's cheeks reddened for a moment, and she raised a hand to her face as though she had just been slapped. But then she recovered herself and turned off the water. "As you wish, my Prince. But I insist you join me in the bath. I need to be close to you, my love."

She placed emphasis on the last two words and gave Prince Edward a look of warning. He understood. They needed to give their invisible audience a show. Besides, Prince Edward was desperate for a bath after a day of sparring and laying in a cell.

He gave a grim nod, as though about to set forth and enter battle.

But this was an entirely different arena. One which tested every inch of his self-control.

He climbed into the warm bath and settled with his legs resting on the sides. Serena nestled between his knees and wriggled down until her bare back rested on his body. She sighed, contended, her dark lashes resting on her cheeks as she arched her neck and let her head fall onto his shoulder. The water rose to the soft peaks of her breasts and drops of water clung to her skin like diamonds.

"At least wrap me up in your arms, my love. I'm

cold," she said, wriggling her bottom. A forbidden flush of excitement ran through Prince Edward's body.

He had never bathed with a woman before. But he'd spent many nights picturing this very moment with his fiancée, Georgette.

He swallowed against the lump in his throat as Serena's long, red hair turned blonde, and her face morphed into Georgette's.

Without hesitation, he folded his arms across her body, holding her like she was a doll. Then without thinking, he placed a kiss atop her head.

"I love you so much, and I promise I will not allow anything bad to happen to you again," he murmured with emotion.

The woman in his arms stiffened a moment, then melted against his body with a delighted sigh. "Oh, my Prince," she said, snapping Prince Edward out of his illusion. Guilt nipped at his insides as Serena came back into view. She looked up at him with misty eyes. "I love you too."

SERENA

Serena's gaze lingered on the sleeping prince in her bed, his chest moving up and down in a peaceful rhythm. The sheets only came up to his stomach, allowing her to examine the sculpted muscles of his torso. She thought about dragging her finger over each line of his exposed skin but hesitated.

She shifted in bed, propping herself up with an arm to watch him properly. Her heart was conflicted. She knew that binding herself to him had come at a cost.

Her father thought she was foolish to give up her immortality for a human, but Prince Edward was no mere mortal. Neither was he a feeble man.

He was the only soul to show her a shred of compassion, even with the knowledge of what she could do to him.

He had taken it upon himself to rescue her from certain doom, and she had watched him day after day as he tirelessly combed the seas in search of his beloved Georgette.

He raced against time to rescue his beloved from the wicked pirate, but when he found her, she had already surrendered her heart to her captor.

Serena's hands trembled as she fought to contain her racing heart. She knew she would never be Georgette, that much was certain. But a small part of her wanted the prince to look at her with the same love he had for his former flame.

A sigh escaped her lips as she gently placed a hand on his forearm. He slept on, unaware of her presence.

His brown hair grazed his forehead, and his full lips were slightly parted. He looked so innocent; it melted her heart.

Her stomach flipped at the memory of his lips on hers during the binding ceremony and she swallowed to still her racing heart.

Since the ceremony, she had sensed a change. Her senses had dulled to a thick silence that wrapped her in a protective cocoon, blocking out the distant cries of her sisters. It was both a blessing and a curse. After so long of trying to keep out their voices, it was finally a welcome reprieve from the relentless noise. But it also left a fearful emptiness in her heart—she could no longer hear her sisters.

She could not hear her brothers either, no longer able to keep track of the chatter amongst them in Atlantis.

She had lied to the prince, convincing him that she was committed to ending the war, but now they were bound, her truest desire could be fulfilled without leaving her home.

Prince Edward was determined to gain Poseidon's blessing and travel to England. With every breath, he shared his ideas on ways to persuade King George and his Queen of their love—no matter how lofty or inane the task was—so that the English royals gave their blessing. Then they could command peace between their two worlds, according to Edward's noble plan. She pretended to go along with it, offering gentle words of encouragement. The prince had believed her, but she knew that if her true form were to be uncovered by the King, the consequences were too severe for her to consider.

Consequently, Serena did not want to abandon Atlantis. She had no interest in rushing into the chaos of a war that seemed to be escalating by the day. No. Her heart yearned for more time with the prince. She hoped he would fall for her affections, as it would make her next move easier.

Even though there was no one watching them inside

her quarters, her brothers did possess the ability to listen to their every word. Atlanteans were known for eavesdropping. The currency of the underwater city was not of gold and silver, but secrets. If they discovered that Prince Edward did not truly love Serena, they would destroy him, ignoring the sacred laws that forbade it.

Another secret she was determined to hold close to her chest was that she had hoped the prince might bed her if he believed they were being watched. She thought he would fear for his life, but she could not have been more wrong about that.

It was not his life he feared for, it was her purity.

Serena was not entirely sure whether she was touched or frustrated by his nobility.

She shifted slightly, a spark of electricity running through her body as she remembered how the prince had held her close in the bath—their naked bodies pressed together in the most delightful way.

He had said "I love you", but she could not be sure if he had meant it.

She settled back on the bed and closed her eyes.

As she drifted off to sleep, Serena dreamed of the prince, his strong arms wrapped around her, their bodies entwined in a passionate embrace. His lips were on her neck, kissing softly and sending shivers down her spine. He trailed his hands down her back as they moved together in perfect harmony. His touch was gentle and caring, exploring every inch of her body as if he was learning all its curves and contours.

The warmth of his skin against hers filled her with pleasure and she shivered under the vibrations of his deep voice as he growled, "You belong to me now."

But the dream quickly turned into a nightmare, as she found herself surrounded by the Tritons of Atlantis. Her brothers were whispering, their voices echoing in her mind, taunting her with their secrets. That she did not belong, she would never belong, and that her foolish wish to become a mother made her weak and pathetic.

They continued to spit toxic sentiments at her as they pressed in, crushing her from all sides.

Serena tried to fight them off, to push them away, but they only grew closer, their scaled skin brushing against hers as they bared their teeth, pointed like fangs.

Suddenly, a hand squeezed her shoulder, and she turned to see the prince standing there, a look of repulsion on his face.

"You filthy little siren, I would never breed with you."

Serena's heart panged and she struggled to swallow against the hard lump in her throat.

"Serena, wake up!" Prince Edward said urgently, shaking her.

She opened her eyes, realizing it had all been a

dream. But she could still feel the lingering touch of the Tritons, and she shuddered.

"What is it?" she asked, sitting up in bed.

She placed a hand over her racing heart and looked at the prince, who was wide awake now. His big eyes were creased in the corners as he looked at her with concern. "You were whimpering, and your skin is exceedingly hot. Are you well, my lady?"

Serena stared at the prince for a moment. She was not used to being called a lady.

Then she nodded, grateful for his concern. "Yes, I'm fine. It was only a bad dream."

He gave her a small smile, reaching over to brush a strand of hair from her face. "I'm here for you, always."

Serena's heart swelled at his words, wondering if they were just empty platitudes or if he truly meant them. She decided to test the waters and leaned in to give him a soft kiss on the lips.

She was shocked at the intensity of his response, her heart pounding wildly as he tangled his hands in her hair and their lips locked. His body pressed against hers, and desire coursed through her veins like liquid fire. She clung to him as he explored her with passionate fervor until their breaths came in short gasps and shuddering sighs. Breaking apart for air was like sweet torture.

Prince Edward rested his clammy forehead against Serena's.

"Serena, I'm so sorry. You must have me under a spell. This is quite unlike me."

Serena pulled back to look in his eyes. "I assure you, my Prince, there is no spell. But I do believe the binding has brought us closer. Here."

She picked up his hand and placed it over her pounding heart, then she rested her palm over his.

"Our hearts are in sync."

Prince Edward's eyes widened at her words, and he looked down at their joined hands. His fingers flexed against her skin, feeling the rapid thump of her heartbeat under his touch.

He leaned in and placed a gentle kiss on her temple, wrapping his arms around her in a warm embrace. "What have you done to me, my beautiful siren bride?" he whispered.

Serena's eyes filled with tears at his words, and she clung to him, savoring the moment.

They stayed that way for a while, lost in the magic of their bond.

Before long, they would earn Poseidon's blessing and have to follow through with Edward's plan. She shut her eyes tight and made a silent vow to cherish every moment they had left before they had to leave Atlantis.

PRINCE EDWARD

The following two weeks were a whirlwind of discovery for Prince Edward. Serena took him all around the mysterious kingdom under the sea, introducing him to all kinds of magical creatures and sights he had never seen before. As they traveled, he became more entranced by her beauty, captivated by her stories, and enchanted by her carefree spirit.

Along their journey, they stopped often to admire the peculiar creatures. Brightly-colored birds sang enchanting melodies from atop coral beds, and schools of rainbow fish flit across the surrounding waters along the city's edge. The prince marveled at the beauty of this strange new world.

As the days continued on, Prince Edward began to trust Serena. So, he told her about his life back home in

England. She listened intently as he opened up about his childhood— growing up in a castle surrounded by bustling courtiers, his years spent in military training, his desire to one day take on a role as a leader for his people. He told her everything, except for two important details; the fact that he had a brother and the tragedy of losing Georgette.

He discovered that even though he truly wanted to believe they were dead to him, he could not merely switch off his feelings. Every time he thought about the betrayal of his older brother, fury blazed in his chest. And when his mind strayed to Georgette and her deception, anguish took hold of him.

It was far easier to avoid the topic altogether.

Serena responded with stories from her own life as Poseidon's youngest daughter. How she had grown accustomed to spending her days exploring the depths with her brothers or tending to her garden of rare plants from all corners of the seas.

"Why were you separated from your sisters? Growing up as the only woman in Atlantis must have had its challenges," Prince Edward mused. He brushed a thumb over one of the sea plants growing in her garden. The blood-red leaves had a silky soft texture, but the flowers were pure white, ball-shaped needles.

He glanced at Serena. She was bent over, tending to a

weed. The red tresses of her hair covered her face but the cheeky way her bottom wriggled made him imagine her with a smile on her face.

She straightened with a toss of her hair and flashed him a charming grin. "It wasn't so bad if I am honest… Having experienced both, I believe I'd rather be in the company of men," she said with a wink. "My sisters would flood the waters with their sensational gossip and enjoyed playing with sailors before dragging them to their doom. This is what they consider sport." She waved a hand aside as if to bat the thought away.

"The Tritons are more interested in testing ability and strength… The strongest in an arm-wrestling competition, the fastest in the water, reciting all forty-two sonnets of Atlantean folklore."

She stopped to chuckle to herself, staring at the ground with a faraway look.

"I won that one, by the way. I love to read. Ajax taught me in secret." She met Prince Edward's gaze with a blush. "I am sharing too much, I am sorry."

Prince Edward shook his head and took her hands. "You could talk to me for a thousand years, and it would still not be enough."

Serena hitched a breath, her hands tensing in his grip. Prince Edward refused to let go.

She had a soothing energy that took away his pain

and terrible thoughts. "Why do the Tritons and Sirens live apart?" he asked.

Serena stretched her arms back and folded them, lifting her shoulders in an awkward way. The flush of her cheeks deepened as she averted her eyes.

"That is a simple question with a complicated answer. I am not sure I am permitted to offer it. Not here."

She bit her lip and looked around them. Prince Edward noticed the Tritons walking afar off had stopped, their shoulders tense and muscles flexed.

"I did not mean to cause you any discomfort, my lady. You must forgive my inquisitive mind. Your world is very different from mine. I am only eager to learn all I can."

Serena beamed at him. "Come, my Prince." She held out a hand. "Let me show you the library. It holds all of our history."

The library was deep inside the palace. It reminded Prince Edward of the Sistine Chapel. The vaulted ceilings were covered with paintings of sirens swimming amongst dolphins and fish, while warrior-like men stood with spears around the temple of Poseidon. The frescoes were so lifelike, it appeared that the eyes of Poseidon on his throne followed Prince Edward everywhere he went. "It is as though Michelangelo was here," he mused aloud.

Serena hummed in agreement. "Yes, my father

inquired who worked on a Venetian palace and commissioned him to create this mural for him."

Prince Edward dragged a hand through his hair with a gasp. "Goodness, Michelangelo *was* here."

Serena hummed as she ran her fingertip along the spines of a row of books. "He may be the last human to enter Atlantis before you, my Prince," she said, smiling to herself. She then made a sound of victory and pulled out a thick, leather-bound book.

"This is my favorite story," she said.

Prince Edward took the book and carefully thumbed through the pages while Serena recounted it. "Thetis was a beautiful goddess. A siren. She was in love with both Zeus and Poseidon. But a prophecy turned their hearts against her, and she was thrust out. Shunned because it was said she would bear a son more powerful than even the gods."

Prince Edward looked at the black-and-white pictures of sea creatures he had recently seen. Then he met Serena's thoughtful stare. "She finally found true love in a human named Peleus." Her eyes dipped to his mouth. "They adored one another. He did not care about such prophecy, for he was both humble and utterly charmed by her." She moved closer until her chest pressed against the book. Prince Edward swallowed nervously as he watched her lick her lips.

"She was immortal, so it couldn't last forever. They separated eventually, and her son did grow up to be the strongest warrior in all the lands—Achilles."

Prince Edward closed the book and backed away clearing his throat. "That is your favorite tale? It has a tragic ending." He scratched his head. "I have heard of Achilles. He died in battle."

Serena crossed her arms. "All mortals die someday." Then she took a breath and reached for his hands. "Which is why we must make the most of the days we have left."

Prince Edward's stomach tightened, and he looked deep into Serena's eyes while he caressed her cheek. "You shall live forever, my lady. There is no need to say we."

When Serena's smile dropped, a sense of dread pulsed through Prince Edward. He frowned. "My lady?" he asked, cupping her face with both hands now. "What is it? I see pain in your eyes."

Serena shook her head, but a tear leaked out and wet his palm. "I have no regrets. I could not watch you hang. You saved my life; I owed you a debt."

Prince Edward held his breath as he processed her words. Then everything fell into place. His heart pounded like the beat of war drums in his ears.

"The binding… After it happened… I was healed of

all pain and weakness. I feel stronger than ever. Different."

Serena's hands found his chest. "And I am weaker. I no longer hear my brothers or sisters. I can no longer sense the emotions of creatures."

Her voice wavered. "I am mortal now."

Prince Edward wrapped her up in his arms in a bone-crushing hug as a flood of guilt ripped through his soul. The siren's sacrifice was far greater than he could have comprehended. And she had done it because he stopped his men from brutally slaughtering her. It was unthinkable.

"You owed me no such debt, and you should not have done the ritual. I would have…"

"Died," she finished, pulling back. Her eyes flashed. "You would have been tossed from the castle walls and fallen until the rope grew taut and snapped your beautiful neck. Then your body would be left there to decay until the stench of your corpse grew too much for my father. Then he'd cast you away for the sharks."

Her face turned magenta as she continued. "That was your fate had I not intervened. And I am glad I did. Because you are here now, alive. Every glimpse of your face is a sweet reminder that it was worth it. If I had to go back and do it all again, I would. In a heartbeat. Do not pity me, my Prince."

Her words wrapped around Prince Edward's heart and gripped it until it bled. "My sweet Serena. I do not know how to repay you, but I vow to you now." He went down on both knees and looked up at her imploringly. "I shall spend the rest of my days thinking of ways to make it up to you."

Serena tugged on his hands, prompting him to stand again. "You can start by kissing me," she said as she clung to his shirt.

Without hesitation, Prince Edward lifted her body, squeezing her waist, then claimed her lips with his own. He held her tight, embracing the rush of delight shooting through his veins.

Serena's kiss flooded him with pleasure until he grew dizzy. Her hands roamed his chest and neck while he moaned into the kiss.

In the back of his mind, he knew this was all an act. Had she not told him that they were being watched?

Perhaps he was being overly cautious, and the siren truly had feelings for him. The way his body reacted to her now, he seemed to be developing feelings of his own.

The carnal side of his brain lit up with all sorts of forbidden scenarios. He wanted her. He yearned to have all of her. And he knew she would gladly offer herself to him.

But Prince Edward considered himself an honorable man. A gentleman.

Though the way he was kissing this siren in the middle of a public place was far from gentlemanly. When she unbuckled his breeches, grasping for him, he lurched back, ripping their mouths apart. He gasped, willing his brain to stop spinning as he recovered himself.

"I cannot do this," he whispered.

Serena's face was a look of a thousand tragedies, and it almost broke Prince Edward to see it. "Have you forgotten that we are under scrutiny?" she whispered, her eyes darting around them. They were alone in the library, surrounded by nothing but rows and rows of tall bookshelves.

Prince Edward adjusted himself and fasted his belt again. "Serena, my lady." He caressed her cheek, so soft under his calloused fingertips. "I have not forgotten. That is why I cannot do this. Not here. Not now."

Serena huffed, her cheeks reddening. "Then let us go back to our quarters," she said.

When they returned to her home, the door had barely shut before Serena's arms were flung around Prince Edward's neck once more.

He grunted as he gripped her delicious hips, grinding against her. He ached to rip her dress from her and claim her.

The desire rose to new heights as he walked her back to the bed. Kissing Serena was a healing balm to all of his wounds. He wished they could stay in Atlantis and hide from all of the worlds' problems for eternity.

He froze again when his values caught up to him. He let go of Serena's hips and stepped back. "I can't dishonor you, no matter how much I want to."

Serena snorted. "Dishonor?" She pushed him onto the bed and lifted a palm in the air. Prince Edward traced the silver line etched into it, then held out his own. They clasped hands, lacing their fingers together. "You are bound to me, my Prince. To deny me now would be the greatest dishonor."

She crawled into his lap, and he reached up to caress her back while they kissed. He wrapped his arms around her and pulled her in, holding her close. "I'm sorry. I'm so, so sorry," he said, stroking her hair. "If we do this now, it would be out of lust. For purely selfish reasons. Because you make me feel… Renewed."

Serena pulled back to glare at him. "I have no qualms over being used, my Prince. Be selfish." She leaned in to kiss him again, but Prince Edward stopped her by clutching her upper arms. "Someday, I do believe I shall ruin you. In the very best way." He smirked. "When the time is right, I will devour every inch of your flesh until you are crying out to all of the gods."

Serena's chest rose and fell at a rapid rate and her eyes darkened with anticipation. "And when will the time be right?"

Prince Edward held his breath as he thought on it. If he were to be honest, it would be when he finally got Georgette's face out of his head. He could never tell Serena, but every time her mouth touched his, it was Georgette's image that entered his mind.

Every time he lay in bed and closed his eyes, he pictured Georgette lying next to him.

He could not in good conscience do anything while his heart still beat for another woman. But he could not bring himself to confess that darkest truth to Serena. She watched him, waiting for a response. He kissed her on the cheek and squeezed her hand. "You will know when. I promise."

Days rolled by as they explored Atlantis and continued to get to know each other. Serena did not make any other advances, much to Prince Edward's relief. His self-control was hanging by a thread. If she so much as tried to kiss him one last time, he was certain his body would take over and go wild.

He grew comfortable having her hand in his. As time went on, the picture of Georgette grew dim in his mind. He almost forgot what she looked like. Almost.

The two shared secrets that neither had ever confided

in another before, relishing each other's company as they nestled side by side in bed each night.

Finally, the day came for them to leave Atlantis, and the two walked along the edge of the city hand in hand, admiring its beauty one last time. All manner of sea life swam along, supposedly unaware of their existence.

"It's almost as if I'm dreaming," Prince Edward said, looking out at the vastness of the ocean before them. "This place is like no other on Earth. It aches to say goodbye."

Serena nodded sadly, squeezing his hand in agreement. "I wish we could stay here forever."

They returned to the temple of Poseidon, and Prince Edward was surprised at how heavy his heart was as they walked up the stone steps.

As they stepped inside the temple, they clasped their hands tightly together. When they reached Poseidon's throne, they bowed, and the god looked down upon them with approval.

"It appears your courtship has been a success," Poseidon declared in his deep voice, a faint hint of amusement in his eyes. He nodded to Prince Edward, who was uneasy.

The all-powerful king of the sea had not been kind at their last meeting. He knew Poseidon would not hesitate to smite him if he made one wrong move.

Serena's colorful description of what would happen to him flashed before his mind.

The god turned to him and inclined his head, offering a sign of respect.

"I have been observing you, Edward. And you do possess royal blood after all. The respect and care you have shown to my youngest daughter are most noble. I daresay it would be hard to find men and gods alike who can resist her the way you have."

Prince Edward bowed to hide the flush of heat rising to his face. He was grateful the god had mistaken his actions for restraint. "I am humbled by your words, King Poseidon. My only wish is to keep Serena safe and make her an honest woman."

Serena squeezed Prince Edward's hand again and he glanced up at her beaming smile. Poseidon cleared his throat and clapped with finality.

"Then you have my blessing. It is time for you to travel to England and complete your mission: Marry and end this bloody war once and for all."

Prince Edward nodded solemnly, amazed that Lord Poseidon had fallen for their ruse. They bowed again before Serena's father, then turned to leave the temple.

As they took the long walk outside of the city gates, scores of Tritons lined the paths, staring. Serena did not so much as glance at a single one of them, which Prince

Edward thought odd, considering these warriors were her brothers.

But in the time they had shared together, she rarely spoke of them. He wondered if there was not much to say, or if she was merely trying to avoid the topic, knowing that every word they shared was under scrutiny.

Soon, his fears gave way to the new problem at hand. A rush of concern flooded his body as they reached the place where they had entered this magical world two weeks ago.

"Are we to reach the surface using the same method that brought us here?" he asked, trying to sound polite and not worried.

He did not fancy the idea of being pulled up to the surface of the sea with Serena's mouth clamped over his.

Serena laughed. "Do not fear, my Prince. You can breathe under water now."

Prince Edward gasped, but before he could press Serena for more information, she yanked on his hand and dragged him through the sponge-like barrier and into the water.

After several long seconds of nothingness, Prince Edward stumbled into the ice-cold watery depth and gasped again.

He expected to choke as the water filled his mouth, but instead, it was cool and crisp. Like sea air on a fresh

December morning. He took a deep breath, letting the new sensation flood his mind with energy.

Serena's hair flowed around her like flames as she grinned at him, her eyes sparkling. "Take my hand," she said, and the words entered Prince Edward's mind.

He was amazed and a little terrified.

Prince Edward followed her lead with haste, the thrill of the unknown making his heart race. It beat faster still when he noticed the deep blue darkness of the ocean giving way to a dazzling array of colors. Blues, greens, and purples sparkled in the light above like a thousand stars, and he was hurtling toward it.

Serena grabbed his hand with an iron grip and pulled him up. He could see the entire ocean now —its beauty and power humbling him as they swam faster and faster up to the surface.

Finally, after what seemed like an eternity, Serena broke through to the air above them with a triumphant cry, dragging Prince Edward along behind her. He gasped for breath as they reached land again, dizzy from the rush of gaseous oxygen in his lungs.

It had been weeks since cold air had slapped his cheeks, and the exhilaration of their journey flooded his body with excitement.

He looked around them. It was night, and there was dark water as far as the eye could see, except for the beach to his right. He recognized the deserted port immediately. It had been the very place he had come to summon Serena weeks ago.

Though only a short time had passed, Prince Edward had returned a changed man.

They stepped onto the shore together, feet sinking into damp sand that glittered in the moonlight. Serena held out her hand and he took it without hesitation—relieved and amazed to feel the soft grains of sand beneath his feet again. He was home.

"I never thought Atlantis was real. I am honored to have been there. Thank you, Serena," he whispered as they looked out toward the horizon together.

He smiled down at her in awe at what she had done for them both—not just for him alone—and silently thanked Lord Poseidon in prayer for offering his blessing. He knew the hardest part of their plan was done.

Serena laughed. "Let us go and fulfill our mission."

Prince Edward nodded, his heart thumping with anticipation. He knew that their journey ahead would be fraught with danger, but he was ready to face whatever obstacles came their way. If they could fool Poseidon, then they could easily convince his parents of their love.

As they walked away from the beach and toward the town of Port Harbor, the cool night air kissing their skin,

Prince Edward had a sense of elation he had never known before.

He was not sure if it was the siren blood running through his veins, or having Serena's warm hand in his, but he was fired up and filled with hope—hope that their plan could work after all.

They would put an end to the war, and he would find peace and come to love Serena.

They walked through the deserted streets of the town, their footsteps echoing in the silence. The moon was high in the sky now, casting an ethereal glow on everything around them.

The once-picturesque landscape was unrecognizable —mangled carriages were strewn across the road, and rows of homes had been reduced to rubble. Fear gripped their hearts as they surveyed the disaster. A haunting silence had taken hold of the streets.

Prince Edward and Serena exchanged terse glances, then she looked behind him, and her beautiful mouth opened in a scream.

Her shriek nearly split his eardrums. He spun around in as much fear as pain.

"This has gone too far," she whispered. "They are vile, heartless monsters."

Edward's gaze landed on the line of wooden poles as tall as buildings, each one with a siren tied to it, slumped over their beautiful tails, and drenched in blood. The sight pierced Edward's heart and he reached for Serena's hand, wondering now how he could even look his father in the eye knowing full well that he was behind all of this madness.

They needed to act fast.

A sound broke the silence. Thunderous footsteps. Coming closer and closer. Serena cried out in shock.

Prince Edward instinctively reached for his knife, but a strong hand clamped over his mouth with a cloth and Serena's screams grew muffled. His vision faded to black, and his knees buckled. Then he fell into darkness.

GEORGETTE

Georgette savored the feeling of her sleek, long tail propelling her through the water as she sped through the sea. She was one with the ocean. Connected to it and its depths in a way she hadn't yet fully grasped. She spread her arms out like wings, slicing through the water in graceful arcs as her tailfin moved her forward in an undulating motion.

Being in siren form was the perfect escape from all of the crushing pain that had been weighing her down. As she darted through the water, scattering schools of fish in her wake, her body lit up with an energy that urged her to move faster.

The ocean seemed to come alive with her presence—the vibrations of the sea in her ears like a collective heartbeat, and the vibrant colors of the coral and sea life blurring in magical swirls as she moved with more urgency.

The salty mist of the waves against her skin rejuvenated her soul, and the shimmer of the sun on the surface of the water warmed her heart.

She took in the vastness of the horizon in all directions and all of her worries were a million miles away.

Georgette never wanted the feeling to end. Out here in the ocean, she answered to no one. She was powerful and free.

Even though there was a brutal war raging on, Georgette felt safe. Underwater, nothing could stop her. And if an enemy happened to cross her path, she was confident she could destroy them with her bare hands.

Captain Stone could not understand. He seemed to think physical healing was enough for her to move on from her grief, but he couldn't fathom the depth of what she suffered inside.

Deep, invisible scars of pain were etched into her very soul, and she was not sure they would ever truly heal. In her siren form, she had found a spark of something else—hope. It washed over and through her with the water, encouraging her to reach out and find the strength to fight for a better life. Even against the most daunting odds, this possibility glimmered like a beacon in her soul.

The island that she had been searching for came into view. Imerta. The magical place her mother Isis dwelled. A mixture of anxiety and excitement swirled in Georgette's chest as she approached, unsure of what to expect when she arrived.

The closer she got to Imerta, the more intense the energy around her seemed to become. It was as if every inch of water in the ocean was radiating with an unseen power. Her body trembled with anticipation.

When she finally reached shore, her tail became a pair of pale, slender legs again. She stepped onto the beach, and it was like stepping into another world entirely; lush greenery lined the coast of white sand beaches; exotic flowers bloomed in the air, and the most beautiful colors of blues and greens danced along the horizon.

There, standing at the edge of the beach, was Isis—her mother. Her long, ice-blue dress glittered on her tall form in the sunshine, and waves of golden tresses fell freely to her waist. Georgette's heart squeezed.

She stood there, frozen and conflicted. She was not sure whether to lash out and scream at the woman for the despicable thing she had done to the man she loved or to crumble in her arms and sob, mourning the years she had lived without a mother.

Isis walked toward her with a proud smile on her face. Georgette watched her wave an arm in an elegant gesture, and a sparkle of silver dust filled the air around them. Suddenly, Georgette found herself in a red gown that clung to her naked form like a second skin.

Isis reached out to hug her, but Georgette pulled away sharply, slightly taken aback by this warm welcome.

Her mother regarded her with an amused expression, apparently unfazed by her rejection. "My dear Georgette. Come, let us retire to my tower. I have been expecting you," Isis said.

A gentle sea breeze wafted past, carrying the salty mist of the ocean. Georgette thought briefly of the comfort of the water. But she fisted her hands and gritted her teeth with determination. She knew what she needed to do. It was only that being face-to-face with her mother had torn open old wounds. Just looking at her almost broke Georgette's resolve.

She followed the graceful goddess through the line of trees, sending all manner of wildlife scurrying about. It appeared Isis was feared by all creatures. A pair of squirrels ran up a tree trunk and stared down at them with unblinking eyes.

Even a rattlesnake shrank back into the undergrowth as Isis strode forward.

"Do not be alarmed, my child. The animals know their place in this world. You will not be harmed," Isis called over her shoulder. Her voice was deep and rich, as smooth as spun chocolate.

Georgette kept her eyes on the grassy path, grinding her teeth as she chewed on her mother's words. It was not the wildlife that had Georgette's heart racing with anxiety.

They walked in silence, passing small groups of beautiful young women tending to the gardens. They had come upon fields of crops and lines of fruit trees as far as the eye could see.

Some of the women stopped what they were doing to watch Georgette, their eyes narrowing in suspicion. She knew they were sirens, and that made them her sisters. But there was none of the warmth she had received from some of them in the past. They only had icy stares for her now.

Isis seemed to read her thoughts as they reached the bottom of her tower.

"You have no need to worry about your sisters, either. They are merely distrustful because you did something they are forbidden to do."

"And what is that?" Georgette asked as she followed Isis up the winding staircase. The stone steps were cool beneath her feet.

Isis hesitated for a moment. Then she pushed open a door and they stepped out into her room. "You married a man, of course."

She walked behind the narrow desk in the corner and picked up a China pot.

"Would you like some tea?"

Georgette frowned. "I did not come here for tea, Mother. I came for answers."

Isis's mouth formed a straight line as she pursed her lips, then she let out a light laugh that did not come across as sincere. "Of course, my dear. But a cup of tea wouldn't hurt, would it?"

Georgette hesitated a moment, then reluctantly agreed as she lowered herself onto one of the plush armchairs in front of the desk. Isis poured the hot liquid into two delicate cups and passed one. Georgette noticed it had been hand painted with pictures of seashells.

They sat in silence, sipping their tea and listening to the seagulls honking over a backdrop of crashing waves.

Isis finally set her drink down and gave her daughter a piercing look.

"Now, Georgette. What is it that troubles you?"

Georgette almost choked on her tea, offended by the

question. "You know what troubles me, Mother. You tried to kill the man I love, with no warning. No explanation. How could you do something so cruel?"

"Ah, yes. I see," Isis replied. "But you must understand, my dear. It was necessary. I had to be sure."

Georgette blinked several times. "Sure of what?"

Isis rolled her lips inward and bit down, something Georgette recognized, with a start, as a tic of her own—it was something she personally did whenever she wanted to take a moment to collect her thoughts before answering a particularly difficult question.

Then Isis leaned forward and rested her elbows on her desk, lacing her fingers together. "I needed to be sure of what you are. Where you came from."

Georgette frowned, then she tugged the locket from under her gown and opened up the locket. "I could have shown you this. And you could have asked me to show my siren form," she said, anger she could not restrain rising to the surface.

Isis shook her head. "You could have stolen that piece of jewelry. After all, my immortality ring ended up in a stranger's hands."

"But I am a siren," Georgette insisted, indignant. "You could have just—"

Isis let out another laugh. This one was far more authentic. She twirled a lock of her golden hair and looked out at the blue skies. "You could have been a shapeshifter. A trickster. No. I needed to be sure that you were truly who you said you were. And..." She stopped to turn back and meet Georgette's gaze. "The only way to know you were my daughter was to see for myself that you possess the power of resurrection."

Georgette stared at her, incredulous. "Resurrection? What do you...?" She looked down at her hands in her lap, at a loss for words. Her hands were trembling. "What a cruel test," she muttered painfully.

Another thought entered her mind. It was a seedling of hope. If Isis was telling the truth... If she truly possessed the powers of resurrection, then perhaps the pregnancy she lost...

"That cannot happen," Isis interrupted her thoughts. Georgette met her hard look with a heart full of desperation. "You know?"

"Of course. I was there, remember? You told that filthy pirate you were having his child," Isis said, her nostrils flaring as her eyes flashed with disgust.

A spark of hatred lit a fire in Georgette's belly at Captain Stone being referred to as a filthy pirate. "You will *not* speak of my husband that way," she demanded. "He is the most honorable, decent man in this world. You cannot just treat him like..."

Isis scoffed. "You left his body to decay on my beach,

wrapped up in the arms of his brother, no less." Her words cut deep, and Georgette shut her mouth, letting Isis carry on. "Meanwhile, I took him, cleaned his wounds, and waited."

"Waited for what?" Georgette asked, hardly believing that Isis could be telling the truth. Captain Stone had never told her what happened on the island after she left. She had assumed that he awoke, healed from his wounds, and took one of the boats off the island without hesitation.

Now that she reflected on it, she realized that was a foolish thought.

But the idea of Isis caring for him after she so brutally ripped his chest open seemed equally absurd. Georgette had come here for answers, but so far, Isis had only given her more questions.

Isis's eyes glazed over as if she were mentally replaying the events. "Your tears did so much more than heal the man. They were a source of life—of the purest form of energy—that bound his soul with his body once more. Then it was just a matter of waiting for the body to heal."

Georgette stayed quiet; her curiosity piqued. "If I can bring him back, why can't I…" She paused and placed a hand over her stomach. It was less bloated than before now, feeling more hollow than it ever had in her life.

Isis cocked her head to the side with a sympathetic tut. "That is my doing, I'm afraid."

The words cut through Georgette like they were knives. Her fury bubbled to the surface again, but she held it in check. She needed an explanation. None of it made sense.

Isis rose to a stand and clasped her hands behind her back.

"Before I met your father, I was with someone else. He was a powerful god with an ego as big as his city." She began to pace the small area by the window and Georgette listened with rapt attention.

"Lord Poseidon, God of the sea, was quite the charmer. We were together for almost a thousand years. Together, we bore scores of sons and daughters. Together, we ruled the world. He reigned over the waters, and I brought life and fertility to the lands." She stopped and bowed her head, her face scrunching up as though her mind had just conjured up a particularly painful image. "Poseidon may have the strength of a thousand men, but his self-control was weaker than a tom in an alley full of cats in heat."

Isis settled in her chair again with a deep sigh. "Blinded by love, I looked the other way for a time. But I continued to hear of his numerous affairs, and the resentment turned into bitterness as time went on. I became unable to bear even hearing his name."

Georgette wrung her hands, wondering how this had anything to do with her miscarriage. Isis's eyes flashed at her.

"I could not in good conscience allow the wretched god's bloodline to continue. So, I did the unthinkable."

Georgette swallowed. "What did you do?"

Isis carefully picked up an old leather-bound book from her desk and lifted it for Georgette to see. "Blood magic."

She handed the book over and Georgette thumbed through the pages of drawings and ancient writings as Isis continued to speak.

"After demanding a divorce from the god—who was glad to be rid of me—I performed a forbidden ritual. Right here on this island. He ordered his sons to stay in Atlantis, protecting it with their very lives, while he surrendered his daughters to me... Casting them aside like a nuisance."

Georgette closed the book and returned her attention to her mother. "What did this blood magic do?"

Isis did not answer right away. Instead, she twirled her hair, thinking.

Finally, she sighed. "I cursed Poseidon's bloodline

with infertility. I could not in good conscience allow the god to keep creating life."

Georgette clutched her locket until the whites of her knuckles were on show.

"But I am not Poseidon's daughter. My father was Lord Harrington."

Isis carefully set her hands on the desk and looked at her daughter with an expression she couldn't read.

"I confess, there was a slight overlap," she said, her voice feebler than before. "I met your father, who was a mere sailor shipwrecked on my island, while I was still with Poseidon." She sucked in a sharp breath and her eyes twinkled as she recounted the story. "Aphrodite brought him to me through fate, as a consolation for the years of my suffering. You see, this young sailor man was sweet and gentle. He possessed a tender soul, and he claimed me... Took my body and heart all at once. I reasoned that if Poseidon could freely bed any woman he liked, he would not mind if I took comfort in the arms of a human."

Georgette's heart quickened as she listened to her mother's story. Her mother was married to Poseidon while she was with her father. It sent a shiver down her spine.

"I crafted the immortality ring so that we could be together forever, but Poseidon returned to my island. He found me in bed with the sailor, a child in my arms. You. In a fit of rage, Poseidon threatened to destroy you both. But I pleaded with him to spare you."

A single glistening tear rolled down Isis's cheek. "I had to let you both go. And watch from afar as you grew up, having no knowledge of your true form nor where you belong."

Georgette's mind spun as she processed the information. "My father told me you died at sea. He mourned for you his whole life."

Isis's cheeks grew crimson as a flush of emotion washed over her face. But then her fingers curled into fists. "I called upon Plutus, the god of abundance, to bless him with wealth and a title. But the fool gambled everything away, spending night after night at the port, mingling with sailors and *pirates*."

She snarled the last word, and her eyes grew dark. "Furious with Poseidon for taking me from the only man to give me happiness in more than a century, I cursed his bloodline so that his seed may never bear fruit."

Georgette shook her head. "That curse should not affect me."

Isis sniffed and sat back in her chair with a sigh. "Shortly before I met my sweet sailor, Poseidon came to my island, as he so often did, for me to perform my wifely duties." Her eyes clamped shut and her fists trembled for a moment while Georgette looked on in horror.

"*Poseidon* could be my father?" she whispered. Isis nodded, finally opening her eyes. More tears fell.

Georgette shook her head. "The doctor told me it is quite common to lose a pregnancy so early. There is still hope that next time…"

Isis stiffened.

"It is time for you to accept who you are, Georgette. You are a siren, daughter of a goddess. You must let your Captain go and come home. This is where you belong."

Georgette rose to her feet, her heart pounding. "But what about my happiness, Mother? Don't I deserve to be happy too?"

Isis did not flinch under her daughter's accusatory stare. "If you are happy with this human, why did you leave him, in the midst of a raging war no less, to see me?"

Georgette sucked in a sharp breath and began to pace the room. "That is not fair. I was grieving. So much of my pain and suffering has had nothing to do with—"

"Really?" Isis cut in, her eyes flashing dangerously now as she rose to her feet. Georgette stopped pacing to stare at her mother wide-eyed.

"Let's go over the facts, shall we?" Isis asked, her nostrils flaring again. "Before you met Captain Stone, you were betrothed to the honorable Prince Edward. The unfortunate mortal was so devoted to you, he scoured the seven seas after you were captured by pirates."

Georgette opened her mouth to argue but Isis lifted a finger to stop her. "This same Prince took you back with open arms when your captor was allegedly killed on my island. He even agreed to marry you, knowing that you were no longer innocent and pure."

Irritation nipped at Georgette's insides as her mother spoke, but she was too humiliated to argue. Isis continued.

"Your so-called husband, Captain Stone, bartered with your father behind your back and tricked him into offering you to him to pay off his debts. He snatched you from the arms of your Prince, cutting down any man who stood in his way. Then he forced himself onto you…"

"Stop!" Georgette shouted, heat rushing to her face. "It wasn't like that at all. He was ruthless on the outside, yes. But he always protected me. He murdered for me. He promised to burn the whole world and all of its wretched inhabitants to keep me safe. And when we did make love, I *demanded* him to do it."

Georgette's heart soared as she thought of all the little things Captain Stone had done to show her love. True love.

"When I was attacked by pirates, he slaughtered every single one of them who touched me. Then he got to his knees and implored me to show him my body. He had to make certain I was unharmed." Tears welled in her eyes. "And when he thought I had died at sea, I found him on the beach, sobbing. He was broken with grief that he could not save me."

Isis listened quietly, her face stone cold and her mouth a thin, straight line.

Meanwhile, a pressure had mounted on Georgette's chest to the point that she could hardly breathe. "When I lost the baby, he never once blamed me for it. He never called me weak. He lay with me each night, stroking my hair... Kissing away my tears."

She wrapped her arms around herself, suddenly thinking about the terrible mission her husband had set himself on. "I've made a horrible mistake coming here. I must go to him. He is going to try to do something unwise."

Isis lifted her palm. "Ava told me of his quest. Do not trouble yourself. Blackbeard is not nearly as powerful as his reputation makes out." She inclined her head. "My child, you have moved me." She walked around the desk and pulled Georgette into her arms. Georgette stiffened, shocked to be embraced by this forbidding goddess.

"I see now that you and your pirate do have a true

love for each other. And I have no doubt that he shall succeed. I have sent Athena to assist him on his quest."

"Athena?" Georgette asked, lifting her head to look up at her mother's face. Isis grinned at her. "She is an old friend, wise and of renowned skill in military combat. Your husband is in good hands. You should stay here and await his arrival."

Georgette thought about it but was not entirely convinced.

When Isis released her, though, she gave her mother a beaming smile.

"Come, my child. You must be eager to speak with him again."

Georgette frowned. "Speak with whom?"

Isis took her hand in both of hers to give her a warm look. "There is a cave on this island, where sacred waters flow. It is where the Underworld meets this one. I have made all the arrangements with Hades. He is anxious to see you again."

"Who?" Georgette asked, her heartbeat quickening. Isis tapped her hand with a light laugh, then touched the golden locket. "Come. He is waiting."

Georgette swallowed hard, unsure of what to expect as she followed Isis out of her chamber and descended the spiral staircase. Clouds rolled over, hiding the blistering sunshine. The hairs on Georgette's arms stood on end while they walked in silence.

The dank smell of moss and damp rock hit Georgette's nostrils as they slowly descended into a hidden path nestled between two willow trees. Their mesh-like vines drew back like curtains as Isis waved her hand, and Georgette looked back to watch them fall back into place.

The air was different now—quiet and still under a canopy of tall willow trees. Georgette's own heartbeat was the only other sound besides the light shuffle of their feet on the stone path.

Finally, they came to the mouth of a cave covered in moss. The strong smell of seaweed clung to her as they passed the entrance. She put her hands out to steady herself and touched a slimy substance on the walls.

The further they descended, the darker it became, until Georgette could no longer see the glimmer of her mother's golden hair. She listened to their breaths and the distant drip from far below. A chill wind thrust her hair back, slapping her cheeks as they moved. Georgette shivered, just as fearful as she was cold.

Finally, the ground leveled, and the narrow tunnel opened out into a vast cave. A flash of blue light illuminated the space and Georgette squinted as her eyes adjusted. Isis moved to an ornate stand made of white stone, holding a torch. She waved her hand in a sweeping motion over it and the torch lit with the deepest blue flame.

Then she motioned for Georgette to join her beside a large pool of sparkling water. "He is here," she said in a low voice, as if trying not to disturb something sleeping within the water's depths. Georgette reluctantly joined her at the edge, her heart pounding hard against her chest in anticipation and dread.

She was not yet certain she trusted Isis, nor believed a word she said. Despite her mother's serene smile, there was an eerie feeling in Georgette's bones. As though someone or something evil lurked in the shadows.

Isis pointed to a large oval mirror hanging between two posts. Georgette walked to it cautiously, admiring the ancient writing etched along the rim. The glass was like water, and the reflection of the blue flames danced across its surface in the most enchanting way.

She turned back to Isis, who stood tall and poised, like a statue. "I do not understand, what am I to do?"

Isis pointed to the mirror again. "This process is called *psychomanteum*. In a moment, I shall extinguish the flames and seal you up in this cavern. Then you shall gaze upon this mirror until you see your father in the Underworld."

A breath caught in the back of Georgette's throat, and she coughed in alarm. "*Seal me up?* Are you going to trap me in this cave alone?" she asked. "You said the water is the entrance to the Underworld and you made an arrangement with Hades?"

"I lied," Isis said, without a shred of regret in her voice.

"Why would you lie? Why can't you stay with me?" Georgette asked, the hairs on her arms standing on end.

Isis blew out the flames without another word, thrusting them both into darkness.

A rush of panic flooded Georgette's body and she began to tremble as a heavy sense of dread took hold of her.

"Mother!" she cried out at the sound of fading footsteps. "How long do you mean to trap me in here?"

A shrill laugh echoed in the cavern, sending another chill up Georgette's spine.

"As long as it takes."

The sound of crumbling rocks made Georgette imagine a stone wall forming in between Isis and the cavern.

Georgette hugged herself, suspended in total darkness.

She reached out to touch the side of the mirror and positioned herself in front of it. It was hopeless.

All that she could see was the black. There was not

even a tiny glimmer of light to illuminate the still water behind her.

Her heart raced and she broke into a cold sweat at the sudden thought that perhaps she had been tricked. Perhaps she was led to her death, and like a foolish lamb, Georgette had followed her wretched mother to the slaughter.

CAPTAIN STONE

Captain Stone stood at the helm of his ship, gazing at the horizon. The ocean breeze whipped at his face. His crew had been sailing for days, looking for the hidden island where the Pirate Lords were meeting. They were going to make a truce and join forces against their common enemy, the British Navy. Captain Stone also had to win the trust of Isis, the goddess of the sea, and the only way to do it was to reveal that he was married to a siren. But Isis would not entertain a discussion without an olive branch—the head of Captain Blackbeard. His stomach knotted as his mind spun with skepticism about his odds and concern for Georgette.

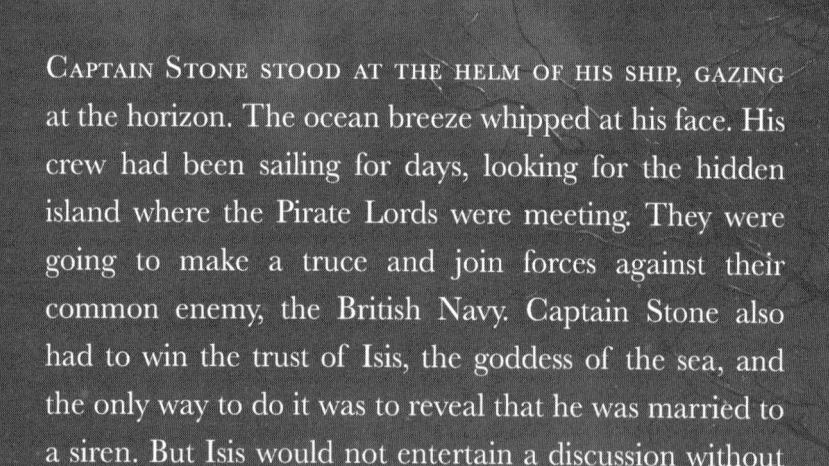

Failure was not an option, and he was eager to return to his wife. He forced his doubts out of his mind as they pressed on.

The pirate isle of Gaza finally loomed ahead; its shoreline visible through the morning mist. Captain Stone's mouth tightened into a thin line as he gave the order to proceed. The wooden hull of the ship groaned and creaked as it advanced toward the shore, and soon they had docked. Captain Stone and his crew stepped warily off the deck and through a fog-shrouded jungle, their booted feet sinking into thick mud. As they trudged on, the air grew thicker with anticipation. Then they were standing in front of a grand clearing. At its center was an enormous wooden table dating back centuries, surrounded by formidable pirate lords. Golden rum made rounds in ornate tankards, and wisps of fragrant cigar smoke filled the heavy air. The pirates' eyes sparkled with mischief as they sized up Captain Stone's team.

The atmosphere in the clearing was electric as Captain Stone made his way to the center. His steely gaze seemed to draw in all the eyes that watched him, and he stood tall with a hand resting on the hilt of his sword.

"Stone? You were dead!"

"How can this be?"

Captain Stone frowned, surprised that the news of his return had not traveled this far. It was a relief in some ways because at least these men did not look at him as a disgraced royal. These wretched men were the ones who stole his treasure after he died and thought they were now looking at a ghost.

"I saw him bleeding out on the beach of Imerta. This is not Stone, but a shapeshifter!" one of them shouted.

All the men rose to their feet then, grumbling to each other. They drew their weapons, and Captain Stone's loyal crew leaped into action, pointing their pistols in the direction of the pirates and growling threats.

Both sides were now facing each other with weapons drawn.

Abruptly, Captain Stone tore open his shirt. The white scars stood out boldly. A hush fell and he gave them all a grim smile.

"You have heard the tales, have you not? I cannot die, or did you numbskulls forget?"

The pirates muttered their misgivings and slowly took their seats once more. Captain Stone began to walk in a vast circle around the table. "I delivered your gold and riches as promised, did I not? Are you not sitting here indulging in your fine wine and admiring your precious jewels because of what I did at Imerta?"

The shoulders of the pirates rose, and the air hung with heaviness as they watched him stroll around them. "And how do you repay me? You leave me for dead and steal my own treasure."

The words cast dark shadows across the faces of the

men. Traitors. Captain Stone held his nerve, resisting the urge to hack them all down with his sword.

"Fear not, my brothers. I am not here for revenge, and I mean you no harm."

A collective sigh of relief followed. Most of them continued to glance warily at Captain Stone's menacing crew lingering in the shadows, their eyes glinting.

Knowing that he now held their attention, Captain Stone nodded to his crew. They sheathed their weapons and stood down.

"Gentlemen," he said slowly, "I am here with an offer. Whether you take it or not is up to you." He paused, scanning the crowd before him. "But I suggest you listen carefully—this may be your only chance."

The Pirate Lords looked at each other, then back at Captain Stone.

"Speak," one of them said. He was a tall man with a spiked mace in place of a hand.

Captain Stone drew in a heavy breath as he began. "I confess to you today... I am married to a siren. Georgette, my wife, is a daughter of Isis and has bestowed her blessing upon me. In order to support our victory in this war, she has consented to be by my side and lend me her formidable power. Pledge your loyalty to me now, for when the battle is won, I shall become the Pirate King and rule with justice unrivaled."

There was a murmur around the table, but it seemed favorable. The Pirate Lords appeared intrigued. They knew the power of the sirens and the importance of winning Isis's favor. Though their fight had been with the sirens, the brutality reached new heights when the Royal Navy got involved. An alliance with Isis would make the difference between life and death.

Blackbeard leaned forward, a big man with slicked black hair, broad shoulders, and hands that looked like they were made of stone. "What proof do you have?"

Captain Stone's heart raced as he beheld the famous pirate, a nemesis of the sea. Skin-like parchment and eyes like two abysses of darkness glared at him, sending chills down his spine. His tar-black beard seemed to smolder with an otherworldly force. There were tales whispered that any man who looked too deeply into those bottomless pits he wore as eyes would be lost in their depths forever, never to return from the clutches of madness.

This was the man Isis sent him to kill. Captain Stone looked upon him and thought that it would not be a terrible thing to do. For he would rid the world of a black evil once and for all.

Blackbeard was prepared for any threat. His crew was fiercely loyal, ready to sacrifice their own lives in order to safeguard his. Their loyalty was born out rather than bravery or allegiance—every pirate had heard the story that claimed Blackbeard would come from the Underworld to take souls and haunt the dreams of every man who had watched him die if he were ever slain.

Fortunately, Captain Stone was an intelligent man and knew the tales for what they were—fabricated stories meant to instill fear and maintain dominance.

He reached into his pocket and pulled out a small bottle. "These are the tears of my wife," he said, holding it up to the light. "They have the power to protect us from the sirens' song."

The Pirate Lords glanced at each other, exchanging silent words of trepidation before nodding in agreement. Seeing this, Blackbeard then shot to his feet with a bellow, smashing an iron fist down so hard that the table cracked. "We accept your proposal!" he roared, saliva flying from his lips as his yellow teeth gleamed in the light. "But there is one condition—you must duel me in combat! If I am bested, you will take the throne. But if you fall by my sword, your wife will become my new lover."

His menacing gaze slid across the room like an icy blade, and he flicked his tongue like a viper.

"Oh, I cannot wait to have her in my arms," he continued slimily. "To ravage every curve of her exquisite body. Tangle my fingers in her silky soft locks. Her screams will resound throughout the cosmos, reverberating even into the Underworld." He cackled darkly as he imagined this night of debauchery.

Captain Stone hesitated, a bubble of fury rose within him like molten lava, burning his flesh as the wretched images crossed his mind.

He did not like the sound of this deal. Georgette had already been lost in a battle of wills. But he was not her father. Besides, he had come to murder Blackbeard. This would be the perfect opportunity to carry out his mission without the other pirates getting involved.

He drew his sword and walked toward Blackbeard, who walked several feet away from the table and unsheathed his own blade. They could waste no time. The duel would happen now. There was a commotion of sliding chairs and shuffling feet as the rest of the pirates got into position.

The two men stood in a wide circle, surrounded by their silent shipmates. Blackbeard's eyes glowed with anticipation as he twirled his curved blade between his fingers, the steel gleaming in the dim light. Captain Stone steadied himself, readying for the attack he knew would come. Then, without warning, Blackbeard lurched forward, thrusting his weapon forward.

Blackbeard was not known to dither. Captain Stone felt the blade slice through the air and instinctively flew to the side—but not fast enough; the tip nicked his arm and warm blood trickled down to his elbow. The pirates around them took in a collective breath.

Painstakingly, the two men danced a deadly ballet, their blades ringing out in the darkness like church bells. Captain Stone leapt and darted around Blackbeard, while the other pirate's brute strength kept him one step ahead. They sparred for what seemed like hours, trading blows as they wrestled for dominance.

Captain Stone's strength ebbed away, and his body began to tremble from the strain of the physical exertion. But he would fight for eternity if that was what it took. This beast of a man was not going to get his black hands on his wife.

Captain Stone slowed his pace. Blackbeard, tireless, seized the opportunity. His sword sank into Captain Stone's shoulder with a sick crunch. Stone's ears rang as an explosion of pain like fire crawled out from his wound to his surrounding limbs.

Blackbeard paused to let out a triumphant war cry. He howled into the sky, arching his back, while Captain Stone panted. A numbness was spreading down his arm, and his fingers tingled as he grew weak.

But Georgette's face filled his mind's eye. With a terrible growl of fury, he wrenched the sword from his shoulder with a bare palm, slicing his flesh in the process, then he kicked Blackbeard back with all his might.

The pirate staggered off balance, giving Captain Stone just enough time to beat the hilt of Blackbeard's sword on his head, knocking him backward.

The ground trembled as Blackbeard fell with a grunt, like a pile of rocks.

Captain Stone tossed Blackbeard's sword aside quickly and grabbed the vial from his jacket. His heart raced and adrenaline soared through his body as he unstopped the bottle with his teeth, spat out the cork, and poured the siren tears onto his wound.

A fresh wave of strength immediately flooded his body, and he rolled his shoulder back, enjoying the renewed sense of vitality. Within seconds, blood had stopped seeping from the wound. Then the gash knitted itself together with an invisible force, and all that was left was a dull ache.

But in the short time he had averted his gaze, Blackbeard had scrambled to his feet and brandished a knife from inside his jacket. His eyes were wild and frenzied as he let out a roar and hacked at air. Captain Stone dodged the attacks, smirking with an arrogance which only riled Blackbeard even more.

After several more fruitless jabs, Captain Stone began to taunt the pirate.

Convinced that his victory was only moments away, he was surprised when Blackbeard gained the upper hand. He kicked Captain Stone in the gut and gnawed on his wrist until Captain Stone cried out and let his sword drop to the grassy floor.

A rush of pain took over his body. Buoyed by pain and anger, Captain Stone head-butted Blackbeard and took out his own knife.

With a savage jab, he stuck the pirate in the stomach and grunted in satisfaction as he twisted it. Then he staggered backward, letting out raspy breaths. For a glimmer of a moment, Captain Stone thought the fight was won.

It was not. Blackbeard's face broke into an evil, wicked grin. He pulled the knife from his body as though it were a pencil, and fresh blood gushed like spilled wine all over his dark clothes. Then he began to hack at Captain Stone with a renewed vigor that forced him back with his own bloody knife.

He had Captain Stone against a tree, knife at his throat. "Any last words?" he growled.

Just then, something amazing happened. In a vision that seemed to only be for him, the goddess Athena appeared. The sun shone brightly upon the gleaming armor of the goddess, making it glow as if on fire. "Captain Stone," she said, her calm voice echoing in his mind. "I bestow upon you this axe. Use it well and aim true."

In a flash, Captain Stone held a heavy golden axe in his calloused hands. He swung it with one powerful motion and cleaved Blackbeard's torso from between his legs to his ribcage. Cries of repulsion and shock spread in a wave around the circle of men.

Captain Stone took no chances. He ripped the axe free from Blackbeard's torso and directed another strong swing toward the pirate's neck, slicing through it so cleanly that Blackbeard's head tumbled helplessly to the ground like a ripe coconut.

Captain Stone heaved for breath as he watched the remains of Blackbeard collapse to the ground. His body stirred up a cloud of dust and a putrid stench of death began to pollute the area.

He growled in rage, his whole body shaking with fury. His eyes burned like torches, and he cursed fiercely under his breath as he spat on the defeated pirate's corpse.

"No one disrespects my wife!" he roared.

He bent and grabbed the head of his defeated foe, then held it before him, a symbol of his absolute power. Raising it up in front of all the Pirate Lords, he bellowed with thunderous authority, "I am the Pirate King—bow before me and I will lead us to victory!"

The other pirates looked upon him in fear and reverence, then knelt to declare their unwavering loyalty.

PRINCE EDWARD

EDWARD CAME TO IN A WORLD OF PAIN. HIS HEAD throbbed. He blinked several times, trying to make out his surroundings. Wherever he was, it was cold and musty. Somewhere to his right, he heard a light scuffle and the familiar squeak of a rodent. Slivers of daylight floated down from the boards above his head, and for a moment, he wondered if he was in the belly of a ship. He did not sense the familiar sway of the sea, but he could hear the roaring waves, like ghouls wailing from outside.

He decided he was beneath a house, in a cellar.

The cellar was dark, lit only by the lone torch. The stone walls were rough and cold, the floor not much better. He shrugged, trying to free his hands, but they were cuffed behind his back with heavy manacles.

Shouting voices came from above and echoed off the walls. Edward immediately began to consider how to get out. He yanked on the chains, but the unforgiving shackles on his wrists sent a jolt of pain to his shoulders.

He knew he was likely chained to the wall, and that it was futile to try to escape by force.

The floorboards creaked above his head and the men muttered curses and accusations about Edward. He distinctly heard the words "filthy siren" and "slit her throat."

He shifted over the hard, dusty floor until he bumped into something soft. A body. As his eyes adjusted, he made out red hair. Serena. She lay deathly still.

Edward's heart stopped as a dreadful thought crossed his mind. Was he too late? Had they already done something unforgivable?

But she stirred. His bump must have woken her. She sat up with a groan, and her hair fell away from her face. To his blessed relief, she blinked at him, her gorgeous eyes glowing in the torchlight.

"What happened? Where are we?" she asked.

The voices above stopped.

The absence of the noise set Prince Edward's heartbeat racing. He shushed Serena but it was already too late. Creaking stairs and approaching footsteps announced the arrival of their captors. Prince Edward braced for the confrontation.

A door opened and a flood of light had him squinting and blinking as the cellar lit up with daylight.

He tried to look around, his vision was blurry and a pressure behind his eyes pounded. As he adjusted to the light, he came face to face with four grizzly-looking men. They had mad eyes, wild manes for hair, and rags for clothes. Prince Edward eyed the gold rings on every one of their digits as they fisted their stubby knives.

But it was the stench of hard liquor on their breaths that told him all he needed to know about what type of men they were.

Pirates.

Prince Edward grimaced, shaking with fury that such wretched souls dared capture him and Serena. Above all the pathetic creatures on the Earth, he *loathed* pirates.

"What is the meaning of this?" Prince Edward asked, scowling. "Release us at once, we have no dealings with you, gentlemen." Prince Edward's stomach flipped as he uttered the last word, but the pirates' grim faces broke into looks of amusement. Flattery went a long way with pirates, and Prince Edward supposed it had been a long time since any of the insipid fools had been referred to as anything resembling human.

"Did you hear that? We're *gentlemen*," one scrawny

pirate said to the others. He flashed a smile and Prince Edward noticed that four of his front teeth were missing.

A dark wave of laughter crossed the men, but the largest one, a brute of a man with two thick legs and a rock-like torso, growled. He moved forward and thrust a rusty knife to Prince Edward's neck.

"Where be ye going at this ungodly hour?" he asked. The puff of air from his mouth nearly suffocated Edward.

His eyes burned and he resisted the urge to cough.

Prince Edward frowned at the unusual question. "Our business is our own. This is a free country the last I heard," he said, keeping his voice steady.

The pirates exchanged looks and laughed so long and deep, it sent a chill crawling up Prince Edward's spine.

"We must have hit the sailor man too hard on the head. He be thinking we're in a free land," he said, sneering.

Prince Edward could not make sense of their words. He had only been gone for a little over two weeks. "I am not a sailor. I am Edward, Prince of England, and by order of King George—"

The pirates' laughter stopped him in his tracks and Prince Edward frowned at them, wondering what had them so amused.

"Prince Edward is *dead*, and we do King George's work now."

A wash of cold dread crossed Prince Edward's soul as he stared into the inky eyes of his captors. "Everyone thinks I'm dead?" he thought aloud.

The night he left for Atlantis; his men were readying the Victory for sail. They had been loading up the frigate with all manner of steel weaponry and he had commanded one of his men to pose as him, wearing the admiral uniform.

Had his disguise failed? Or had sirens got to the Victory and sent her to the bottom of the ocean?

Prince Edward's stomach knotted, but he refused to show any sign of weakness.

"My men will come for me. The Royal Navy—"

"The Royal Navy is dead and gone," one pirate spat.

Prince Edward's ears rang as he processed the information. Even if the Victory did sink, there were scores more men in the Navy. How could an entire army perish in such a short space of time?

But the filthy pirate had the answer to that as well. "I don't know who you are, young sailor. Nor what you're doing walking the streets with this beautiful lady, but let me fill you in on a few details."

He leaned forward, and the stench of him almost choked Prince Edward. "The King commanded his

Naval army to hunt down sirens in the Pacific. Consumed by paranoia that the deceitful sea witches might infest our waters, he sent more and more fleets of men. And he had them do *terrible* things to the sirens. Things that even us, humble pirates, would never do. The mission was in vain, for the Navy drove the sirens to the Atlantic and the waters between England and France are red from all of the bloodshed. The sea is no longer safe for us, so we're forced to forge a life on the land. With no one left to enlist, the King turned to us. *We* are his army now. The men chuckled darkly.

Serena trembled beside Prince Edward, and he longed to reach for her hand. But he held firm and kept a steady eye on the pirate.

"Lies! My father would never work with pirates."

The very thought of it made his skin crawl. King George was bereft when he learned that Prince Mannington had turned his back on the throne for a life of piracy. But then a dreadful thought filled him with fear, and he wondered if the formidable Captain Stone had returned and somehow driven King George to insanity.

Were he and Georgette calling the shots, now?

He wondered if things were even more bleak and Captain Stone had killed their father in cold blood, commanding his pirate crew to take over.

But before he could process any of the information further, one of the pirates stepped forward and withdrew a long, thin blade. The scrape of the metal rang in the air, and everyone fell to silence.

"It is a pity to defile such a fine thing. But on order of the King, we have to be sure you are human and not one of *them*…"

The pirate was not speaking to Prince Edward. His beady eyes were focused on Serena, who eyed the blade with a cold look.

She was staring danger in the face, but she had gone as steely as the iron in the pirate's hand. After a moment, she merely spat, "Do your worst. *Pirate.*"

The pirates exchanged looks, none of them smiling now. "She's got the spirit of a siren, gents. A simple woman would cower with fear. But look at her eyes. They are blazing."

Prince Edward's heart pounded as he desperately thought of a way to break out of the situation. "Wait. I demand answers. *Who* is your king?" He asked this with a certainty that the pirates were not talking about his father.

It was the only conceivable way pirates could be roaming the lands, working in the name of a king. But the question washed off the pirates like water off a duck's back. Their attention was now set on Serena, and a sickly sensation swirled around his stomach as they edged closer to her.

One of them took a lock of her hair and hummed in delight. "Don't worry, my dear. We will not kill you... Y*et*."

They chuckled to an inside joke and Prince Edward's blood boiled.

"Keep your hands off her," he growled.

They ignored him. Another pirate took a fistful of her hair and yanked until her ear met his mouth. He mumbled something inaudible into it and leered.

Serena scowled at him. "I will chew you up and spit you out, *pirate*."

The pirates' excitement rose, and they shuffled around her until Prince Edward could hardly see Serena's face between them.

"I said, get your *disgusting* hands off my woman!" Prince Edward roared so loud the floor seemed to tremble. The pirates halted and finally turned to look at him, their eyes wide with confusion.

The largest one seemed bored with the prince. "I will make you a deal," he offered.

The other pirates glanced at him warily. They did not seem to like the sound of a deal.

Prince Edward was happy to distract them.

"What is this deal?" he asked.

The main pirate stroked his shaggy beard. "You will allow us to perform a simple test. If she is a woman, it will not harm her at all."

The other pirate with the thin, steel blade raised it, and it glinted in the sunlight.

Panic washed over Prince Edward. He knew what was coming next.

"Sirens have a weakness. *Steel*. It burns their skin… I've heard their guts sizzling as I stuck my blade into their bellies."

Prince Edward swallowed the buildup of saliva in his mouth but kept a poker face as the pirate continued. "If she does not react to the steel, we shall admit our wrongdoings and let you both free."

The last word hit Prince Edward square between the eyes. He pictured them getting out of there, far away. He even considered going right back to Atlantis. These wretched lands were doomed if they were under the reign of pirates.

The main pirate continued, snapping him out of his thoughts.

"If the steel burns her skin, you shall watch as we each take turns with her. Then when we are bored, we shall cut her throat and you can watch this pretty silver gown turn red. Do we have a deal?"

Prince Edward seethed as he imagined the pirates

laying their filthy hands on Serena. Every atom in his body began to tremble with fury.

"If you so much as *breathe* on my lady, I shall tear one of your limbs from your fat body and beat you to death with it," he growled.

The pirate's left brow lifted, but the others were not affected by his words. One of them was still holding Serena's hair. Just as the one with the blade approached her, an almighty roar ripped from Prince Edward's lungs and he wrenched his wrists, snapping the chains connecting his iron manacles. The pirates lurched back, the whites of their eyes on show as Prince Edward lurched for the pirate with the steel dagger. Like a wild beast, Prince Edward snapped the neck of the pirate in one quick motion. Then he took the steel blade and slashed the throat of the other.

The largest pirate remained frozen where he was. Things had happened so fast; shock had prevented him from making his escape. Prince Edward let out another roar, grabbed the pirate's arm, and yanked upward until there was a terrible crunch. The pirate yowled in pain. Prince Edward carried out his promise and tore the arm from its socket. The pirate collapsed to his knees twitching. The pain and disbelief in his eyes turned to a hollow resignation as he bled out. He let out a moan. The last pirate—the scrawny one—stood by the door. His mouth had formed a perfect o. He watched the dismembered pirate fall to the ground with a thump before he remembered to scramble for the door.

He threw a ring of keys over his shoulder as he fled. Prince Edward caught it, scowling, and bellowed after the hastily retreating figure, "Go and tell them that Prince Edward has returned. And he brings with him a new bride."

When the last sounds of the coward's scurrying faded, the air grew still and heavy.

Prince Edward went to Serena, who looked up at him with glistening eyes. Admiration lit her face. "My Prince! I had no idea you had it in you to be so…." She looked around the dead pirates on the floor while Prince Edward freed her from her chains. Then she rose to her feet and touched his cheek. "Brutally dominant."

"I'm sorry you had to see that, my lady," he said, breathing hard. His hands trembled until Serena took them in hers.

"I am not. That was the most beautiful thing anyone has ever done for me."

Prince Edward's heart was still pounding, and he looked down at the broken shackles on his wrists. It was as though his rage had given him the strength of one hundred men. He looked back up and cupped Serena's face, looking deep into her eyes. "I was not going to sit and watch them harm you, my lady. No one can lay a hand on you."

Serena's eyes lit up at his words. "And why is that, my sweet Prince?"

Prince Edward's eyes dipped to her lips and the overwhelming desire to claim her took hold. "Because you belong to me."

Serena rose on tiptoes as Prince Edward leaned in and kissed her right there in that dirty cellar.

The sweet, familiar taste of her washed away the repugnant stench of the pirates, and pleasant tingles scattered all over his body as he wrapped his arms around her waist, pulling her up off the floor.

Their noses nuzzled as they kissed, losing themselves in each other. Prince Edward almost forgot about their surroundings. He held Serena tight, pressing her soft bosoms against his hard chest. He caressed her tongue with his and moaned into the kiss, while Serena ran her hands through his hair. When they finally broke apart, Prince Edward was lightheaded and painfully charged.

He thought about holding her against the cold cellar wall and taking her right there and then, but then he caught another whiff of the stench and set her down instead.

"Come on, my lady. We must take you somewhere safe."

He needed to get Serena as far away as possible. She did not argue as they hurried up the staircase and out of the old home.

"Do you think those men were telling the truth? Could they have been working for King George?" Serena asked as they ran hand in hand along a grassy lane leading back to the town.

The cool sea air rejuvenated Prince Edward's soul and he filled his lungs with deep breaths. Then he looked up at the palace in the distance, his stomach knotting. "I am not certain. But if there is anywhere in this world that has answers for us, it's the palace."

Serena tugged on his hand and stopped walking. "Your parents… What if they don't believe our story? What if they put steel on my skin as a test?"

Prince Edward cupped her face once more, sweeping his thumbs across Serena's pink cheeks. "Serena, princess of Atlantis. There is no conceivable way my parents will not adore you. I vow to protect you until my dying breath."

Serena nodded between his hands, and they walked up the hill arm-in-arm to an unknown fate. Prince Edward held no fear in his heart. He felt alive with the hope that whatever terrible challenges unfolded, they would face them together.

SERENA

SERENA WALKED IN SILENCE AS SHE FOLLOWED EDWARD TO the stone wall surrounding the palace. She could not stop replaying the events in her mind of Prince Edward breaking free of his chains and killing the pirates.

She saw him in an entirely new light now.

He had fought like her brothers would have—merciless, unrelenting, and possessive. All to defend her honor.

Serena could not help imagining what all that energy would feel like in the bedroom. If he even showed an ounce of the passion he exhibited in that cellar, Serena knew she would spiral in complete and total bliss.

Her stomach fluttered and she blushed.

As they reached the palace, Prince Edward let go of her hand. "It is customary in my land that we walk two feet apart, my lady."

He cleared his throat and fell into his formal character. She thought it laughable to even try and go back to formality after the way he handled himself in the cellar.

He was no more a gentleman than those pirates.

But she reminded herself that they were on an important mission. It was her turn now to convince his parents. She had to play the part of a shipwrecked princess. A human one. And she would have to pull it off so well that they would be moved to offer their blessing over their union. Then their marriage would be recognized, and a truce could be made.

There were many delicate steps to their plan and multiple opportunities for things to go terribly wrong.

Serena swallowed as she thought about the atrocious scenes on the beach. The line of dead sirens, like trophies facing the sea. It was so indecent. So disrespectful. So *vulgar*.

She could not fathom a moment that Poseidon or Isis would ever consider making a peace treaty with such people.

But they had to try. If the war had escalated this much in such a short time, there was no telling what would be left of the world should things be left to continue.

They approached the main entrance of the palace.

Before Serena could even prepare herself, she was standing in front of a pair of royal guards.

Visible relief flashed across their faces when they recognized Prince Edward. They bowed and opened the gates. Without a word, Prince Edward hurried up the path and through vast gardens. It took all of Serena's power to keep up. There was no time to take in the sights of manicured hedges and stone statues littered about.

Guards and ladies-in-waiting gasped as they passed, but Prince Edward did not stop to greet anyone. Serena gave them a shy wave as she ran to keep up with his broad strides.

Finally, they entered a throne room with vaulted ceilings and windows depicting scenes of battles and noble deeds. The sun came in through colored panes of glass, filling the air within with swirling prisms of color. The people assembled looked up in surprise as Prince Edward and Serena walked boldly into the room.

"Mother. Father. I have returned from my quest, and I bring good news," Prince Edward announced formally. He straightened his back and made a short bow to both thrones.

King George and Queen Charlotte's faces were gray as they looked upon Edward. Serena felt for them as she imagined their inexpressible shock. "This meeting will continue at another time. There are far more pressing matters to attend to," King George announced, rising to a stand. Wise men and advisors mumbled to each other in hushed tones as they vacated the room. When the door shut behind the final courtier, King George's sharp expression softened, and he turned to Prince Edward.

"My son. When we heard the Victory had fallen, we feared the worst."

Queen Charlotte walked over to Prince Edward in graceful strides and pulled him in for an embrace. "Are you real? I can hardly believe it is you."

Serena stepped back to offer them their privacy, a little envious of seeing Prince Edward's parents standing side by side, embracing him with such tenderness.

She had never been in the same room with both of her parents. In fact, the times she had even seen her mother were few and far between. She could count each moment on one hand and each one had been from afar.

Of her father's numerous qualities, *warm*, *kind*, *and loving* were not among.

But as she watched Prince Edward talking to his parents, she thought back to the ugly pirates who had them captive only hours before.

One of them said they were committing their atrocities under the name of King George. And Prince Edward had said earlier that his father commanded his men to hunt down sirens. Now there were dead sirens lining the beaches, and many more bobbing in the seas. She marveled at how this man, King George, who looked upon his son with sweet relief and joy, could be the same man to condone such violent acts.

Prince Edward's bright eyes caught Serena's attention and she snapped out of her thoughts, realizing all three of them were now looking at her.

"After the Victory went down, I was lost at sea on a piece of driftwood. I stayed there for days before Serena found me. She escaped on a small dinghy when pirates took over her ship and murdered her parents."

Serena was not sure whether to smile or nod along to the rehearsed story. They had gone over the details almost every night from the moment they arrived in Atlantis. She thought neither smiling nor nodding would appear sincere. A grieving young woman would not smile and nod when recounting her deepest horrors.

She opted to look at the delicate patterns on the mosaic tile floor instead.

"Oh, dear me. You have suffered so much loss, I can only imagine the awful things you witnessed," Queen Charlotte said, taking Serena's hand. She almost jumped back in surprise at the woman's tenderness. She met the woman's gaze and noticed her bright eyes were the same almond shape as Prince Edward's.

"It was truly awful, Your Majesty. I never learned to

row. If I had not happened upon Prince Edward, who handled the oars with such unrelenting strength, I would not have survived."

Serena leaned closer and widened her eyes to share a horrified whisper. "I cannot stop thinking about what might have happened if the sirens found me all alone."

King George and Queen's expressions turned stone cold for a moment and Serena wondered if this was a sign of their masks slipping, but Queen Charlotte's face lit up with a sunny smile again.

"Edward tells me you are a princess, where are you from?" she asked.

"Endorra," Serena replied, a little faster than she intended.

"Endorra," King George repeated, his brows knitted together. "I can't say that's a country I am familiar with."

"It's a small island off the north coast of Norway," Prince Edward explained. They were on route to the Caribbean islands when they were attacked."

King George looked at Prince Edward with a frown as though he did not believe a word he said, while Serena clasped her hands together to stop them from shaking. She could not imagine what would happen if the plan failed. What would the prince do if his father commanded his men to kill her?

There was no doubt Prince Edward possessed the

strength to kill a man with his bare hands, but could he do that to his own father?

Unlikely.

King George's face broke into a warm smile. "We are humbled to be at your service, Princess Serena of Endorra. Please, make yourself comfortable in our home and stay as long as you need."

A rush of relief flooded Serena as she curtseyed. "You are too kind, your Majesty. I am most grateful for your hospitality."

Then Queen Charlotte stepped in, the mass of curls pinned around her face bobbing as she moved. There was a sparkle in her eye.

"I shall have the housemaids prepare you a bath, and I do believe I have a few gowns from my younger years. They will be very fine on you indeed." She linked her arm through Serena's and began to lead her away while talking at top speed. Serena glanced over her shoulder to catch one last glimpse of Prince Edward's apologetic smile. Then they were out of the throne room, and he was gone.

Queen Charlotte led her to a room with simple fixtures, nothing but a four-poster bed and armchair. A metal tub sat in the middle of the floor. The windows were tall and thin, covered in gauzy curtains that let in rays of glittering sunshine. Serena could not believe the sun could shine so brightly. She had to turn away from it before the light blinded her completely.

"I shall leave you in the very capable hands of my ladies-in-waiting, Serena. I cannot wait to get to know you a little better at dinner."

Serena bowed her head and curtseyed in respect to Queen Charlotte before she took one last glance around the room, feeling awe and perhaps a hint of fear wash over her. Queen Charlotte closed the door behind her as she stepped back out into the hall.

"May I help you undress, ma'am?"

Serena spun to look at who had addressed her. It was a short, young woman with broad shoulders and muscular arms. Her sleek brown hair was pulled back tightly into a bun, secured by dozens of hairpins that glimmered in the light. A white lace cloth sat atop her head - an accessory that added an air of delicacy to her otherwise stoutly features.

"May I help you undress, ma'am?" the woman repeated, this time with a hint of impatience in her voice.

"Thank you," Serena said, on autopilot. Prince Edward had forewarned her of their customs. Ladies had handmaidens, called ladies-in-waiting, who did everything for them. Even the oddest things that Serena thought were perfectly ordinary to do by herself. Like, take off her clothes.

She also knew to expect the maidens to style her hair and lace up her stays—though she did not know what *stays* were.

When she pressed Prince Edward on it, his face flushed with color, and he changed the subject.

The ladies-in-waiting helped Serena out of the simple gown that had been torn and dirtied. A messy blood stain had two of the ladies-in-waiting raising their brows, but they did not comment. Serena was grateful for their silence. She did not enjoy telling lies, and she thought it best not to mention the fact that a band of pirates had tied her up in a cellar and planned to rape her. It seemed inappropriate to share such horrid revelations with strangers as the sun shone so bright. It was the type of story that should be whispered in the midst of old confidants under the blanket of night.

She tried to come up with another topic of conversation, but every time she thought of something, she decided against bringing it up. After all, she had burning questions and all of them were likely to be met with odd looks. For example, what was the porcelain pot she spied poking out from under the bed? She wondered if someone had left it there by mistake.

What was the strong-smelling rock they scrubbed all over her body? And why did it make her skin so dry?

But when it came to dressing, she soon discovered what a *stay* was. Much to her dismay.

The ladies-in-waiting mentioned the word as one of them lifted a strange piece of white fabric with holes down the middle. Long ribbons weaved through the holes and when the maid turned it over, Serena noticed it was actually in two pieces. They wrapped the strange piece of clothing around her torso and suddenly it became exceedingly tight.

Serena gasped as the material molded with her body, pushing up her breasts until they piled out like two plump mounds under her chin.

It was the most ridiculous sight.

The ladies-in-waiting tugged on the ribbons and her ribcage became so restricted, she was forced to take short breaths.

"What torturous device is this? It is so tight," she said as she panted.

One of the ladies-in-waiting looked sheepishly to the other before she bobbed. "I'm sorry, ma'am. It is how Queen Charlotte likes it."

The door creaked open once more, and a maid stepped in with a gown draped over her arm. The light pouring through the windows illuminated the bright yellow fabric of the dress, which was trimmed with white lace around the cuffs and neckline. It glinted as if it were made of pure gold.

The material was as warm and gentle as sunlight in the sea, and when it was handed over to her, she was relieved to find that it wasn't as coarse as her undergarments.

She touched the skirt, running her thumb across the silky soft material in admiration.

As the ladies-in-waiting dressed her in it and fastened the small, round buttons up the back, she looked down and noticed the exaggeratedly low neckline. She could feel the cool air upon the tops of her restricted bosoms, a sensation both unfamiliar and uncomfortable. "Is this really what women wear in England?" she asked.

No one heard her, for they were too focused on their next job; taming her hair.

With each tug of the comb through her long locks, Serena felt more and more a prisoner. They twisted her long red curls around strange tools she'd never seen before and pulled them into tight ringlets that fell in disarray around her face.

Serena shuddered as she watched the ladies transform her into a different person in the wall mirror. The pastel yellow gown was beautiful, but the strange material was unfamiliar and alien on her body. When she inspected her reflection, she almost gasped.

Her usually wild hair was now up in a neat bun. She didn't recognize herself at all. In spite of the strangeness and discomfort, a part of her wished she could stay this way forever and pretend that all of the ugliness in the world didn't exist. But then she forced her mind to focus on what was important.

While she was being pampered in the palace, a savage war was raging outside.

She recounted the steps she needed to take to calm her nerves.

Her quest was to convince the royal court to offer their blessing on her relationship with Prince Edward. Only after they were married could anyone know she was a siren. It would force King George to stand down and form an alliance with Isis and Poseidon.

For now, she had to pretend to be human. She bit her tongue, trying to hide her disdain of her look, but when a maid pulled out an odd-looking device made of all manner of jewels and white feathers, Serena could not hold back a laugh.

"Is something wrong, ma'am?" the maid asked.

Serena's face heated. "Forgive me, but what is that? And where do you propose to put it?"

The maid lifted the strange object so Serena could get a better look. Sparkling rows of beads and jewels reminded her of the coral reef. "It's an aigrette, ma'am," she said, touching the feathers with reverence. "They hold the curls in place and are quite popular here in Europe."

Serena frowned at the aigrette. "I have never seen anything like this in my own country," she said, looking closely at the decoration. She could not understand why anyone would wish to use fowls for fashion.

They set the headdress atop Serena's hair, and she watched as they carefully twisted it into place. The white feathers stuck up above her like a crown, and Serena thought that she looked most peculiar. She touched them with her fingertips as if to make sure they were real.

"Will the prince find this pleasing?" she worried aloud. Her cheeks flamed at the question, but the ladies-in-waiting swooned anyway.

They patted her shoulder and told her that of course he would. It seemed that above all of the differences between her world and the human one, the notion of pleasing a man was universal.

"Oh yes, my lady. You look very fine indeed," one maid said. "Do not worry yourself, Princess Serena. When we are done with you, no one will be able to resist you."

After her transformation was complete, Serena was escorted down to a room where King George and Queen Charlotte waited with Prince Edward. Serena remembered her training with Edward and curtsied before them all, greeting them politely. As she bowed her head she could feel the prince's eyes upon her, and when she looked up their eyes met.

"My lady, you look exquisite," he said, holding out his arm for her. Serena flushed with happiness at the compliment. But also, from relief that the prince did not laugh at her appearance, thinking she looked like a goose.

As they proceeded to the grand dining room, Serena gasped, surprised by its magnificence.

The table was lavishly decorated with gold-trimmed porcelain dishes and crystal glasses filled with fine wines.

A large chandelier hung from the ceiling and sent glimmering light over the entire room. The smell of roasted duck, potatoes, and rosemary wafted through the air and made Serena's mouth water. She watched in wide-eyed awe as servants brought out course after course of sumptuous food—poached salmon with lemons and capers, braised beef with root vegetables, and for dessert, a selection of fresh fruits flavored with honey and brandy that Queen Charlotte said had been imported from France.

They kept their conversation light as they ate, and soon Serena cursed her tight clothes for preventing her from indulging in the food to her heart's content. The sight of it all spread out before her had her mouth watering.

Food in Atlantis was simple in comparison.

Once the servants left and the doors were closed, Queen Charlotte turned to Serena.

"Tell me about where you are from?" she asked.

Serena bit her lip as she thought about how best to answer the question. She remembered that Prince Edward said her library reminded him of the Vatican. So, she decided to be as honest as she could.

"My father's palace is very old. He had Michelangelo paint murals on the vaulted ceilings."

Queen Charlotte *oohed* and *ahhed*. "I should like to see that someday."

Serena smiled at Prince Edward and set down her fork. He nodded to her to keep going, so she placed her hands in her lap and laced her fingers together as she thought about what to say next.

"My country is peaceful but fiercely protective. We keep to ourselves, mostly. For we are small and rarely have visitors."

"What is the weather like? Do you have fair summers?" King George asked.

Serena was startled to hear his deep voice, for he had remained quiet for the duration of the dinner.

Now his eyes were burning into her soul as she smiled back at him. She sensed suspicion in those eyes.

But she shook herself mentally, reasoning that it was paranoia making her imagine things.

"It is quite pleasing, yes. We do get a lot of rain, but I must say, I am in awe of how beautiful your gardens are."

Queen Charlotte clasped her hands together with a joyful purr. "Thank you. We must take a turn in the gardens tomorrow. My rose hedges are my pride and joy."

"I should like that very much," Serena said, surprised by how formal she sounded.

The setting sun cast a gorgeous orange glow over the table, and soon the servants walked in to light candles around them.

"May I ask, what are your talents?" Queen Charlotte asked, leaning forward. Her eyes glistening as she looked upon Serena like a new toy.

Serena swallowed. She was unprepared for such a personal question. In truth, her main talents involved tearing ships apart with her bare hands and how fast she was able to swim.

But she did not think those were the type of gifts Queen Charlotte would be impressed by.

"I am fond of tending to plants myself, as a matter of

fact," she said, dabbing her lips with the corner of her napkin. "And I can sing, your majesty."

King George hummed. "I should be very keen to hear that," he said. Serena stiffened at the tense tone in his voice and glanced at him.

His eyes were fixed on her. Prince Edward coughed to break the tension.

"It is getting late, and we have been on a long and arduous journey. May I suggest we retire for the evening?"

Queen Charlotte's face fell, like Prince Edward had just canceled Christmas.

"Why don't we retire to the chamber? We can have our musicians play us a little music so that Serena may bless us with her singing?" she suggested.

Before Serena could argue, King George rose to his feet with a sound of agreement. "To the chamber," he announced.

Serena's heart raced at the jarring sound of the chair legs dragging along the marble floor as everyone rose to their feet.

Prince Edward's face paled, and he kept a firm gaze on Serena.

She was unsure what to do and reprimanded herself for talking about her voice. King George strolled happily into the next room. Serena was certain now that he was suspicious of her.

If he discovered the truth, that she was a siren, she dreaded to think of what he would do about it.

The chamber room was much smaller than the banquet hall. Tall tapestries hung on the walls, and a large rug stretched across the room, muting the sound of their footsteps. King George settled into a large armchair beside a roaring fireplace while Queen Charlotte spoke to one of the servants before she seated herself at her husband's side, perching on the edge of a delicate stool.

Prince Edward took Serena's hand and placed it in the crook of his arm as he guided her to a strange, bed-like chair with a scooped back.

"What happens if you sing? Can you do it without casting a spell on us?" he muttered into her ear. Serena resisted the urge to laugh.

There was no spell needed. On the seas, a pretty woman's face and a songbird voice were enough to charm men without magic.

In fact, she was certain that the tales of men who had heard the sirens' song were just fairy tales.

But she could not be entirely certain. For all she knew, her voice *did* possess magical qualities, although it was not something she was aware of.

They sat together and Queen Charlotte's eyes

narrowed for a moment before she gave them a stiff smile. Serena jumped, realizing she was still clinging onto Prince Edward's arm like her life depended on it.

She broke contact and shuffled away to give some space, but the damage was already done. "May I be bold?" Queen Charlotte asked while a group of musicians filed into the room. "I cannot help but notice that there seems to be a spark between the two of you. Did something happen on your adventures?"

Prince Edward cleared his throat and he and Serena exchanged looks. To her relief, he took charge of the situation and handled the question.

"We faced terrible dangers on the open waters. There were many days I did believe we would not make it here alive. You could say something happened. Many things happened and I am a changed man because of it."

Then he gently took Serena's hand by the fingertips and placed his other hand on top of hers as he smiled deeply into her eyes. "I was going to wait to talk about this, but now seems as good a time as any… Mother, Father. It is my intention to marry Princess Serena."

The musicians began to play a stirring, haunting song. One that Serena did not recognize. The instruments they played were made of wood and strings. She looked at King George and Queen with anticipation. They stared back, their faces impassive and blank.

"Goodness, Edward. This is not the way we do things…" Queen Charlotte began. But when the music started a new song, one that Serena *did* know, she mustered the courage to stand and began to sing.

King George's expression had grown hard, and she thought for a moment he might order his guards to take her away.

So, she sang as sweetly and quietly as she could, trying to emulate a human's ability rather than her own.

Queen Charlotte's eyes glazed over, and her mouth opened as Serena let the music flow into her body and come out in an ethereal song. The words rolled off her tongue and danced in the air, casting a light over King George's dark face. The line between his brows disappeared and he smiled, giving a faraway look as though her singing had transported him to another world entirely.

Prince Edward looked up at her, his eyes like two diamonds, deep admiration was written all over his features.

It was difficult to catch her breath in the tight dress, but Serena thought that to be a benefit, for it suppressed her abilities. In her own mind, she thought she sounded like a mere human maid singing along in a field as she picked daisies. But everyone in the room became enchanted, and Serena realized the stories were true after all.

There *was* something magical about a siren's song.

When she was done, the musicians shook themselves as though they had been asleep, and Queen Charlotte took in a sharp breath. "That was beautiful, Serena. Just beautiful."

Then she clapped her hands and jumped to her feet. "You have my blessing, Edward. Serena will make a fine wife for you, indeed," she said, beaming at them both. Serena curtsied, her cheeks flushing. But King George had a hard expression on his face. The side of his jaw jutted out, and Serena knew that was not a good thing. Prince Edward did the same when he was in the presence of Poseidon and thought he was about to face execution.

When he got to his feet, Serena held her breath.

"I am not feeling well. I think I shall retire to my room," he said, and he strode out of the chamber before anyone could speak.

Queen Charlotte's brows knitted together as she watched the door shut behind him, then she turned back to smile at Prince Edward and Serena.

"I shall go and make sure my husband is well. It was a pleasure to spend time with you, Serena. I will show you the gardens in the morn," she said, walking over to Serena to grasp her hands. Serena jumped to her feet and bobbed as Queen Charlotte squeezed her fingers. "I look forward to it, your Majesty."

Queen Charlotte beamed back, then her eyes grew misty as she looked upon Prince Edward. "The gods have smiled on our family, my dear. Not only did they bring you home safely, but they have brought a beautiful wife to make you happy."

She embraced him and then left the chamber.

Serena held her breath until they were alone with the musicians, then she glanced at the two ladies in waiting standing quietly in the corner of the room. She supposed they were her chaperones.

She turned to Prince Edward, who exhaled long and deep.

"I do believe that went well," he said, sounding far too polite to be normal. Serena understood. There was no privacy in his palace. They were not free to talk openly.

"I am so relieved your parents approve," she said, matching his tone.

"Your father, though…"

"Do not concern yourself with him. He is old fashioned, that is all," Prince Edward replied, resting a hand over Serena's again. His gaze dipped to her mouth. Like a moth to a flame, he leaned in until his hot breath clouded Serena's cheeks. But an abrupt cough came from the corner, and he let her go again in an instant.

"Forgive me, my lady. I forgot my manners," he said, lurching back.

Serena froze, her heart thumping wildly against the tight gown. She longed to break free from the restrictive clothing and wrap her arms around the prince's neck. Wild and scandalous thoughts crossed her mind, but before she could make a move, Prince Edward made his excuses and vacated the chamber, leaving Serena in a frustrated state of confusion. She tugged on the neck of her gown and took a deep breath, wondering how long they would have to keep up the charade and when she could be truly alone with her Prince again.

GEORGETTE

Georgette had no sense of time in the dark cave. The only hint that offered her any idea of the sheer volume of hours that passed was the gnawing ache in her stomach, and how her limbs began to tire of holding her weight.

She gazed at the mirror—or at least, where she knew it was—but there was nothing but pitch black. Sometimes she would catch a glimpse of two hollow eyes glinting back at her, but she knew they were her own.

Fatigue and malaise took hold of her not too long after she began to pace. Her other option was returning to the mirror to stare unblinking until her eyes grew dry.

Slowly, a kind of madness crept in, and she began to hallucinate. She clamped her palms over her throbbing eyes and watched a flash of different colors explode before her. When she pulled her hands away, the colors danced in the dark like fireworks in the night sky.

She stumbled back, nearly falling into the pool of water, and when her foot dipped inside, it was like millions of daggers biting her skin.

She hissed, lurched, and fell forward, grabbing the frame of the mirror on her way down.

"Father!" she cried out, her voice raspy and dry. Her skin was tight over her knuckles and her tongue was like sandpaper scraping the roof of her mouth when she swallowed.

A bitterness flooded her heart as she thought about Isis leaving her there to die. For all she knew, the siren goddess had spouted a pack of lies to manipulate Georgette and lead her to her doom.

She chewed her lip furiously, wondering how she could have been so gullible. So foolish. But another side of her mind wrestled against the idea with the defense that she was just a young woman who had suffered much grief and loss. More than anything in the world, she wanted to believe that her mother did not abandon her. That she was not evil. She wanted to believe that there was one person in this wretched world that loved her unconditionally and did not want to control her.

Captain Stone's face flooded her mind. Yes, he had done despicable, wretched things. She had seen with her own eyes what brutality he was capable of. But when it mattered, did he not always give her the gift of free will?

Every time she wanted to leave, he let her. Even if the action splintered his heart, shattering it into a million pieces. He respected freedom above everything.

Georgette clung to the mirror, her knees digging into the hard rock floor, wishing that Captain Stone had forbidden her to leave him. Clearly, this was a trap. There was no deal with Hades in the Underworld. Or if there was, Isis forgot to mention the part that involved Georgette having to die in order to get there.

The salty water sitting a few feet away taunted her like a honey trap. More than a few times, she thought about cupping her hands and gulping it down to end the maddening dryness in her mouth. Or to soften her lips.

But she knew that consuming sea water would only quicken her death.

"Father, please," Georgette whispered, gazing into the mirror one last time.

She clung onto hope for as long as her body could sustain her, but as a terrible weakness dragged her limbs down to the floor, she slumped sideways, until her arm collided with rock. Her head hit the ground so hard, she saw stars in her eyes.

She did not know how long she lay there. Was it

minutes or hours? But she held the mirror by its frame, resting sideways until her shoulders grew numb.

She was just about to loosen her grip and finally succumb to despair when a soft blue light began to dance in the center of the mirror.

Georgette watched it float around from left to right, then it spun in a circle, faster and faster, the light growing brighter and brighter, until the blue light took the form of a familiar face.

Thin lips, a narrow jaw. Neat brown hair tied back into a low ponytail, and a distinctive moustache that curled at the ends. Georgette sighed at the sight of a pair of glowing eyes.

"Father," she whispered.

There was a stillness in the air as a rush of peace washed over her. For a moment, Georgette wondered if the bittersweet sting of death had come for her. But her father chuckled softly, as though he had heard her thoughts.

"You are not dying, my sweet Georgette. Not yet," he said. But then his smile vanished, and his eyes glazed over. He seemed to be lost in thought. "I must apologize to you. I am responsible for so much of your suffering," he said in a hollow voice.

Georgette forced herself to sit, grateful to have a small source of light so she was no longer laying in the dark. She looked at her father's face and wondered which question to ask first. There were so many, they swam around her mind like a school of fish. While she tried to gather her thoughts, her father took the time to make a confession.

"Upon reflection, it seems ludicrous now. But at the time I believed I had no choice."

Georgette held her breath with anticipation, waiting for her father to tell her the truth. But the sound of his voice summoned grief like a sleeping monster and a sickness began to swirl inside of her stomach as she looked upon his face. In that moment, she didn't care about the past. Or what he did or didn't do. She didn't even care if Isis was right and he wasn't her birth father.

She was and would always be the daughter of Lord Harrington.

"My sweet Georgette. I should not have done it. But I lost your dowry in a game of cards to a ruthless pirate… And you know what happened next."

Georgette shifted her weight, her body groaning and aching like she'd never known. "I fell in love with him, Father. I do not hold any resentment for what you did," she said.

"You love Captain Stone?" Lord Harrington said, aghast. "Well, that is something I never foresaw." He hummed in thought, but then his head shook like he was trying to be rid of the thought altogether. "I must speak to you concerning your mother."

"I know my mother is Isis, the siren goddess of Imerta," Georgette said, nodding.

"You must be wondering why I did not tell you the truth. Isis is both unpredictable and highly dangerous. But I did truly love her," Lord Harrington said. "And it was far easier to tell you that she died than to reveal the horrors…"

Georgette sucked in a sharp breath as a question burning within her came rushing to the surface. "Is Poseidon my true father?"

Lord Harrington did not reply right away, he pressed his lips together tight until they disappeared under his bushy moustache. Finally, he uttered one syllable as a whisper. It smacked Georgette with a deafening blow.

"Yes."

When Georgette did not respond, he sighed. "I am sorry, Georgette. I can only imagine how difficult this is to hear. But there is more."

"Is it true that I have a twin?" Georgette asked.

Lord Harrington nodded. "Your mother gave birth to twin daughters. One with golden hair and the other with hair like fire."

Georgette hugged herself as she recalled Isis's words. "I have a sister."

"Poseidon took the redheaded child, and I took you. It was his punishment to Isis for being unfaithful."

Georgette frowned at Lord Harrington's words. "But he bedded women all the time? How could he be so…"

"Poseidon is a god who believes he may do whatever he wishes with no consequences, and I'm sorry to say this, but in his world, gods rule over everyone. Even goddesses. But listen to me, Georgette. Poseidon only spared my life under one condition… That I take you and never let you near the water. I was forbidden from telling you what you truly are."

Georgette frowned deeply. "But why did he separate us?"

Lord Harrington's voice grew quiet, and she had to lean in to catch his next words. "Isis is desperate to reunite you with your sister. She will stop at nothing until she succeeds. And it is not a mother's love that drives her will." He stopped to draw in a deep solemn breath while Georgette's heartbeat quickened.

"What is it? Why does she want to reunite us?" she asked, clutching the frame. But the ground suddenly began to tremble, and Lord Harrington's face grew faint. A sense of panic rose in Georgette. With every answer he gave her, two more questions were born. She feared they could have talked for an eternity, and she would never be content. The cave continued to shake. Rocks crumbled away from the walls and a sense of danger flooded Georgette with the knowledge that their visit was coming to an end. But she clung onto the frame, desperate to find out what she could in the little time she had left with Lord Harrington.

"Isis is determined to fulfill a prophecy. A prophecy around you and your sister," Lord Harrington's face disappeared into a blue flame once more and his whispers echoed in her ears. Georgette wrenched the mirror from its stand and screamed at it. "What did the prophecy say? What could make Isis so desperate to have it fulfilled and Poseidon so determined to stop it from happening?"

Suddenly, the ground jolted violently, and Georgette dropped the mirror. It crashed at her feet, the glass scattering in millions of tiny shards and sparkling like glitter.

Georgette backed away until the ground sloped, and her feet met with the water. Large chunks of rock dropped to the ground, and an eerie whistle flooded the cave, sending a chill up Georgette's arms.

Thrust into darkness again and knowing that there was no use in waiting any longer, Georgette waded into the water and transformed. His legs shifted into a strong tail once more, and the seawater flooded her body with strength.

She swam deeper, hoping that wherever the water

was coming from, the gap would be large enough for her to squeeze through.

But it was just as dark underwater as it was in the cave. She was forced to feel her way along the rocky floor, following her instincts as she tried to find a way out. As she felt around, moving her fin to propel her faster, a single thought kept repeating in her mind—she needed to find her twin sister. Maybe she knew more about the prophecy, and perhaps she was the key to ending Isis's curse on their bloodline.

CAPTAIN STONE

Captain Stone gripped the railings as he looked out at the open water. It was unnaturally still, and the sun's rays dazzled him as they scattered across the water.

His body ached to hold Georgette again. To cup her face and caress her cheeks while he lost himself in her pretty eyes. He missed her kiss, and the press of her fingertips on the back of his neck.

He shut his eyes and pictured the moment they would be reunited. The rush of relief on her face when she saw him walking toward her, alive and well. Perhaps her cheeks would redden as she stared in awe at his prize. He not only survived a battle with the notoriously wicked Blackbeard, but he succeeded in killing him too.

He might not even go to Isis right away. He'd take Georgette to a secluded part of the forest instead. Or perhaps not secluded at all, for he did not care who might choose to watch as he roughly took his wife. He would hold her up against a tree as he thrust into her, and her cries would echo across the whole island so loudly that even the mountains would blush.

He kept the head of Blackbeard in a sheepskin bag tied to his belt, carrying it with him wherever he went.

His crew had been obedient before they reached the pirate's cove, but after witnessing the brutal fight with Blackbeard and upon seeing just what dastardly things Captain Stone could do with his golden axe, they were particularly agreeable and subdued. Every man was quick to follow his every command and no one, not even Smythe, would look him in the eye.

None of this mattered to Captain Stone. He would have gladly cut up a thousand pirates from groin to crown in order to forge a better future for his wife. Georgette consumed him. Her safety was all that mattered in the world. He did not need anyone else to understand it, and he was more than happy for his crew to look at him like he was a monster.

He knew that so long as he had Georgette, who saw who he truly was deep down, it did not matter what anyone else thought.

If Georgette loved him, nothing else in the world mattered. She was his most precious treasure.

The quiet gave him peace to think about what to do next. He knew that Isis was scheming and unpredictable by nature. The head of her enemy would merely grant a meeting with her. But would she agree to his offer?

He suspected she was unlikely to agree to peace with the humans. Not after the savage way King George and his men had hunted down the sirens, displaying them like trophies in the sea.

But now he was Pirate King, perhaps there was another deal that could be made. He had to hold onto hope. Without it, the future was too bleak to bear. The tiny island soon appeared on the horizon, glinting like a jewel in the sunshine. Captain Stone paced the deck in anticipation, willing the ship to sail faster. He commanded his men to take to the oars and row like their lives depended on it.

The crisp, sea air soared over him, ruffling his hair, and flooding his lungs in the most glorious way. He stood strong, emboldened, and ready for whatever challenges lay ahead.

Suddenly, the sky grew gray, and clouds shrouded the brilliant sunshine, casting them all into darkness. An ethereal siren song flooded the air and the crew stopped rowing. The ship slowed and Captain Stone dashed to the lower deck as lashings of rain came down. "Pick up your oars and row or I'll gut you and feed you to the sirens!" he bellowed, his voice crackling in the rising storm.

When he climbed back up to the deck, an icy-cold wind howled, nearly knocking him off his feet.

He raised the sheepskin bag in the air. "Isis, I know you can hear me. I have the head of Captain Blackbeard and I wish to speak with you."

As though they had dropped from the sky, two sirens flopped on the deck, transformed into women, and stood tall and dangerously beautiful before them.

Their long, flowing locks covered their naked forms, but the sight of them startled Captain Stone long enough to set him off guard. He was not prepared for a confrontation with sirens, and when a floorboard creaked behind him, he did not turn quick enough. There was a smack, then a dull throbbing ache in the back of his head. His knees buckled and he sank into blackness.

When Captain Stone came to, his temples throbbed. He blinked several times as he made sense of his surroundings. His wrists were bound together and tied to the wall. The roar of the tide was faint in the distance, but he could still taste the salt in the air. He looked around the dimly lit room. It looked like a log cabin but with walls made of earth and wood. Creeping insects scuttled along the walls, and he could see soft peaks of light through the cracks in the ceiling.

"Good. You're awake."

Captain Stone jumped at the sound of a woman's voice and looked to his left. Isis stepped out of the shadows, her hands cradling something like a baby.

When she reached him, he saw that it was the head of Blackbeard. Thick congealed blood dripped to the dusty floor. Captain Stone grimaced as the stench of decay wafted over to him.

"I am disappointed, Captain Stone," Isis said with a tut. She held out the mangled face of Blackbeard for him. "I expected you to make a clean job of it. How am I to know for certain that this is the face of Blackbeard?"

Captain Stone scowled at her. "Are you calling me a liar?" he snapped. "After everything I've done for you?"

Isis's eyes flashed dangerously, but she set the head on a small wooden table and wiped her hands on a piece of cloth from inside her pocket. "Done for me? Let's see, shall we? First, you steal my immortality ring…"

"I won that fair and square in a game, I didn't ask your former lover to gamble it away," Captain Stone cut in. Isis lifted her palm.

"Then you steal my daughter."

"I didn't steal—" Captain Stone began but he shut his mouth under Isis's cold stare. He wanted to put his point across and clear his name, he also needed to be on her good side, and arguing with her was not the way to achieve that.

"You think cutting off some filthy pirate's head is going to make up for all of the pain you have caused me?" she asked. For the first time, Captain Stone saw some emotion in her face. He swallowed.

"I am sorry. I had no idea my actions had caused you any suffering," he said. It was true. As far as he was concerned, Isis did not care about Lord Harrington or his stone ring. Neither did she care for the child she abandoned.

His apology seemed to soothe Isis a little. Her shoulders lowered and a small smile crept across her lips. "But you did send her back to me, thank you for that."

Captain Stone's ears pricked up as Georgette's face flashed before his mind's eye. "Where is she? Let me see her," he said, wrestling with his binds.

Isis laughed. It echoed like a bell. Shrill and sharp. "She is gone, and you will never see her again. I'll make certain of that, *pirate*." She spat the last word like it was poison. "I know why you're here. I heard you muttering it, rehearsing the speech in your sleep as you sailed over to my island."

Isis clasped her hands behind her back and strolled around the room, humming to herself as though she found it all highly amusing.

"Now, don't you worry. I told your men that I have agreed to an alliance. They are to inform all the Pirate Lords that Isis is on their side, so long as they join me on the docks of England in three weeks' time."

Captain Stone frowned. "What are you planning?"

Isis stopped. Her smile grew wide, and her eyes glazed over. "Oh, something I should have done a *long* time ago." She looked up at the ceiling and traced her fingertips along the cracks. "Human children have treehouses… But we sirens make our houses in the ground." She chuckled warmly to herself. "When my girls were little and just learning to transform, I would tie them up in these underground rooms, and wait for the tide to come in." She turned to face Captain Stone. "You see, the quickest way to teach a siren how to tap into her powers, is to let her natural preservation instinct kick in. If she failed to shift, she would drown."

"You sound like a wonderful parent, Georgette truly missed out on an experience," Captain Stone said, his voice dripping with sarcasm. Isis pressed her lips together for a moment and blinked, giving him a cold stare.

"I believe you have a little under an hour before this room is completely flooded. Seeing as I'm not letting you out, I shall let you in on a little secret." She bent down to him, and her long golden hair fell around their faces like a curtain.

"There is a pathetic man who calls himself King, who has ordered for my beautiful daughters to be mutilated in ways I have never seen in all my years on this Earth. He and his precious lands shall be destroyed by the army you have gathered for me. Then I shall order my sirens to turn on their new allies and rip their ships into pieces. They shall tear every limb from limb until the seas run thick with human blood."

Captain Stone's wrists burned as he tugged on his binds. "What is this? Revenge? Isn't ripping my chest open and leaving me to die enough? I will speak to King George; he is my father. I will *kill* him if that is what must be done. Have I not proven my honor? I returned the ring to you, I cut off the head of Blackbeard on your request, and I even told Georgette—"

Isis pulled back, glaring at Captain Stone. "Whatever you told Georgette wasn't enough to help her trust me. I could see it in her eyes, and you would have loved to hear the sickly-sweet things she said about you. She truly believes you can do no harm."

Captain Stone's chest throbbed at her words, hoping she was being honest. After their fight, he was not sure how Georgette felt about him. But then a horrible nausea took over him as he thought about Isis's vile plan and the fact that he had unknowingly aided her in it.

Isis began to walk away, but she stopped when

Captain Stone shouted out, "Why are you leaving me here? You saw how bereft Georgette was, that day on the beach when you attacked me. And after she left, you promised never to harm me again."

Isis blinked slowly as drops of water began to seep through the cracks in the ceiling, pouring like rain. Then, she opened her mouth and uttered four words that turned Captain Stone's blood cold.

"I changed my mind."

The door shut behind her with a bang and Captain Stone gritted his teeth at the decapitated head of Blackbeard. He'd made a grave mistake.

Isis was never to be trusted. From the beginning, all of this was an elaborate trap. He was merely a pawn in Isis's dreadful game, and if he did not find a way to break out of his prison, he would not be able to warn the other pirate lords that they were sailing right into a trap as well.

Then what would happen to Georgette? There was no telling how far Isis's vengeful heart would take her and what she would do.

He grunted as he wrestled with the thick rope binding his hands and set his mind to think of an escape plan. He had no intention of dying like an animal beside the head of his enemy. No, he would get out of this watery grave, find Georgette, and sail for England to warn the others. Before it was too late.

PRINCE EDWARD

Prince Edward rapped his knuckles on the walnut door of King George's office and waited for his father's voice.

"Come in."

His chest grew tight as he entered the room, wondering how to approach the conversation. It was a tremendous relief to see that Mannington had not taken over the throne, but he could not understand why the pirates said they worked under King George. He refused to believe it was true.

He found his father seated behind his desk, poring over a stack of papers. A pair of spectacles sat at the tip of his nose. He looked over them as Prince Edward approached. "I cannot deny I am surprised by the revelations at dinner last night," he said after Prince Edward took a seat.

"Revelations?" he asked, taken aback. His mind had been spinning as he replayed the horrible events that took place before he arrived at the palace. His concern for the future was like a sickness in his heart. Dinner was the last thing on his mind.

King George set down his glasses and laced his thick fingers together with a sigh. "I had thought after the way things turned out with your last fiancé, that you would have taken some time…"

Prince Edward gripped the sides of the armchair as a fresh wave of humiliation flooded his veins. He would likely go down in history as the Jilted Prince. Despite their formal announcement that he and Georgette parted ways amicably, everyone who attended the wedding saw her running off with Captain Stone.

Captain Stone—who had revealed himself to be the Lost Prince of England, his older brother. He glared at his father. "Do you not think we have more important matters to discuss than who I will marry, Father?"

"I do not," King George snapped. "Who you will marry affects the future of the monarchy and that impacts this country. Tell me, Edward. What do you know about this woman?"

Prince Edward prickled under his father's

accusatory stare. He spent his entire life heeding the man's counsel, leading the Royal Navy, and setting aside his own desires to fulfill his duty to his country. Still, he would never fill the void that his older brother left behind when he walked away from royal life. Even though he was considered a disgraced member of the family, there was a way King George looked at Prince Edward that never matched the way he gazed upon Prince Mannington. Even when he charged into the palace during the wedding ceremony. King George looked on, quiet and unmoved by Captain Stone's outrageous declaration that he had already married Georgette.

It was never said with words, but Prince Edward always had the sense that King George looked at him as the inferior son. The weaker son. The one who did not have the backbone to fight for what he wanted.

The whites of his knuckles were on show as his fingers curled over the edge of the armrests. That would change. After all, he now had siren blood running in his veins. He had slaughtered grown men like a savage beast in order to protect his woman. Now, he was going to fight to win his father's approval. No matter the cost.

He sat forward and looked his father in the eye, unblinking. "I know that Serena will make a fine princess of England. You worry about this country? Tell me why there are pirates roaming the streets, terrorizing the people, and doing so in the name of King George?"

His eyes stung at the bitter memory of seeing Serena tied up in the cellar, with the pirates eyeing her up like a steaming plate of meat. King George's nostrils flared.

"I know nothing about that," he said, his voice curt. But he averted his gaze, seemingly unable to look Edward in the eyes.

"I hear that the entire Naval fleet has been destroyed. Is it true? Are they all dead?"

King George stiffened in his chair and wiped his nose with a handkerchief. "It appears so," he said, clearing his throat. Then he rose to his feet and looked out the tall windows overlooking the gardens. Prince Edward hurried to his side, his heart pumping. "All of them? Every single —" He cut off, holding a hand over his chest as an ache spread across it. "Then it is over. You will stop hunting sirens and put an end to the horrors."

King George puffed out his chest and looked at Prince Edward, his eyes blazing. "Have you forgotten that the sirens have been attacking our men for years, long before we finally retaliated? Until you revealed their weakness, we were powerless against them, and they were swarming the Pacific Ocean like wasps. If I didn't do something, it would only be a matter of time before they came to the Atlantic Ocean. Tell me, Edward, what would our country do if we could not trade with our neighboring countries? What if the sirens cut us off from the world?"

Prince Edward shook his head, unable to comprehend his father's logic. "I have seen the dead sirens lining our beaches. This has gone beyond protecting our country. It is sickening."

"It is a clear message—that England shall not tolerate their existence."

"*Existence?*" Prince Edward's blood boiled as if thousands of years of memories had come rushing to the surface. He could almost hear the endless wails of suffering from the sirens at the hand of his people.

Shame flooded his soul, threatening to rip his chest open. "*Listen* to yourself, Father. How can you decide who may or may not exist?"

"*I am King!*" his father roared. The whites of his eyes were on show as he squared up to his son. But Prince Edward did not recoil under his father's reaction. Surprised at the lack of fear, King George deflated.

He regarded his son a moment, then turned to look out the window again. Prince Edward followed his line of sight. Serena was walking through the garden in a pale blue dress, arm in arm with Queen Charlotte, who was showing her the roses.

"I have hired privateers to take up arms and fight for

our country. The French army will aid us in our mission. I am now waiting to hear from Germany, but I expect they shall be on board also."

Prince Edward scowled. "What about the people here? You're sending all of our men out to open sea when our own towns and villages are being attacked by pirates."

King George sighed and turned away from the windows. Then he hummed.

"You say Serena will make a good princess. Prove it."

"Excuse me?" Prince Edward asked, ripping his gaze from Serena.

King George met his inquiring gaze with a grim smile. "Take Serena to the nearby orphanage and introduce her to the people as your bride. She is very beautiful, indeed. And her voice is, dare I say, *enchanting*. But can she win over the hearts of the people?"

King George returned to his desk and looked at his papers once more. "If she does, then we shall arrange for a royal wedding imminently. This time, we shall open the gates and allow the whole kingdom to witness it."

Then he gave Edward a cold stare. "If you want to do your duty for your country, you will stay away from the sea and play your part."

"And what is that, Father?" Prince Edward asked, his

skin crawling at the idea of having to stay at the palace while the war raged on outside its walls.

King George smiled but it did not reach his eyes. "You are to distract the people from their miseries. Parade around with your new wife. Have her bear a son as soon as possible. That is your duty now."

"But, Father, the war—"

"Has nothing to do with you now. I shall build up a new Navy and find someone else to be Admiral."

The note of finality in King George's voice set Prince Edward's ears ringing. "You're stripping me of my title?" he asked, unbelieving.

"Edward, I do not understand you. I thought it was your wish to marry your princess. I am merely giving you exactly what you want. I'll make you a Duke if that pleases you."

"But what about the pirates? They—"

"They will do whatever I say," King George snapped. "Thanks to your brother and his reputation."

And there it was. The sense of pride in King George's eyes as he talked about Mannington. Prince Edward's hands balled into tight fists. If King George only knew what the pirates had done to him and Serena. If he knew the brutal things which they planned, and would have carried out, had Prince Edward not intervened.

But somehow, the words would not come out. He could no longer trust his father. He now sensed a wickedness in his father that had him on edge.

He gave a curt bow, his jaw jutting out as he did so. "As you wish, Father. I shall have my carriage ready and take Serena to the orphanage."

"Very good," King George said, looking back at his papers. "We all have our roles to play, Edward. It is well that you know your place and do what is expected of you."

"Yes, Father," Prince Edward said through gritted teeth. Then he left the office, his arms trembling with fury.

When he joined Serena in the gardens, his heart swelled as her gaze landed on him. Her hair was pinned up and a cascade of ringlets fell down her neck. The neckline of her gown fell dangerously low, leaving little to the imagination, and her waist nipped in so far that when she turned sideways it was almost non-existent.

His mother's face broke into a warm smile upon seeing him. "There you are, Edward. Serena and I have been having a most pleasant morning together," she said, releasing Serena and stepping aside.

Prince Edward inclined his head to them as he addressed them both. Then he held out an arm for Serena to take.

"I am glad you two are bonding," he said. "But I must steal her away from you, Mother, as Serena and I are to visit the orphanage."

"Orphanage?" Serena repeated as her arm slid along his. When her hand clutched the crook of his arm, a delightful shiver ran down his body. Her fragrant scent was calming. He longed to hold onto her forever.

"King George has arranged for our first outing to introduce you as my bride," he explained.

Queen Charlotte clasped her hands with a joyful squeak. "I shall write up a formal statement and have the message spread throughout the whole kingdom!"

She hurried up the winding path back up to the palace, muttering things about flower arrangements and having too much to do. Prince Edward looked at Serena, breathing in her scent and basking in her glow for a moment.

"How do I look?" she whispered.

Prince Edward looked around them and was happy to see there were only two ladies-in-waiting further up the path and well out of earshot. Nonetheless, he guided her to the hedge maze at a pace that had Serena running to keep up.

When they were alone, Prince Edward clutched her waist and looked deeply into her eyes. "You look timeless, my lady. I can hardly steal a breath whenever I look at you."

Serena's face flushed with happiness as she beamed at him. Her hands found his collar and she looked him up and down. "I confess I do like the way your trousers show off the delightful bulge between your legs. Do you bundle something down there or is that all you?"

Prince Edward froze under the words and stiffened against her gaze as she eyed his crotch. He had never been spoken to in such a manner.

"Thank you," was all he could muster as her fingertips slipped under the fabric of his shirt and grazed his collarbone. Her breath misted his cheeks as they leaned into each other. They stood still, just breathing one another's air for several moments. The tension between them rose, heating their bodies, and Prince Edward broke into a nervous sweat as he clung to Serena's tiny waist as though he would drown if he let her go.

"I wish we did not have to leave," Serena whispered, rising on tiptoes until her lips brushed against his. A rush of tingles scattered throughout Prince Edward's senses and his eyes rolled back at the delightful graze of her decolletage against his chest.

The siren had him enchanted, and suddenly, he

forgot his manners or their surroundings. "After the orphanage, I may be able to convince my driver to take us to my country home."

Serena's index finger trailed up his neck and she ran her fingers through his hair as she hummed. "Will we still have chaperones to keep us out of trouble?"

Prince Edward swallowed, allowing his hands to slide up the laces on the back of her dress and then rest on the lower swell of her breasts. Their breaths quickened as all of the horrors and pressures of expectation set on them melted away. A raw, animal magnetism took hold instead.

Each brazen touch was a healing balm on his invisible wounds. Siren or not, Serena made Edward feel more alive than ever. His body ached for her. Even with her pressed up against him, she was too far from him.

He needed to be enveloped in her. To touch her skin to skin. He pressed his lips to the sensitive part of her neck, and she threw her head back with a sigh at his feather-light touches. "I am certain I can bribe our chaperone to stay in the carriage for a short while," he murmured against her ear.

Serena shivered under his words, her body rippling with pleasure against his torso. As the front of her gown caressed his length, he became all too aware that his "delightful bulge" had now grown considerably in size.

He panted as pent-up frustration rose to the surface

and without thinking, he reached down and picked up Serena's leg, pinning it to his waist as he forced her back against the hedge.

"Oh, my Prince!" Serena gasped, arching against him with a shuddering sigh. "What has made you so primal?"

Prince Edward tore his lips from her silky soft skin to look into her eyes again. He caressed her cheek and grazed his thumb along her bottom lip. "I think I've wanted you for longer than I'd dare to admit. Even when I shouldn't have."

Serena captured his lips again in a kiss, rolling her tongue along his and moaning low and deep. He wrapped her up in his arms and nipped her bottom lip. She mewled softly, as though tamed.

When they broke apart to take a breath, Prince Edward rested his forehead against hers and clamped his eyes shut. "Seeing you in that cellar, surrounded by those filthy pirates… Hearing the vile things they planned to do to you… I cannot get any of it out of my mind."

Serena put her leg down and placed her hands on his chest. "You saved me, my Prince. Again. Do not let those thoughts torture you…"

Prince Edward took a steadying breath and nodded. "It is just that… If anything were to happen to you, I do not think I could bear it. I vowed to protect you, my lady, and I take my vows seriously—"

A cough interrupted the moment and Serena jumped back, putting some distance between them. Prince Edward silently cursed the young maid who dared to intrude on such a private moment. But then he remembered that it was customary to be watched. The palace did not know that according to Atlantean law, he and Serena were already married.

He had to show restraint for a little while longer.

He offered Serena his arm once more. "Let us go to the carriage. The orphanage is waiting."

The biggest orphanage in Port Harbor was in a convent. The old church had high ceilings and the air was bitter cold, even when the sun blazed outside.

There were at least fifty children under the age of eleven, and they sat cross-legged on the stone floor, surrounded by nuns, as Serena told them mythical tales of the sea.

Prince Edward watched her with rapt attention, just like the children. Her face lit up as she spoke to the sea of innocent eyes, and when it was time to leave, she took a moment to hug each and every one of them.

"Serena is indeed the people's princess, Your Highness. We thank you for this great honor of your visit," the priest said as they began to leave.

Outside the church, a large mass of people had gathered. Word had already spread that the prince had chosen a new bride, and everyone was there to catch a glimpse of the Princess.

When Serena stepped out into the sunlight, her hair flamed red and the crowd gasped, wowed by her beauty. Prince Edward let a broad grin cross his face as they waved to the crowds. Serena took in all of the attention with her head held high—a quiet confidence that inspired Prince Edward.

In all of their experiences together, he had never once seen Serena shaken. It seemed she was able to take anything in her stride. The only tell-tale sign of her nerves was the way she clutched his arm. Her grip was so tight, he was certain her fingertips would leave a bruise. But he did not care. She could cling to him for all eternity.

As promised, he ordered his driver to take them deep into the countryside. They sat in silence with their chaperone watching them, beady-eyed across from them.

Serena looked out of the window, pointing out all of the ordinary things that seemed peculiar to her. A fluffy-tailed rabbit. The lush green foliage lining the rocky path. Even the little rows of wooden houses on the hill in the distance, their chimneys smoking.

When the carriage rolled through the open gates to the manor, Prince Edward handed a bag of coins to the young man sitting across from them. "Mind the carriage, we shall not be long," he said. Then he helped Serena out onto the path. Her hand fit neatly in his as they walked up the gravel path to the house, and a rush of anticipation flooded Edward's senses as they entered the manor.

He could not wait a moment longer. He needed to be connected to her, in a way only a husband could be. Being back in his own kingdom and under the suppressive rules and customs was like a chokehold on him. He was starving of oxygen, of happiness. Serena was the breath of fresh air that he needed.

The door had barely closed behind them when he swiveled Serena on the spot and kissed her roughly, gripping the tops of her arms with urgency.

She kissed him back and melted under his touch, and Prince Edward knew that finally, nothing could stop what would happen next. He was ready for it.

SERENA

Prince Edward's rough hands roamed over Serena's exposed skin and his hot breath heated her body in ways she had not experienced before.

They had kissed before now, yes. They had even caressed each other in Atlantis. But the way Prince Edward looked at her now was different. He gripped her arms like he was confirming she was not an illusion. And he nipped the flesh just above her cleavage with a hungry growl. Serena shut her eyes as he pressed her up against a wall and held her wrists above her head with one big hand, while he fondled with the laces on the back of her dress with the other.

To her surprise, Prince Edward knew exactly what he was doing and soon single-handedly had her gown undone.

He released her wrists and her heavy dress dropped, pooling at her feet. Then he set his heated gaze upon her undergarments. If looks could burn clothes, Serena was certain she would have been naked in an instant and her undergarments would be on the floor, smoking. He flicked his tongue across his bottom lip, eyeing her like a predator. She bit against a smile. *This* was how she wanted him to look at her.

"I do not wish to dishonor you, my lady," he said as he ran his thumbs underneath her corset, grazing her skin. "But in my eyes, you belong to me just as I belong to you," he said. He gave her another rough kiss, moving with urgency and greed. Serena's eyelids drooped as pleasure rushed through her. "Nay, my Prince. On the contrary, it is my desire for you to *utterly* defile me. Right here in this parlor."

Prince Edward did not need to be asked twice. He yanked up her underskirt and pulled her cotton shift down, releasing the blazing heat between her legs.

Serena hitched a breath, hardly believing that after all of this time, he was finally going to fulfill her deepest wish.

She had not imagined him taking her in such a fashion. Not for their very first time, at least. For all his talk, she had imagined rose petals scattered over a bed, and the golden flicker of candlelight casting shadows over them while he caressed and kissed every part of her body...

But he was ravishing her against a wall instead, grunting. His breaths hot and heavy while he released his hard length from his breeches and nudged the tip to her core.

He picked up her other thigh and nestled it in place, and before Serena's mind could scramble any thoughts, he pushed inside her until she cried out in shock.

She crossed her ankles behind him and held onto his shoulders while he thrust into her further, hard, and deep.

Serena shuddered at the rising tension inside of her, the friction was agonizingly sweet. These sensations were new and welcome.

"Oh, Edward," she whispered between rough kisses. Their connection was full of yearning, desperate. Like two star-crossed lovers stealing a bittersweet moment in the darkness of night.

His eyes were closed and his brow sweaty as he quickened his pace. Serena throbbed and her legs trembled. She was grateful that he held her because she was certain to collapse in a heap on the floor should he let her go.

The pictures on the walls rattled until one of them came crashing to the floor. Neither of them paid any attention, too lost in the pleasure of each other's bodies.

Serena surrendered to him in every way, willing him to keep going until he emptied his seed.

But then he uttered a word that showered Serena in ice-cold dread.

"*Georgette*," he gasped, his eyes clamped shut.

As soon as the word escaped his lips, his eyes flew open. He lowered her to the floor, shaken and weak.

Serena looked at his ashen gray face as though he had slashed her throat. She held a hand to her neck just to be sure it was still intact. "What did you say?" she whispered in horror and disgust.

Prince Edward tucked himself away and dragged his hands through his long hair with a sigh. "Serena, I'm so sorry. I have no idea why I said that…"

"I do," Serena snapped, picking up her gown and slipping her arms through the sleeves. "I know exactly why you said her name."

She struggled to lace up the gown for a few moments before she finally gave in and let Prince Edward do it for her. But as his fingers worked, her body seethed with hurt and fury.

They were so close. So close to a blissful, happy ending. And he had to ruin it all with that wretched name.

"I thought you had moved on," she said, averting her gaze when he was done.

"So did I…" Prince Edward replied. "Truly. I promise she was not on my mind."

Serena lifted her eyes to give Prince Edward a hard look. "Tell me the truth, have you ever held me and thought about *her?*"

When Prince Edward looked down, his brow red, her heart sank. "She broke your heart, left you at the altar, and ran off with your brother," Serena spat, appalled by the situation. "How could you not be over her yet? I thought we had something real."

Prince Edward looked at Serena imploringly, grabbing her hands, but she yanked them free, unable to bear his skin on hers. He continued to plead with her. "I *am* over her. And we *do* have something real. I told you I will protect you from harm."

Serena fixed her hair and walked to the front door, resting her palm against it. Then she looked at Prince Edward over her shoulder. "And yet, here I am, spoiled. Taken while you thought of another woman. You just did me more harm than any of those pirates could have managed."

Then Serena threw open the door and walked out of the manor. She marched toward the carriage with her eyes and the back of her throat burning.

The ride back was long and awkward while Serena fantasized about hunting down Georgette and killing her in every possible way. But even then, the memory of her would still haunt Prince Edward. Would he ever be released from her spell?

Serena wondered what could possibly be so special about Georgette that Prince Edward could not let her go. She knew that while his heart still belonged to someone else, her dream of becoming a mother would ever be out of reach.

She did not want to create new life as her lover uttered the name of another woman. She had more self-respect than that.

And she could not bear to even think about bedding him again unless it was to choke him to death. He said he was sorry for it, but she would make him truly sorry. She ground her teeth, staring at the blurring countryside out of the window. Her mind kept swinging from wanting to destroy the prince's former fiancée to attacking him instead.

But they were bound to each other. If she killed him, she too would meet the same fate.

Then she would be destined for an endless journey through the Underworld, never to hold a babe in her arms. Never to enjoy the experience of rearing her own child.

She clenched her fists as she set her mind on the mission at hand. Queen Charlotte approved of their union. Soon, they would be married and then they could negotiate a peace treaty with King George.

Although now that she had met King George, Serena had the suspicion that those negotiations would not go as smoothly as Prince Edward insisted.

But she could not allow herself to have any more negative thoughts.

So, the prince did not love her. They still had to go through with the wedding. Too much was at stake, and she had sacrificed too much to back out now.

She could only hope that one day she could tolerate him enough to allow him to give her the one thing she yearned for in the world: a child.

The next day, Serena woke to a huge array of red roses in vases, set all around her room. The ladies-in-waiting bobbed, bowing their heads to her, and beaming from ear to ear. "From Prince Edward, Your Highness," they said. "He wishes to see you in the breakfast room."

Serena sighed as she looked at all of the flowers. It was a pitiful attempt to earn her forgiveness. "Tell the prince I am unwell."

She rolled over in bed but turned back when she heard a cough at the door. "Oh, dear. Shall I call for the doctor?" Queen Charlotte stood tall and regal, her hands placed carefully at her sides. "We have made all of the preparations for your wedding tomorrow. I do hope you are well enough for that?"

Serena sat up, her heart racing. In her disgruntlement, she had forgotten herself and the mission at hand. "No, your majesty. I have a mild headache is all."

Queen Charlotte relaxed. "Then you shall join me in the gardens. Nothing treats a headache like fresh air, and it is quite a beautiful day today."

Serena nodded, her mind reeling as Queen Charlotte left her room. Slowly, her ladies-in-waiting approached her, like circus men surrounding a wild bear.

Serena sighed. "All right, here we go again," she huffed under her breath. Then she got out of bed, ready for the ladies to work their magic on her once more.

Prince Edward sent one of his messenger boys to pass her a note, with his official wax seal to keep it shut. Serena refused to look at it.

In the afternoon, he sent the musicians to perform a romantic song, supposedly written by him. The harmony was pleasing, but nothing could take away the knot in her stomach.

Once again, she declined his invitation to join him.

Instead, she spent the day with Queen Charlotte—admiring her flower beds, choosing her wedding cake, and finally, standing on the plush foot stool surrounded by seamstresses, who were busy creating formal clothes for the wedding.

By the time late evening came, Serena had successfully avoided the prince all day. But when her ladies-in-waiting left her room at night, there was a soft knock on the door. Serena knew exactly who it was.

She tried to ignore it, but the tapping grew constant and obsessive.

When it became too much to bear, Serena slid out of bed, pulled on her robe, and marched barefoot across the stone floor. When she yanked the door open, her furious expression faded at the sight of King George standing in the hall.

Her eyes widened and she pulled her robe tighter around her body. "Your Majesty, I was not expecting you," she said, with a curtsy.

King George stepped inside without invitation and Serena staggered backward. He closed the door behind him. "As it is your wedding tomorrow, I am most certain you are full of nerves," he said, pulling out a bundle of cloth from his pocket. "But I came to tell you there is no need to be anxious. My son is an honorable, decent man who will treat you well," he continued.

Serena wanted to mutter something under her breath, but King George began to unwrap the bundle in his hands. "And as per our traditions, I wish to bestow upon you a family heirloom." The cloth fell away, revealing a small dagger with intricate patterns painted on a bone handle.

"It is exquisite," she said, looking at the knife.

King George held it out for her, but she hesitated. He leaned forward to give her a piercing look and the air grew cold. She resisted the urge to shiver. "The handle is made of ivory, imported from Africa. And the blade itself, well, it is the finest steel from the north."

Serena swallowed as she met King George's stare. She wondered what had given her identity away. In her fury with the prince, had she slipped and done something siren-like in front of the ladies-in-waiting? She supposed he had eyes and ears in all of the palace, perhaps she had muttered something in her sleep?

What if it was Prince Edward who had let her secret out?

Whatever it was, King George was now looking at Serena with eyes like hot pokers, holding out a steel blade for her to hold.

When she did not take it, he picked it up in one hand and held it up to eye level. "Do you ever wonder why a siren's weakness is steel?" he asked.

Before Serena could summon a reply, King George thrust the knife up an inch away from Serena's neck and fisted her hair.

"I have to know," he said in an acid whisper. "Are you really Serena of Endorra? Or are you a filthy little imposter, posing as a human so you can stab me in my sleep?"

Serena scowled at King George, wishing she had indeed gone to his quarters and murdered him. It would have been far easier than all of the pretending and she would not have ended up with him in her room and a steel blade to her neck.

"If you are who you claim to be, this won't hurt at all…" he said, yanking on her hair to force her head back. Serena resisted the urge to hiss, knowing that if King George saw her furious side, the charade would be up.

However, as soon as the steel blade touched her skin, it would sizzle and redden, as though she had been touched by a burning rod.

There was no escape. Serena wished Prince Edward had decided to come. Her anger faded as she silently screamed out for him, willing him to burst through her door in a rage and tear his beastly father from her.

No one came to her rescue. She was alone with King George, and he had her right where he wanted her.

He sucked in a breath of anticipation and pressed the edge of the knife to Serena's neck. She shut her eyes, bracing for the pain. But the burning never came. All she felt was hard, cold metal. No burn, no sting. She opened her eyes and watched King George withdraw the knife. He frowned. After a moment, he swallowed and cleared his throat, then stepped away.

"Are you satisfied now?" Serena asked, summoning all of her courage to keep her voice steady and use the turn of events to her advantage.

King George forced a smile back. "You may not be a siren, but that only means it will be even easier for me to slit that pretty neck of yours. And believe me, I shall not hesitate to do so, should you tell a soul about any of this."

He handed her the knife. For a flicker of a second, Serena thought about slashing King George's throat with it. But something held her back and she gave him a cold stare as he vacated the room once more.

When the door shut, leaving her alone, she trembled all over.

GEORGETTE

An earthquake shook the ground and threw Georgette down. She heard the crash of rocks and a rumble, as if boulders were tumbling into the sea, then silence. When she caught her breath, she drank some of the sea water for more strength and swam across the bottom of the cave to a tiny opening, where she peeked out. The coast was littered with stones and sand, and a pile of rubble blocked off the passage where the water had been gushing in before.

This was going to be more difficult than she thought.

She felt around for another opening, but there was nothing. She returned to the small gap in the rocks and blinked into the setting sunshine.

A rock fell from above and splashed into the water, scraping her elbow on the way down. Georgette cried out in fury and balled her hands into fists, determined not to die in this godforsaken cave.

As her determination grew, so did her strength. A force flooded every fiber of her being. Her fingernails began to grow, and she felt her ears stretch. The transformation would have been terrifying were she not in the grip of a terrible rage. Finally, her nails were as long as claws and her hearing was enhanced. Now, she had truly transitioned into a siren like the ones she had seen attacking pirate ships in the past.

In her new form, Georgette was connected to the world. She became acutely aware of the life around her and had the ability to draw power from it.

She took deep breaths, listening to the rushing waters outside. Then she paid attention to the creeping scorpions scuttling along the ground above the water. She sensed a group of hogs snuffling about and envisioned feeding on their life source. She inhaled their strength until they collapsed, and she was fully restored. With renewed strength, Georgette smashed her fists against the small opening, and it broke through as if it were a stack of playing cards.

She continued to smash the opening with her clawed fists until it was big enough for her body to squeeze through, and when she did wriggle through it, her vast fin propelled her forward, following the flow of water out to the open sea.

The exhilaration of freedom made her heart soar. She flew through the water as fast as she could. But as her anger dissipated, her ears and nails returned to normal. As she drew close to the beach, sounds grew muted and her newfound energy drained until she could barely move a muscle.

Slowly, she floated back to the shoreline, and when she crawled onto land, she collapsed, resting her left cheek on the coarse grains of sand.

The tide rolled over her body like foam as it crawled back and forth, while the setting sunshine warmed her exposed body.

The last of her energy faded away until she closed her eyes and succumbed to sleep.

When Georgette came to again, she was wrapped in a warm blanket that came to her neck. Crickets chirped in the distance and the sky was inky black above her. The whisper of the ocean soothed her racing heart, and she looked up at the stars dotted along the night sky between the trees looming over her.

To her left, a soft orange glow drew her attention. A

crackling fire licked the darkness with its flames. When she saw a pair of eyes between the flames, she sat up, clutching the blanket to her chest, and backed away.

"Who are you?" she snapped at the stranger.

Slowly, a woman leaned into the light, mousy blond hair flowing past her shoulders. "No need to address me in that manner, sister," she said with a note of amusement in her voice. She walked around the fire to sit beside Georgette. Then she picked up a coconut full of steaming liquid and handed it to her. "Drink. You need to recover your strength."

Georgette eyed the woman with suspicion for a moment. Having called her sister, she reasoned she was a siren.

It came as no surprise. The only people who dwelled on the isle of Imerta were sirens. The fact did not ease Georgette's distrust.

"Here," the siren said, sensing Georgette's suspicion. She blew the steam and took a sip of the liquid before handing it back to Georgette.

"If I had wanted to kill you, Georgette, I would have left you on the beach," she said, hugging her knees.

Georgette took the coconut to her lips and gulped the hot soup. It burned all the way down, but she didn't care. She was too desperate to have sustenance.

"What is your name? And how do you know mine?"

Georgette asked, wiping her mouth with the back of her hand. The blond lowered her knees to sit cross-legged and began to play with her long hair, humming to herself in thought. "You may not know us, but we know you, Georgette. After you came here with the pirate and resurrected him with your tears, we learned all about you."

The siren smiled, serene and calm, until she jumped as though struck by an idea. "I am Ava. Your pirate husband saved me. So, when I saw you at death's door, I thought it only right to intervene."

She held out her hand, but Georgette remained still, her brows knitted together. "My husband? Captain Stone?" she asked, eager for more information.

"The one and only," Ava replied, beaming. "He's got a funny sense of humor. I like a man who makes me laugh. Not that I'd show it of course. Men are intolerable at the best of times. The last thing you want to do is stroke his ego."

Georgette dropped the coconut, grabbed Ava's thin upper arms, and gave her a shake. "Did he succeed in his mission? Where is he now? Is he talking to Isis?" She fired questions at Ava like darts. The siren seemed amused.

"First things first, what happened to *you*? I thought you and Isis were getting along… How did you end up washed up on the shore looking like bait?" she asked, both brows raised.

Georgette took in a breath and gazed into the campfire, watching the dancing flames. "I was foolish. I trusted Isis when I shouldn't have."

Ava hummed in agreement. "One thing to remember about Mother is that she always has her own agenda. She is the queen of manipulation, so don't be too hard on yourself for falling for it. She can be incredibly convincing when she wants to be."

Georgette rubbed her throbbing temples and shut her eyes. "I just can't believe she would lock me up in a cave and leave me to die."

"Ah," Ava said, raising a finger in the air. Georgette looked at her again.

"Let me guess. There was an earthquake and the cave flooded."

Georgette frowned. "Did you feel it too?"

"Oh dear," Ava said under her breath. She rose to her feet. "It's an age-old trick, I'm afraid. She's done it to us all at one stage of our existence. I suppose it was your turn."

Georgette scrambled to her feet, holding the blanket around her to block out the chill of the ocean air. "She's done it to you too?"

Ava walked over to a pile of clothes and picked up a

simple cotton dress. "Here, put this on," she said, tossing it to Georgette.

"Listen, first rule of being a siren. Trust no one. Not even the goddess Isis. Being honest is not our way of life," she explained as Georgette pulled the dress over her head.

"Then how do I know you're telling me the truth now?" she asked when she had straightened the dress over her body. Ava shrugged. "You don't."

She began to pace. "Humor me for a moment and say that I am being honest. May I ask a question?"

Georgette sighed, trying to make sense of her thoughts. Her silence seemed to prompt Ava to continue. "How did you do it?"

"Do what?" Georgette asked, frowning again.

Ava scratched her forearm with a bashful smile. "How did you get a pirate to fall for you? Did you sing and seduce him in bed?" Her eyes glowed like two moons as she looked at Georgette with a hopeful expression on her face. "Did you hypnotize him with your voice? Perform a blood ritual?"

Georgette shook her head and shut her eyes as her mind began to spin. It was the first time a siren had shown so much interest in her. Let alone ask about pirates.

"No, none of those things. He captured me and

forced me to marry him," she said, irritated by all of the questions. Ava puffed out a breath, blowing a lock of hair away from her face. "You are so lucky. I wish that happened to me."

Georgette squinted at Ava, seeing her in a whole new light. "You want a pirate to force you into marriage?"

Ava squealed, as though the words flooded her with excitement. "Between you and me, Georgette, the thing I wish for more than anything in all the world, is for a strong man to fall in love with me."

Georgette stared at Ava, wondering if this was a joke or if the soup was poisoned after all. Ava looked back at her, dead serious. Georgette thought back to Captain Stone. "My husband. Where is he?"

Ava's smile fell. "Now? Dead, probably."

The words hit Georgette like a smack to the face. She lifted a hand to her mouth. "What do you mean? Ava. You must take me to him immediately."

Ava shook her head. "Oh no, Isis forbade it. None of us are permitted to help him."

Georgette grabbed Ava by the shoulders. "What are you talking about? Where is my husband?" Ava shrugged.

"You can get a new pirate husband. It is too late for Captain Stone. Isis lured him into a trap. He was captured and Isis says he shall never see the light of day again."

Georgette gripped Ava's shoulders with all her strength and her nails dug into her skin. Ava yelped, her eyes growing wide like saucers.

"Take me to him," Georgette growled. She made herself as big as she could, holding Ava so tight, her bones began to creak. It was clear that Georgette was more powerful than her sister. Ava seemed to know it too because she swallowed nervously. "All right, no need to crush me to death. I will take you to your dead pirate."

"Don't say that," Georgette snapped, letting her go. "He is not dead."

Ava rubbed her upper arms with a disgruntled frown. "How do you know?" she asked, picking up a bucket and covering the fire in dirt. Georgette closed her eyes and took in a deep, steadying breath.

"If he was dead, I would feel it. Now take me to where he is at once, or I will tear your head from your body for wasting my time."

Ava snorted, undeterred by Georgette's gruesome threat. "You sound more and more like a siren, sister."

CAPTAIN STONE

WATER GUSHED INTO THE SMALL DWELLING AS CAPTAIN Stone tried and failed to free himself of his bonds. He gritted his teeth and placed a foot against the wall. Then he tugged and pulled until the skin on his wrists bled.

He prayed to Athena, cursing her for aiding him. "Were you working for Isis, then?" he spat into the air. "Since when do you side with bloodthirsty sirens?"

To his dismay, Athena did not present herself to him again. He sorely wished for the golden axe. It would have so easily cut the rope like blades of grass. As soon as he was free from this place, he would hunt Isis down, rid the world of her once and for all.

The water rose to his knees as he looked wildly around him for anything sharp that he might use. The room was utterly empty, save for the decapitated head of Blackbeard, now bobbing mere inches from him.

Captain Stone kicked the wooden wall with all his might, roaring furiously. A small voice entered his mind. "Look down."

When he looked, his gaze landed on the head of Blackbeard once more, but this time, he caught sight of a thin, black blade hidden in his locks of hair. Captain Stone could have kissed the dead man. Of course, Blackbeard would hide a knife in his braids. Now Captain Stone only needed to reach it and cut himself free.

That was no easy task.

He lifted his knee and dragged the head around to his hands behind him, then fumbled blindly through the dead pirate's tangled locks. Going by touch made the process almost impossible, and congealed blood made it all the harder to divide the hair and get access to the handle of the knife. All the while, the sea poured into the room at an alarming rate.

The water had risen to his waist by the time he got a hold of the blade. He set his focus on the painstaking work of cutting his binds. His heart hammered in his ribcage as he struggled to keep the blade in his grip. If the blade dropped, that would be the end.

Finally, one of the binds snapped, freeing a wrist. Captain Stone swiveled around to free his other one and tried to ignore the throbbing pain in his wrists—red raw from rope burn.

The water had reached his chest now, and the knife struggled to cut the damp rope underwater. Captain Stone pocketed the knife and worked on untying the knot instead. The air stank of rotting flesh and seawater.

Finally, the rope pulled free, and he wriggled his hand out of his bind. The water was now at chin level.

Without hesitation, he spun around and swam toward the steps leading to the door. Of course, when he tried to open it, the door would not budge.

Captain Stone swore and rammed his forehead against the door in anger. There was no lock to pick, so he supposed it had an iron bolt on the other side. Trying to smash his way through would be a waste of energy.

He took a breath and swam under the surface of the water, exploring all the corners of the room. He found nothing.

He clawed at the wood beams in the ceiling in a desperate bid to wrench them apart and find a means of escape. It was pointless. The beams did not budge. As the water rose to the top, he sucked in a final breath and sank to the bottom, praying to whatever god hated Isis the most.

He offered a silent prayer. Should someone come to

his aid now, he would be their humble servant and carry out whatever brutal designs they desired.

It was the desperate, final plea of a doomed pirate, but just as his lungs began to ache, a blue portal opened in front of him, and he looked out at a vast and open field on the other side.

He had begun to see stars with blackening edges, but his body moved of its own accord. He lunged forward through the portal.

As soon as he spilled out on the other side, Captain Stone took greedy gulps of air—gasping and spluttering. He lay still for a moment, relishing the solid ground and the presence of air. Eventually, he sat up to look around him. The sun was low in the sky, but he recognized the trees in the distance and Isis's tall tower further north.

He was still on Imerta. Sudden remembrance struck him, and he looked wildly around, searching for his rescuer. His eyes landed on a lone cow grazing in the field. The beast had beads of every color draped over it in the form of a headdress, and Captain Stone took that as a sign to walk over to it. As he approached, the cow transformed into a tall woman with black hair and sun-kissed skin.

The hairs on his arms stood on end. Captain Stone went down on one knee and bowed. "Hathor," he murmured. A part of him wondered if perhaps he had not been saved after all.

"Are you here to assist me into the afterlife?" he asked, wary.

Poised and regal, Hathor blinked slowly. "No. I heard your prayer and have spared your life, Prince Mannington."

Captain Stone noticed her thin lips did not move. He was hearing her in his mind. She pointed at Isis's tower. "You must ensure that Isis's tower falls."

Captain Stone followed her line of sight and looked upon the structure. The magnitude of it would require crates of dynamite to bring it down, and he was skeptical about what good that would do, beyond irritating Isis. Nevertheless, he turned back to Hathor and bowed. "As you wish. May I request one last favor, so that I may be able to carry out your task?"

Hathor remained silent but held eye contact. Captain Stone took it as permission. He cleared his throat. "I need a boat and supplies. That I may sail back to England and warn my brother of Isis's devious plans."

Hathor blinked again and the air grew still and muted. Captain Stone could no longer hear the waves of the ocean lapping the rocks on the beach. Or the crickets that chirped endlessly.

Then a sudden rushing sound turned his attention to

the shore, and he jogged that way, watching from afar as a plain sailboat rose from the water. It was barely big enough for three grown men but had stacks of crates on one end and several bottles of wine. Captain Stone bowed to Hathor once more. "Thank you. I shall not let you down, I promise."

A gust of ocean wind blew back his hair and the goddess vanished before his eyes. He made his way to the boat.

When he had the thick rope of the boat in his hands, he hesitated. He wondered what Isis meant when she said Georgette was gone. Had she sailed off to find him at the pirates' cove? Did she come into trouble? Or was she exploring the seas in her siren form, embracing her true nature?

His heart ached as he thought about her and when they might see each other again. But right now, he needed to return to England as quickly as possible. A simple sailboat would never get him there in time, but he had been granted help from the gods thus far. He knew he needed to try, and only hoped that someone would help him on his way before it was too late.

PRINCE EDWARD

Prince Edward bit his tongue and pretended to be calm all the way back to the palace, while his mind screamed at him like a feral animal berating his betrayal.

In the throes of passion, his tongue slipped, and he uttered the last word either of them expected to hear. It echoed in his mind.

Georgette.

His mind chanted Serena's name over and over, in a desperate bid to erase his error. But nothing could change things now.

He cursed himself in his head as he walked silently from the carriage to the palace doors. When he entered, he made his excuses to Serena, who would not so much as glance in his direction. Then he made for his room, ignoring the inquiring stares of his servants.

Once he was in his private quarters, he kicked his chest and punched his bed until feathers filled the air and floated all around him like ash falling from the sky.

His anger spent, he heaved, panting through his nostrils, and struggling to make sense of what had happened.

He was over Georgette. He was sure of it. He had refused to bed Serena until he was certain. But just as his body reached a pinnacle of ecstasy, his mouth betrayed his unconscious mind and decimated the mood.

He paced his room with balled fists, cursing Georgette. Once again, she destroyed his happiness. Just when he was beginning to believe he could find peace in the arms of Serena, he hurt her in a way that he feared could never be repaired.

With no work to distract him, and his father's words ringing in his ears, he set his mind to make it up to her.

He did everything he could think of to soothe the suffering.

He ordered for her room to be filled with red roses before the morning, so she would wake up surrounded by them.

Then he arranged to have a banquet laid out in her honor.

She refused to attend, of course. So, he had his men send the food out to the poor people in Port

Harbor, in her name, instead. Word had spread of Serena's visit with the children at the orphanage and he was certain the people were already in love with her, but this charitable act would certainly seal their approval.

With their wedding just around the corner, Prince Edward began to question if he might become the Jilted Prince for the second time, and whether to call off the nuptials altogether to save his crumbling reputation.

He penned a song for Serena and instructed the musicians to serenade her. Even that did not earn him a response. No matter what he tried to do, Serena refused to leave her room.

Prince Edward paced from dusk until dawn, thinking of all of the ways he could rectify his mistake. He made a silent promise that the next time he took her to bed, he would growl her name over and over.

Serena. Serena. Serena.

Until then, he would follow her on his knees everywhere she went, begging for mercy, if that was what it would take to earn her forgiveness.

When the morning of their wedding arrived, he looked out at the gardens and thought about the sheer humiliation he'd face should Serena leave him at the altar. It would be a most terrible—but possibly appropriate—punishment for his actions.

And he reasoned that perhaps that was Serena's plan after all.

Guilt squeezed his heart until it bled as he washed and began to dress for the wedding. Knowing full well the fact he ran the risk of becoming the laughingstock of England, and the joke of the British monarchy for all its history. Prince Edward did not care.

He deserved to be ridiculed. Nothing could make him feel worse than he did about his actions. And he reasoned that if Serena wanted to humiliate him, so be it.

Resigned to whatever fate was before him, he finished dressing for the wedding and made his way to the grand hall, his heart pumping wildly.

Whispers flew as the crowds gathered in and outside the palace walls. All manner of fine ladies and important guests were seated in the pews lined up in the great hall. Meanwhile, the musicians played a whimsical song, as Prince Edward found his spot near the front.

His father and mother sat on their thrones, overseeing the room with matching smiles on their face.

Prince Edward nodded to his parents, then stood with his hands clasped in front of him, looking at the rows of guests looking back at him.

A few heads turned and there were quiet mutterings. He wondered how many people had placed bets on whether this time the bride would say "I do."

Seconds stretched into long minutes, and Prince Edward stood stiff. He kept his jaw clenched as hundreds of eyes bored into him. The crowds outside the palace were talking loudly now and the air flooded with rising anticipation that any moment now, the double doors would open, and the bride would enter.

As the minutes ticked by, Prince Edward grew more nervous. His nostrils flared and he tugged on the collar of his shirt as he stared at the brass door knobs, willing them to turn.

The mutterings grew louder, and the anticipation turned into anxiety. The people were exchanging theories on what might happen next.

Had Serena come to her senses and run back to the sea? Perhaps she was still in her room, penning a farewell note which would be passed to him by one of her ladies-in-waiting?

Just as Prince Edward started to think of a suitable speech to offer the guests, the brass knobs turned, and the doors were thrust open.

The musicians promptly stopped mid-song and started to play a dramatic number. Trumpets flooded the air and there was a collective gasp in and outside the palace.

"All rise," the priest called out.

There was a commotion as everyone jumped to their

feet. Prince Edward paid them no attention. His gaze was locked on Serena as she stepped into view.

Her white gown was immense. The bodice fit snugly against her body with a soft lace overlay covering her collarbone and shoulders. The skirt was a large structure made of organza, with hundreds of white roses pinned to the material. Her red hair fell in waves to her waist, free and wild, and her bright eyes sparkled like the jewels in her tiara.

She clutched a small posy of red roses like the ones he had sent to her room, and to Prince Edward's relief, she was smiling at him.

The music played strong and loud as she approached, but soon every other sound was drowned out by the thunderous beating of his heart. He placed a hand on his chest, his eyes prickling.

She reached his side and handed her flowers to a maid, then she turned and held Prince Edward's fingertips.

He hitched a breath. "You came," he whispered, swallowing against the lump in his throat. "I'm so glad you came."

A soft wave of laughter followed. The guests must have heard his words.

The prince couldn't care less that was being laughed at. Serena was beautiful and she was looking at him. Not like a despicable human being, or a foolish man who broke her heart. No. She looked at him like an adoring bride, happy and excited to exchange vows.

When the priest prompted Serena to speak, she said "I do" so loud, her words rang through the halls of the palace and were met with an explosion of cheers from outside.

The musicians played triumphant music as they kissed. King George stood and held out his arms to call the attention of everyone. "With great honor, I introduce to you, Prince Edward and Princess Serena, Duke and Duchess of Port Harbor."

Prince Edward glanced at his father and mouthed his thanks to him. Then he turned back to smile at Serena.

They played their roles perfectly, moving from table to table at the royal banquet to strike up polite conversation. Lords and Ladies, Barons, Viscounts, and all manner of rich members of the society were in attendance. Serena complimented the ladies' apparel, or hairstyles, while Prince Edward exchanged pleasantries with the men. To his surprise, no one uttered a single word of the war. The fringes of it were creeping up the beach, from the lines of dead sirens on pikes to the houses reduced to rubble along the port, but it seemed as though no one cared, or perhaps they had been instructed to steer clear of unpleasant topics of conversation. He noticed that several of the gentlemen glanced at King George, who kept his gaze steady on the newly wedded couple the entire day.

Serena clung to his arm, but occasionally her gaze would hover on King George as well. Had he spoken to her? Was that the reason for her sudden shift in attitude?

Finally, the evening rolled in, and Prince Edward and Serena were permitted to leave the palace without a chaperone. They smiled and waved at the cheering crowds as they walked down the path, and Prince Edward helped Serena into the carriage that was waiting for them.

When the door closed behind Edward, the cheers were muted. He turned to Serena, who was looking out of the window with her back to him.

The carriage rolled forward and the gentle clip-clop of hooves hitting the cobbled streets was a soothing contrast to the commotion outside.

"Serena," Prince Edward said, touching her shoulder softly. She flinched under him and turned her head but let out a laugh. "I'm sorry, my Prince. You startled me. I was miles away."

Prince Edward's heart leaped at her words. It truly seemed she was no longer upset with him. He took her hand, and she did not pull it away.

"My dearest Serena," he said, lifting her hand to kiss

her knuckles. "About the other day… I want to apologize again…" he began, but Serena pressed her finger to his lips with a hard look.

"Let us not speak of it again, my Prince. It was a mistake, and I am quite certain it shall never happen again."

He wrapped an arm around her, and she rested her head on his shoulder. Then finally, Prince Edward relaxed and fell into a blissful sleep as the carriage rocked them side to side.

It was entirely dark when the carriage came to a stop, jolting Prince Edward awake. Serena stirred in his arms. "Are we back at the cottage?"

Prince Edward clenched his jaw at the question. Under no circumstances was he going to take Serena back to that place. He had half a mind to burn it all down after what happened.

"No, we're at Walnut Manor, in a small village further inland."

Serena yawned as she sat up and shuffled along the bench, following Prince Edward out of the carriage door. "My goodness, how many homes do you own, my Prince?" she asked while taking his hand. Prince Edward chuckled but did not reply, tucking her delicate hand into the crook of his arm.

It struck him then that they had finally succeeded in their mission. They were married.

When they entered the manor, Prince Edward went about lighting the lamps. He found Serena running her finger along the spines of old books in the study.

The floorboards creaked under his boot as he entered, prompting her to look at him. "Have you read all of these books?" she asked.

Prince Edward swaggered over, loosening his tie. "There may be a couple of tomes in there that I have been unable to finish. But mostly, yes."

A flash of memories crossed his mind's eye and Prince Edward was transported back to Atlantis—the nights they spent reading to each other from the old books they'd found in the palace; The secrets they whispered to each other in the dark.

It seemed a simpler time, and they had since been through so much.

He reached around her and pulled out a thick book. "Would you like me to read to you, my lady? We can pretend we're back in Atlantis and far away from this kingdom."

He tried to smile warmly at Serena, but her mouth was sloped into a frown.

"What is it, my lady?" he whispered, setting the book on the table, and cupping her face.

"Will you not say my name, anymore?" she asked, blinking up at him. A single tear rolled down her cheek.

Prince Edward's chest grew tight as realization dawned on him. It was not just the fact that he had called out Georgette's name earlier that hurt her.

She pulled away and walked to the door, clutching her arms. "You used to whisper my name in your sleep. Back when you were on your quest, looking for *her*."

A flush of heat rose to his temples. Serena turned on the spot to give him a brazen look, her cheeks pink.

"Have I not always done everything you asked of me?" She did not wait for him to answer before she continued. "After you lost your ship and crew during the maelstrom, I saved you. And whenever you called out my name, crying for help, I never hesitated to show up. When my father sentenced you to death, I gave up my immortality and bound myself to you. And now, even though your heart still belongs to another woman, I have agreed to be your wife."

She lifted up her left hand, the gold ring glinting in the dim light. Prince Edward's heart thrummed in his ribcage as she moved toward him. Her long hair flowed like molten lava down her elegant white dress.

A waft of her sweet floral scent washed over him as she drew near.

Prince Edward looked at her as though it was for the very first time.

All of the time he was chasing Georgette, Serena was there.

And even when he was focused on carrying out his royal duties, thinking of ways to end the brutal war between sirens and humanity, she was at his side.

"Do you not find me desirable?" she asked, pulling her hair away from her shoulders. "What does she have that I do not?"

"I do not care for her anymore," Prince Edward said, struggling to swallow, his throat suddenly dry.

Serena frowned. "Then why will you not even say my name?"

Serena.

The word screamed in his mind, but for some reason, his tongue seemed to grow twice its normal size and he could not force the word out.

He gripped her tiny waist in desperation, dragged his thumbs over the lacy material, and let out breath. Serena reached up and opened up his cotton shirt, the tips of her fingers grazing his chest. Her breath tickled his neck as she rose on tiptoes and whispered into his ear, "Tell me, was any of it real? Or were you always pretending for the sake of your duty?"

A rush of heat traveled south, leaving Prince

Edward's mind to spin. He licked his dry lips, trying to remember how to form a sentence. Serena was already pulling his jacket off his shoulders and tugging the bottom of his shirt out of his trousers. When her fingers touched his lower abs, his body set alight in need.

He longed to find the words to tell Serena exactly how he felt about her, but it was almost impossible at that moment. He could not make sense of it all. The line between reality and make-believe had been blurred for so long, he was no longer certain what to think.

He shut his eyes and took in a deep breath as he tried to straighten out his thoughts. "You are the most beautiful person in this whole world," he began, opening his eyes again. Serena stopped touching him and drew back to look into his eyes. He took her hands in his. "And not only on the outside. It is your soul that shines the brightest. You are right. You have always been there for me, even when I did not deserve it."

He held her hands between his, reached up, and rested them over his heart. "My heart only beats for you. It races when you look at me. It skips a beat when you smile. And I fear that if something terrible happened to you, it would stop beating entirely."

"Then say it," Serena insisted, her thick lashes fluttering. Prince Edward frowned as he tried to guess what she was meaning.

"I love you," he said.

But Serena shook her head and leaned in to brush her lips over his. "Say my name."

Prince Edward lost himself in the pools of her eyes, then he finally whispered, "I love you… *Serena*."

Serena melted against his body and Prince Edward wrapped her up in his arms as he kissed her. First, it was chaste and sweet. But then he let go of her and tangled his fingers through her hair as his mouth found her ear. "Serena," he growled.

He chanted her name over and over as he left a thousand kisses over her neck and décolletage. Then he picked her up and carried her across the hall to the master bedroom.

The servants had decorated it for their honeymoon. Dozens of candles burned in the corners of the room, and the four-poster bed stood proudly in the center. Hundreds of red rose petals were scattered across the sheets.

"Serena, with your permission," he said, lowering her gently to the bed. "There is one duty I must fulfill as your husband. I'm going to spend all night uttering your name until I lose my voice, while I worship every single inch of your body."

Serena looked up at him with heated eyes. "Nothing would give me more pleasure."

SERENA

Serena fell back against the bed with a sigh, sending a cluster of petals flying into the air. Prince Edward removed the last of his clothes and crawled over her like a wild beast.

Surrounded by fine furniture, sweet-smelling flowers, and plush sheets, it was the perfect setting for their wedding night.

Serena refused to let her mind think of anything unpleasant as she gave into the pleasurable flutters in her stomach every time the prince's lips met her skin.

His hands found the top of her gown and he tore the lace overlay in two. Serena arched her back, ready to be freed from the restrictive bodice of her dress. There was no time to fiddle with intricate fastenings or ties. Prince

Edward ripped the gown away from her body like it was Christmas morning and she was his main present.

When he ripped her corset open, the release of pressure left her gasping.

The cool air struck her with a delightful rush, and the contrast of Prince Edward's body heat made her ache.

"Serena," he said for the hundredth time before he kissed her on the mouth again. His hand found her throat and flexed, sending a thrill down Serena's spine.

He moved with more urgency now, supposedly eager to be skin to skin. Serena was reminded of the man who saved her in that wretched cellar—when he had killed the pirates who threatened her.

She wanted to be ravaged by the man who saved her from the pirates. Not the gentle, sweet prince who always did what was right.

To her delight, Prince Edward bit her thin cotton undergarments and tore them off with his teeth.

When she was naked, he let out a hungry growl. "Serena, Serena, Serena," he repeated between long, sucking kisses down her abdomen. Every time he trailed his kisses down her body, he would return to grip her throat and give her a hungry kiss on the lips.

His body burned against her skin, and she clung onto his bulging shoulders for dear life while he nuzzled her neck.

Still, he grunted her name. Over and over. It was almost like a ritual. Each time he said her name, Serena's heart swelled.

Suddenly, nothing was complicated anymore. There was no war raging outside, and for the first time, she felt she truly understood what it meant to be bound.

Serena became acutely aware of Prince Edward's racing heartbeat. It matched the speed of hers as their clammy torsos touched. They sucked on each other's lips, grinding hips, and Serena was not sure where she ended, and Prince Edward began.

Everything about this moment felt right. It was the most natural, beautiful thing she had done in all her life.

She gasped against his mouth as his hard length nudged between her thighs and teased her throbbing core. Serena arched her back again, pressing harder against his chest and urging him to satisfy her need.

"Complete me," she demanded, unable to hide the desperation in her voice.

Prince Edward pulled back to look into her eyes, and she paused to look back. He watched her for a moment, then he nodded, resolute, and took hold of her hips as he positioned himself.

He slid in with so much ease, a deep groan ripped from his throat and his eyes rolled back. He filled her. They clung to each other for a moment and breathed as one as Serena adjusted to the feeling. She wanted more.

Prince Edward fisted her hair and gave her hard, commanding kisses all over her neck, his stubble rubbing her skin raw. Serena did not care. She had never felt more alive and cherished.

He rocked his hips slowly while he tugged her hair, forcing her head back. She clung to him for fear of falling into an abyss.

After all of the horrors and heartache, they both needed this, Serena thought. There was something about the way Prince Edward thrust into her with such urgency and passion, that had Serena lowering all of her defenses.

She knew there would be a time when they would have to talk about the terrible thing his father did to her on the eve of their wedding. And she was still not convinced he deserved her forgiveness. But right now, he needed to be close to a woman, and she yearned to bear a child.

Was it an expression of true love, or just a mutually beneficial act? Serena didn't know, but she didn't need to. The answer would not change anything.

After some time, Serena fell against the bed again, panting. Prince Edward gripped her hips and picked up speed.

He pushed himself into her with an almost savage

abandon, and Serena lost herself in the beautiful, primal moment. Fire blazed in his eyes, and a film of sweat covered her like dew. His own sweat clung to him like drops and Serena licked her lips, trailing her fingers over the contours of his beautiful body.

His dark hair fell over his face, tousled and damp with perspiration as he made love to her. Even in the dim light, the desire in his eyes was as clear as day.

Those eyes were possessive, dominant, and heady. She knew that in that moment, he was looking at her, and only her.

The word *Serena* escaped his mouth in another growl and another ripple of pleasure took over her body.

She could see the pressure building in him by the way his breathing became short and labored. He gripped her waist so hard, it stung.

He was close and they were almost at the finish line. Serena was so close to reaching her dream, she could almost taste it.

He slowed his pace, as though trying to regain some control and draw things out, but Serena bucked against him, willing him to release.

Just when she thought he was going to crash over the edge, he pulled out and crawled over her, kissing, and sucking on every piece of her exposed flesh.

Shivering from the sudden absence of him inside of her, Serena felt oddly hollow and off balance.

She reached for him, but he moved away just before she could curl her fingers around his length. "No, Serena," he said, grinning wickedly as he gave her a sharp spank on the bottom. "I am not done with you, yet." He took her wrists and pinned them to the bed as he hovered over her, the space between their heated bodies sizzling.

Frustrated, Serena clenched her jaw and frowned. Prince Edward let go of her wrists and began to explore her body with his mouth. Then he did something that made her toes curl. A wave of pleasure she could not control followed, and she let out a mind-numbing scream. She was certain her voice reached all the way out to the sea.

By the time Prince Edward found her core again and slid in, she was weak. Her body crumpled under him, utterly melted under his blazing heat. Her soul lifted from her body as he claimed her once more. He picked up pace, grunting and fisting the sheets while Serena was lost in the ether, a faraway land of swirling patterns in multicolor where she had stars in her eyes. Then when he bit her neck and let out a shuddering breath, she fell back into her body with a jolt.

He collapsed next to her, panting, and utterly spent.

They rested in each other's arms, basking in the afterglow of their lovemaking.

It was everything Serena had hoped it would be—and more.

She hoped that something equally wonderful would happen inside her. One that would change her life forever.

When their breathing returned to normal, Serena saw that the curtains on the tall windows were pulled back. If anyone had been outside, they would have seen everything. Her mouth twisted into a wry smile. The thrill of other people watching only made her want to do it again.

She was still suspicious of Prince Edward's true feelings and skeptical that he was truly over Georgette. But in that moment, she did not care. She had what she wanted. "Well, you were true to your word, my dear," Serena said, stroking Prince Edward's dark hair as he lay with his cheek resting between her breasts. "You pleasured me all night. The sun is starting to rise."

Prince Edward looked up sharply, his brows knitted together. "Already?" he said, frowning.

Serena pointed at the tinge of orange in the distance outside the window. "Look," she said.

Prince Edward pulled the sheet around him and

edged out of bed, then he strode across the room to look out the window.

"What is it?" Serena asked, watching his shoulders rise and all of the muscles in his back tense up. He did not answer but hurried to the pile of clothes on the floor. After a few moments of rummaging, he retrieved his pocket watch.

"Something has happened," he said.

Serena sat up, unnerved by the serious tone in his voice. "What do you mean?"

She watched him dress hurriedly, his face flushed red, and his brows tightly knitted.

Serena ran to the window and squinted. The sky was dark. She could just make out the silhouettes of trees and houses. An orange and red tinge of light hovered over a cluster of buildings Serena supposed to be Port Harbor.

"If that is not the sun… Then—" she broke off as a horrid thought crept into her mind. Prince Edward returned with a spyglass and looked out for a moment. He sucked in a breath.

"Port Harbor is under attack," he lowered the spyglass and cradled Serena's cheek with his broad hand. "I have to go. Stay here, you will be safe."

Before Serena could argue, he gave her a rough kiss on the lips. "I love you, Serena," he said and pressed his forehead against hers.

Serena was confused and frightened by the turn of events. This was not how the evening was supposed to go.

"We must both go together and stop this war once and for all," she said, waving her hand over her and conjuring a simple silver gown on her body.

Prince Edward's jaw bulged as he shook his head. "Not yet. I fear that our marriage will not be enough to end this war."

Serena followed him out into the hall. "I am not sitting here in a strange land while you go out on a suicide mission," she said with her hands on her hips.

Prince Edward huffed and dragged a hand through his hair. "I can't protect you and fight—"

Serena hissed. Her fingernails grew long like talons, and she bared her pointed teeth in irritation. "I can take care of myself, or have you forgotten?"

His expression darkened as he looked upon her, but he did not cower. Instead, he lowered himself to his knees and gripped her by the waist. "Serena," he said. Serena calmed, transforming back into her normal form as he drew circles over her hipbones.

"I know you can destroy a whole fleet of ships without even breaking a sweat, but we don't know who is out there. If they have a new weapon… And if something were to happen to you, I would carve out my own heart to put an end to my agony."

Serena paused, conflicted by his tortured plea. Then a bubble of annoyance rose to the surface. "You underestimate me, Edward. Whatever danger lurks out there, I am joining you in the fight. You cannot stop me."

Prince Edward heaved a sigh and rested his forehead against her stomach. "*Please* don't do this. I just can't lose you too."

The words made Serena recoil. She pushed him backward. "Is that what this is about?" she asked acidly.

She began to pace the room. "You're afraid I'm going to leave you like *she* did."

Prince Edward rose to his feet, his face hollow. "It's not that, not at all. I only—"

"In case you haven't noticed, I am *not* Georgette," Serena snapped.

Prince Edward blinked several times. "I know that."

"Do you?" Serena asked, walking up to him, her fury rising to the surface as she gave him a steely look. "Because you keep treating me like the pathetic, weak little woman she is."

Prince Edward squared his shoulders and frowned at her. "Don't say that," he said sharply.

Serena laughed. "Oh? What is it, my Prince? Can you not bear to hear how vile of a creature your precious Georgette is?" They glared at one another for a moment before Serena continued. "Well, I guess you have a type. She's a siren too, after all."

The crease between Prince Edward's brows told her that he did not like being reminded of the fact. He opened his mouth, but no sound came out, and Serena kept going, all of her pent-up frustration flying out like daggers.

"I will not be her decoy anymore. I got what I want…" She placed her hands over her stomach. "We will put an end to this war, and I will go home to Atlantis with my child. You can tell everyone I died at sea. Then you can go and kill that pirate and claim his wife for your own."

She hissed her words, and Prince Edward's eyes grew misty. He shook his head as though trying to break from a spell.

"What do you mean… child?" he asked.

Serena straightened her spine, looking defiantly at him. "I see the torment in your eyes. So, allow me to make things easier for you." She crossed her arms with a sigh. "I do not care about the war. I married you so that you can give me the one thing I want in this world."

"A child?" Prince Edward replied, his brows rising. "Wait. All of this… It was seduction so that I would get you pregnant?"

Serena nodded. It was a lie, of course. What started

out as a simple plan became complicated as her feelings for Prince Edward grew. For a blissful moment or two, she truly believed they could have it all. But then he did the unthinkable. She lifted a finger to point at him.

"You really think I'd forgive you that easily after you did what you did?" she hissed. "I only wanted to fool you into bed so that I could get what I want before I leave you."

"You think it's that easy? That it only takes one time?" Prince Edward laughed a haggard laugh, then dragged his hands through his hair, a look of horror on his face. "I cannot believe this." He shook himself. "No. I won't believe this. You're trying to hurt me so I will stop protecting you."

Serena gritted her teeth. Was it so obvious? Her feelings and emotions were a tangled web of lies that she could no longer decipher. Regardless of the way she truly felt, one thing was certain.

"I'm coming to Port Harbor," she said, a note of finality in her voice.

Prince Edward's jaw jutted out as he looked at her. "Fine," he grunted.

GEORGETTE

Georgette followed Ava through the thick forest, watching her long dress sparkle like glitter. She walked with grace and poise, and her mousey hair fell to the small of her back.

Despite Georgette's frequent threats to quicken the pace, Ava kept her speed relaxed and casual. They were headed for the other side of the island, and it took them hours to cross the tricky terrain. Twigs snapped underfoot and the overgrowth rustled around them. A distant howl broke the constant sound of crickets chirping and Georgette jumped, but Ava paid it no attention.

Georgette reminded herself that there was no reason for them to be alarmed. On Imerta, sirens were top of the food chain.

But her heart wouldn't stop racing as they walked.

With each step, her sense of dread increased. What if they were too late?

She clutched her stomach, praying to all of the gods she knew by name that her husband was still alive. She could not bear the thought of seeing him lifeless. Not again.

But even if that was all she found, she held onto a hope that she could bring him back. After all, she had resurrected him once. She could do it again.

"Here," Ava said as they reached a large sycamore tree. She pulled back a curtain of vines to reveal an ornate door with a black iron bolt. "Welcome to the *Epistrepho*." She grabbed the iron bolt and tugged it back with a grunt.

Georgette watched, and when Ava caught the confused look on her face, she tossed her hair back with a sigh. "Ancient Greek. It means, *to turn*. Isis brought us down here when we were young to awaken the siren in us."

Georgette would have asked more questions, but her ears were ringing. All she could think about was what she might find behind the door.

When Ava pulled it open, a rush of water poured out, nearly knocking Georgette off her feet. But Ava stood immobile and strong. She looked back at Georgette with a sad smile. "Are you ready?"

The words curled around Georgette's neck like fingers and squeezed. All she could do was nod.

They waded down a flight of stone steps until the water rose above their heads. Then they turned into siren forms and swam deeper until they came out in a small room.

Ava gasped, and Georgette's heart jolted as she looked around the empty space. A bundle of ropes floated near the surface and there was a mass of dark hair attached to a decapitated head.

"No!" Georgette screeched, swimming to it.

She clutched the head, hardly daring to breathe as she turned it around in her hands.

The face was battered. Its features were twisted into something almost unrecognizable. The cheeks and chin had swollen, and the skin was blue with a green tinge.

But Georgette's shoulders sagged in relief. It was not the face of her beloved Captain Stone.

She let the head float back up to the surface and joined Ava in inspecting the floor. There were patches of bloodstains on the ground, and scuff marks all along the wall beside an iron loop.

She could see a struggle, but other than the decapitated head of an unknown man, there was nothing else to be found.

Georgette and Ava swam back up the staircase and returned to the forest.

After she shifted, Ava waved a hand and conjured a simple blue dress on Georgette's body. Then she gave herself a dusky pink dress and they walked in silence for several minutes.

"I am sorry," Ava said. "It appears Isis already killed him."

Georgette rubbed her damp arms with a disgruntled hum. "No. That head belonged to someone else."

Ava frowned and gave Georgette an odd look. "Unless your husband is a Triton, there is no way he could have survived it in there. You know that, right?"

Georgette frowned deeper. "He is not dead."

"Isis could have taken his body so you would not be able to bring him back," Ava argued, voicing Georgette's deepest fear.

Georgette looked out at the dark blue horizon, listening to the waves crashing against the rocks. She shut her eyes and willed her senses to reach out and pick up on any sign of Captain Stone.

It had been too long since she felt his hot ragged breaths on her cheeks, or the roughness of his hands roaming her body. She should never have left his side. Now, there was no telling when or how they would be reunited.

Georgette balled her fists and turned to see the top of Isis's tower poking out from the trees.

"Ava, I need you to teach me how to be a siren," she said.

Ava's eyes widened for a moment, then she let out a derisive laugh. "You transformed perfectly, just now."

"Yes," Georgette said. "But I cannot hear like you can, or magic clothing from thin air."

Ava hummed, crossing her arms. "Well, it's not from thin air. We manipulate water," she said, flicking her wrist to make a bubble float above her palm.

"Water is in everything. It gives life, and it takes it away." She snapped her fingers and the bubble popped. "But learning to tune into the water around you and manipulate it takes years of practice," she said.

Georgette waved her hand, picturing a bubble to form, but nothing happened. She huffed. "What about my hearing? Sometimes it seems I can hear a mouse scurry across the ground from a mile away. Other times, it is as though I cannot hear my own heartbeat."

Ava pressed her lips together as her eyes narrowed on Georgette. "Emotions cloud our abilities. It is why Isis forbids us from—" She stopped and looked out at the sea, suddenly clinging onto herself as though she was trying to stop her body from falling apart.

Georgette touched her shoulder. "What is it?"

Ava flinched at the touch but looked back at Georgette, a small crease between her delicate brows. "You are not the only siren with questions and desires."

Georgette swallowed. "You are lonely."

Ava shrugged her hand away and took a few steps. Her hair fell like a curtain over the side of her face as she turned her back to Georgette.

She let out a heavy sigh. "I confess, I have been observing you and your pirate."

She turned back, her eyes glistening. "It was my job. From Isis, you see. I was to follow you and report back what I found."

Georgette's mouth fell open. "You spied on me?"

Ava shrugged, averting her gaze. "You know what Mother is like, I had to. Besides, the more I watched you both fall in love, the more curious I was."

"Curious about what?" Georgette asked, clutching her throbbing temples.

Ava picked up two sticks from the ground and made them hover in the air over an open palm. "You were enemies, but over time, you turned into lovers. And I have never seen a man commit such brutal acts for a siren."

Georgette scratched her arm as she looked away. "He did not know what I was. Maybe things would have been different if he did."

Ava's laugh drew Georgette's attention back to her. "Goodness, Georgette, are you really that ignorant?"

She tossed the sticks aside and sighed. "I have been keeping a keen eye on both of you." She smoothed her hair, her eyes glazing over.

"You may call me your guardian angel, if you like."

Georgette stared dumbfounded. "Why? How—?" Questions tumbled through her mind, but she could not form the words.

Ava continued to play with her hair, and she smiled at the ground with a faraway look. "Isis was bereft when Lord Harrington took you. She had me watch over you both. When a scheming pirate came along, winning the resurrection stone in a game of cards, Isis had me follow him too." She began to pace as Georgette listened with rapt attention. "Captain Stone had a secret. Born of nobility, he walked away from the crown—a disgraced royal. He changed his name and sailed the seas, searching for something."

"What was it?" Georgette asked, her breath catching in her chest.

Ava stopped pacing and met Georgette's inquisitive stare.

"What does any man want? Fulfillment." She turned away and began to walk through the trees. Georgette had to jog to keep up with her.

"You said I am ignorant. What do you mean?" she asked.

Ava stiffened but recovered herself. "Isis and Captain Stone have had a few run-ins over the years. She wanted her ring back. He evaded death time and time again, never allowing himself to draw close to Imerta. In Isis's mind, it was a mockery. That ring did not belong to him. So, she hatched a plan. She commanded me and our sisters to steal all of the pirate's treasure and plant the idea that if a woman were onboard a ship, sirens would leave them be."

Georgette frowned as she took it all in. "I know he targeted me because my father owed him a debt. But that doesn't mean he knew that I was a siren."

Ava halted. "No. But he figured it out much sooner than you. And even though sirens were his greatest enemy, he fell in love with you."

A knot formed in Georgette's stomach. She longed to see Captain Stone again. She scowled at the tower looming over them. "Ava, I need you to go and find my husband. If he has escaped, he will presume that I am dead and return to the sea. Find him and keep him safe."

Ava hesitated. "Will you not come with me?"

"No," Georgette said in an acid whisper. "I have to speak with Isis, one last time."

Ava grabbed her by the shoulders. "You must not.

Please, Georgette. After all these years, I have become fond of you. Please, do not walk into a trap. Get away from here. Isis cannot follow. She is bound to Imerta."

Georgette let Ava shake her, but she gave her a look of determination. "I need to be certain she is not keeping him somewhere," she said. "It is as you said. If she succeeded in killing him, she would hide the body."

Ava nodded slowly. "Very well. Make haste. I shall meet you in the seas."

Georgette gave her a final smile before she picked up a run and flew through the forest toward Isis's tower.

After running some distance, she bent over to catch her breath. Her lungs were screaming, but she had made it to the tower. She rested against the bottom of the structure; her palm pressed against the cool stone.

Then she began to climb the spiral staircase, and her mind raced.

When she pushed through the door, it swung open with a squeal. The fireplace was roaring, and the heat of the flames fanned Georgette's cheeks.

She found Isis curled up by the window, a blanket over her knees and a steaming mug in her hands. Her long hair glowed like gold, reflecting the flames as she turned to smile at Georgette.

"You took your time getting here," she said, setting the mug down. "Tea?" she asked.

Georgette scowled at the goddess, furious at her calm.

"How can you look at me after what you did?" she spat. "You left me in that cave to die."

Isis blinked, her expression neutral, then she gestured to her. "And yet, here you are. Alive and well."

Georgette scoffed. "With no help from you. There was an earthquake and—"

The corners of Isis's mouth twitched. Georgette stopped. "That was you, wasn't it? You caused the earthquake."

Isis raised her palms. "Guilty."

Fury boiled in Georgette's chest and the palms of her hands began to tremble and buzz.

Isis leaned forward, her green eyes glowing brightly. "Did you see him? Lord Harrington?"

The blazing fury faded as Georgette remembered her conversation with him.

"Yes," she said, lowering herself to sit on the ornate chair by the fire. A sudden chill took over her. "He told me about a prophecy. About me."

Isis hummed deep with a beaming smile. "Now you see why I did not help you out."

Georgette's head snapped up and she looked incredulously at her mother. "You wanted me to die?"

Isis waved a hand with a scoff. "No, darling. I wanted

you to *grow*. There is simply not enough time to enhance your abilities through teaching."

Georgette swallowed. "Enhance my abilities?" she whispered.

Isis pulled the blanket away from her knees and joined Georgette beside the fire. The goddess clasped her hand in hers and a sickly-sweet smell washed over Georgette.

"My dearest Georgette. I would never harm you. Everything I've done thus far has been for your growth. I need you strong for what I have planned for you."

Georgette trembled, a cold shiver crawling up her spine as her mother looked down at her lovingly. "Tell me about the prophecy. What is it, exactly?"

Isis sucked in a breath. "I do not know for certain. But whatever it is, Poseidon is determined to stop it from being fulfilled."

Georgette eyed her mother with scrutiny. It was impossible to tell if the goddess was lying or not. "Tell me, Mother. Have you always told me the truth?" she asked.

Isis brushed Georgette's hair from her face and cradled her cheek. Her palm was softer than velvet. "Always, my dear."

Georgette touched her mother's hand and warmth

spread through her body. She wanted to believe that she had it all wrong. Isis was her mother, after all.

Perhaps her methods of teaching were brutal, but maybe that was the siren way of life. So far, she had always ended up stronger.

Maybe Poseidon was the true villain in this story. Maybe she needed to start trusting Isis and fulfill her destiny. Whatever that may be.

Georgette sucked in a breath. "Has my husband returned with the head of Blackbeard yet?" she asked.

Isis's eyes stayed perfectly steady, and her smile never wavered. Her answer crushed Georgette's spirit. "No."

It was a lie. Georgette knew it.

"Then I must go," she said, rising to her feet. Isis frowned.

"You are not ready, my child. You must complete your training."

Georgette forced a smile and shook her head. "I'm ready for answers. And there is only one place that I'll find them now."

"Where?" Isis asked, rising to a stand as Georgette headed for the door.

Georgette rested her hand on the brass handle and turned to give her mother one last look. "I must go to Atlantis."

PRINCE EDWARD

Prince Edward's mind spun as he unbridled the horses from his carriage. Serena stayed quiet, careful to avoid making any eye contact. They had settled into an angry silence.

They mounted the horses and charged toward the fire, but the horses were soon tired, and they slowed to a canter. Unable to bottle up his feelings anymore, Prince Edward broke the silence.

"You must care about the war. Look what awful things are happening to your sisters," he said, keeping his gazed fixed on the road ahead.

Serena made a noise of contempt. "My sisters do not know me. My father kept me hidden from them for almost all my life," she said. "They are foolish and weak, carrying out all of Isis's evil plans."

Prince Edward looked at her and saw that she was scowling.

"So, you were just using me all this time?" he asked.

Serena's eyes burned into his very soul when she finally looked at him. "We both had our reasons for this arrangement. And we've both ended up getting hurt, don't you think?"

Her words cut Prince Edward and he swallowed at the sting. He dragged his bottom teeth over his upper lip and bit down until it burned. The physical pain was a welcome distraction from the dull ache that throbbed within his chest.

Serena was right. He was not over Georgette. The scars of the past had made him paranoid and possessive. He was desperate to cling onto Serena and keep her from any harm, but his real motivation was a fear of losing her the way he lost Georgette.

True, Serena was not Georgette. She was nothing like her. But she was wrong about one thing—as he made love to her this evening, Georgette never once entered his mind. He had savored the taste of her on his tongue. It was her eyes that held him captive. And it was the softness of her own fiery hair tangled between his fingers that made his heart soar.

When he lost himself in pleasuring Serena, he was

utterly devoted to this siren. He had made a silent vow to be bound to her for the rest of his days.

Physically, emotionally, and mentally bound.

But the words could not escape his mouth. In their absence, Serena looked ahead with a cold expression, shielding her pain from him.

No amount of pretending could conceal it from him, however.

He knew what suffering a broken heart brought. He had also tried to put on the same brave face for months.

"Serena," he said, softening his tone. "I—"

The horse *nayed* and picked up its front hooves at the sound of shouting in the distance. Husband and wife exchanged worried looks before they urged the horses to press forward.

Smoke clung to the back of Prince Edward's throat as they approached a blazing fire. Its flames reached higher than the clock tower in the square.

He held up a handkerchief, coughing as they entered a scene of utter destruction.

Entire rows of houses were burning. Screams flooded the air.

They found hundreds of men, women, and children rushing toward the open sea, desperate for cleaner air. A crowd of pirates waited for them on the beach.

"Pirates!" Prince Edward barked over to Serena. She nodded back.

"I see them. I'll put out the fire and meet you on the beach."

Before Prince Edward could ask Serena how she supposed to put out such a tremendous fire, she had moved a few steps away. Prince Edward looked around him quickly for a weapon and his eyes fell on a woodcutter's axe leaning against a well. He dropped from his horse to grab it as the sky grew unnaturally dark.

Prince Edward grabbed the axe and turned just in time to see Serena with her hands above her head and a look of pure concentration on her face. The sky rumbled with thunder.

He watched, momentarily dumbstruck, as lightning crackled across the sky and a downpour of torrential rain flooded the town in an instant.

Within minutes, Serena was at Prince Edward's side again. There was no time for questions. They raced to the beaches.

Shrieks and cries clawed at Prince Edward's eardrums as they abandoned the horses and pushed through the thick crowds of people.

Finally, they reached the front to see a row of brutish men wrestling with women, while others shot any man who dare to approach them.

Prince Edward took his axe in one hand and swung bodily. The arm of the nearest pirate fell. More screams followed.

The pirates turned at aimed their pistols at Prince Edward, but the pouring rain doused them, rendering their weapons useless.

They brandished rusty swords instead, and a bloody battle ensued.

Heartened by the supposed grace of gods, men from the village picked up their spades and knives and charged toward the pirates.

Two women dropped to the ground; their throats cut before the men could get to them. It only enraged them even more.

Prince Edward slashed and cut with the blunt axe, not caring whether his blows were fatal or not as he aided the men in fighting the pirates.

He had lost sight of Serena in the crowds at some point, but he knew that she was nearby. Whenever a pirate got the upper hand, a wave of water would curl over them like a small tsunami and smash him to the ground. Prince Edward had never been so grateful to be on the beach.

When they killed the last of the pirates, the storm promptly ended. Dazed villagers stood drenched and unsure. Was the ordeal over?

The town was smoking, but the fire was out. Seeing that there were no pirates left standing, men, women, and children fell to their knees and began to cry.

Prince Edward looked at the chaos around them with an aching heart. This war had become far more complicated. With the Royal Navy gone, pirates were attempting to take over.

He needed to return to the palace and speak to his father.

On his way, he found Serena carrying a small girl to her father.

The child screamed, "Mama won't wake up!" pointing at a woman lying face-down in the sand—a pool of blood around her head like a halo. The father cradled his daughter and sank to his knees, tears cascading down his hollow cheeks.

Sickened by the sight, Prince Edward's gaze met Serena's. They nodded in mutual agreement. This war would end, whatever the cost.

Back at the palace, Prince Edward and Serena stood before King George, who paced in his office, nostrils flaring.

"Extensive damage to the town, scores of families

homeless, crime on the rise…" he muttered as he paced. Then he stopped to look at them. "What are you both doing here? You should be on your honeymoon."

Serena cleared her throat. "We saw the fire, your Majesty."

King George slammed his fist on the table. "All the more reason to keep far from it."

Prince Edward cleared his throat. "Father, allow me to take a ship. I need a small crew of men."

"You think I'm keeping frigates up my sleeve, boy? All we have left are doggers and fishermen."

"So long as they can sail, it is enough," Prince Edward said firmly.

King George crossed his arms across his broad chest. "And where are you planning to go?"

Serena coughed and the two men turned to stare at her. "My father has an army, far stronger and greater than anything you have ever seen," she said.

King George looked at Prince Edward, who held his breath for a moment. It was true. The Tritons were formidable, with iron strength and endless stamina. But would Poseidon allow his army to fight a battle above the sea? He looked at Serena, who gave him an intense look. It was one that said: *play along*.

Prince Edward finished for her. "It is true, Father. I

shall bring back an army to fight off the pirates and sirens and restore peace once and for all."

King George hummed long and deep as he thought on it. "Princess Serena shall stay here, where it is safe," he said. Serena opened her mouth to argue but Prince Edward cut in. "Of course."

"Then it is done. The sooner we have this army, the better."

Edward wasted no time. He turned on his heel and marched out of his father's office, Serena hot on his trail.

"You know my father will never let you have the Triton army," she whispered. Prince Edward nodded. "I know."

He barged through the open doors and into the cold night, marching down the garden path. Serena grabbed his arm, forcing him to stop.

"Then what are you planning to do? Are we not going to negotiate a peace treaty now that we are married?" she asked. Her eyes were wide and demanding.

Prince Edward shook his head. "Do not let them know who you really are just yet. First, we need to take back control of the piracy. Then we shall use our union to negotiate peace."

Serena's eyes grew so wide, they were like two moons. "How do you propose to control the piracy?"

He swallowed the lump in his throat. "Pirates need a strong, ruthless leader to keep them in line."

He took a breath, nodding at Serena's look of understanding.

"He's long gone, probably hiding on some godforsaken island with *her*," she whispered, grabbing his arms.

Prince Edward took in another breath with a grim look on his face. "I know. But I have to try, Serena. I have to find my brother. Or we are all doomed."

Serena's hands flexed on his arms, and she looked like she was about to pull him in for a hug, but she seemed to change her mind at the last minute, biting her lip instead. "Just promise me you won't die," she said, edging away.

Prince Edward forced a smile. "I will do my best."

CAPTAIN STONE

CAPTAIN STONE SAILED FOR DAYS IN THE OPEN SEA, USING the sky as his only source of navigation. He rowed tirelessly, stopping only briefly to drink and regain strength. He thought of Georgette constantly. He called out to her until his throat became dry. And when he slept, he dreamed of seeing her again.

But Georgette did not come.

He thought about turning around and scouring every inch of Imerta, looking for his beloved. But if he did not get to the shores of Port Harbor, his home country, his family, and all of the pirates in the seven seas would be destroyed.

Georgette would have to wait. He only prayed that wherever she was, she was safe and her feelings for him were unchanged.

He came across another shipwreck. It bobbed in the water, sinking slowly. The belly of the ship stuck out as though it had been struck by a monumental canon ball.

He found a compass, a spyglass, and a pistol on the body of a dead captain. Then he returned to this boat and rowed with a renewed strength.

Though the task was doomed to fail, he would not stop until his body finally failed him. The scorching sunshine burned through his thin cotton shirt and the film of sweat across his brow was itchy. He wiped his sweat with the back of his hand every few moments. On the third day, he sagged over the oars and exhaled, shutting his eyes.

Vultures circled the air and Captain Stone wondered what they were doing so far from land. Exhausted, he squinted into the distance. A small island was on the horizon. Captain Stone was not sure if it was an oasis or an illusion. But he headed for it anyway.

As he approached the shore, his heart leaped with joy at the sight of a vast ship washed up on the beach.

It was a beautiful sight—perfect, with billowing sails intact. He was certain this was a gift from one of the gods.

He climbed out of his small boat and ran across the shore to take a closer look at the ship. He sang praises to the gods, skipping and running his hands across the smooth wooden planks on the sides of the ship. But then he reached the port and noticed it had a giant hole in it. It was filled with sand, and dozens of crabs scuttled in and out of it.

Captain Stone kicked the belly of the ship and shook his fists at the heavens.

"You think this is amusing?" he howled to the skies. "You think we're all just pawns in your sick, twisted games?"

He pulled his hair back into a ponytail and paced around the spot, oblivious to the scorching sunshine.

With Georgette gone, and Isis planning to destroy everything, he had never felt more frustration in his soul. If only he could transform into a creature with wings, or step through another portal that would take him straight to Port Harbor.

He looked around. High cliffs surrounded him on the small beach. There was no conceivable path for him to climb onto the island. The tide moved in with such force, it would have been a waste of energy to try and sail out to sea until it died down.

Captain Stone fell to his knees and clutched the sand as his heart bled. He called out to Georgette with every part of his soul. Willing her to come back to him.

He looked out at the vast horizon, hopeless. Where was she?

He stared bleakly for a few minutes and realized a distant shape was growing bigger. Thinking he had finally gone mad, Captain Stone rubbed his eyes and shuffled forward.

The figure soon turned into a dogger boat with vast ivory sails, heading for him. Captain Stone waved his arms in the air, flagging the boat down and hoping that the fishermen were friendly. He did not have the strength to fight.

Slowly, the ship approached the beach, and Captain Stone paced, impatient as he waited.

Finally, the boat landed on the beach and a man scaled the rope ladder on the side. He hopped down and turned around to face Captain Stone. When their eyes met, Captain Stone's heart sank.

"Edward? What in the blazes are you doing here?"

He sized him up, grabbed his brother's left hand, and ogled the gold band. "Is that a *wedding ring*?"

Prince Edward sighed, eyeing his brother like a father looking upon his wayward son. "You have to come back with me. This war is—"

"I know." Captain Stone said. "It is worse than you think, though. We need to get back to Port Harbor."

Prince Edward scratched the back of his neck and began to pace. "The beaches are crawling with pirates, and they are committing vile atrocities."

Captain Stone's insides clenched. "I am Pirate King now. They will listen to me."

"King?" Prince Edward stopped pacing and a shadow of a smile crossed his face. "I thought you went to piracy to *avoid* becoming king."

Captain Stone pointed at Prince Edward's wedding ring. "And I thought you'd never get over me stealing your fiancée. Yet, here we are."

Crack.

Prince Edward's fist met with Captain Stone's jaw in a jarring punch.

"You have no idea what torment you have put me through!" he roared at his older brother. Captain Stone staggered back, seeing stars. His brother punched him again, this time in the gut.

He quickly raised a hand. "Whoa!" Captain Stone coughed blood. "Steady on, little brother," he said. He spat more blood out on the beach and stumbled backward. His brother grabbed him to stop him from falling and patted his chest.

"God's graces, I'm sorry. I forgot my own strength," he said.

Captain Stone took deep breaths while his vision returned, and Prince Edward's concerned eyes came back into view. "Since when did you possess such brute strength?" he asked.

Prince Edward smirked, but his expression turned serious once more.

"You must call all the pirates to order. They cannot go around pillaging towns. Many are now either dead or homeless."

He proceeded to tell Captain Stone a most unbelievable tale.

One that involved a magical city under the sea, where they would find a god with a tremendous army. And a beautiful siren who had cast blood magic, surrendering her immortality to bind herself with Edward.

Captain Stone listened, hardly believing that the story could be true. But Edward grew vehement as he told him of a time when pirates held him and the siren captive and threatened to rape her right in front of him.

"I tore them limb from limb and took great pleasure in smashing their pathetic, vile bodies."

Captain Stone smiled, a flush of pride rising as he looked at his once meek brother, now protective and fierce. "Edward. I never thought you had it in you," he said. "You must really love this siren. What is her name?"

The question made Prince Edward's eyes flash dangerously. He scowled at Captain Stone. "You," he growled, shaking a fist at him. "You made me—" he cut off, his face paling.

Captain Stone lifted his brows. "Made you... What?"

he asked. Then he lowered his gaze to his brother's crotch for a second and winced. "Impotent?"

Prince Edward's mouth fell open in horror. "No!"

Captain Stone sighed with relief, for he could think of nothing worse than that. "Then what? What did I make you?"

Prince Edward's shoulders sagged, and he turned away. "Her name is Serena. But, while we were..." he coughed, uncomfortable.

"*What?*" Captain Stone asked, impatience rising again. "Can't we talk about this on the boat? We really need to be getting back to—"

"I said the wrong name," Prince Edward finished.

The words hung in the air as Captain Stone chewed on them.

"You said the wrong name..." he repeated blankly.

Prince Edward winced and dragged a hand over his face. "When we were..."

He motioned with his fist against his palm. The captain nodded with understanding. "I said Georgette... Instead of Serena."

"WHAT!" Captain Stone lunged at Prince Edward, fury blazing in his whole body. Prince Edward grabbed his arms at the last minute, so he could not punch him. Captain Stone kicked him in the gut instead, prompting Prince Edward to stumble back with a groan. "Now she hates me," he said through the pain. "I think she'll never forgive me, and it's all your fault!" he yelled.

Captain Stone shoved him. "Oh, for heaven's sake! Man up and take responsibility for your actions. I didn't make you say the wrong name. That was you!"

Prince Edward held Captain Stone's shirt collar, tears leaking from his eyes. "You *stole* her from me. For years, I was preparing to marry Georgette. We were friends. There was not a day that went by that I did not see her. There were times when she begged me to kiss her, and I held restraint. Because it was the right thing to do. But you came along and forced her to marry you. How could she choose you over me? Are we not the same?"

"No," Captain Stone hissed. "Listen, Georgette may have begged you to kiss her, but she begged me to *ruin* her. You and I are not the same. While you played the gold-hearted prince, always doing the right thing to protect the crown, I became the villain to protect *her*."

Prince Edward puffed out his chest, affronted. But he exhaled and looked down. "I finally understand what that means. The way I feel about Serena brings out a side of me that is monstrous. Carnal. Terrifying."

He looked up again to meet Captain Stone's stare. "Still, I cannot stand here and tell you I have no feelings for Georgette."

Captain Stone stood still, too stunned to move. "But you said we were both dead to you."

Prince Edward let Captain Stone's collar go and shrugged. "I guess it's not that simple."

He walked toward the sea, dragging a hand through his hair. "I love Serena, I am certain of it. The way I feel about her reaches deep into my soul. Loving her is both maddening and comforting all at the same time. But she believes that I will never get over Georgette. And I am beginning to think that she's right."

Captain Stone was quiet for a moment, and the two brothers listened to the soothing sounds of the ocean rolling in and out of the beach. Finally, Captain Stone placed a hand on Prince Edward's shoulder.

"I am sorry, Edward. For the pain I have caused you."

Prince Edward took a sharp breath and exhaled deeply with his eyes closed.

It was as though the weight of the world had lifted. Then he finally looked at Captain Stone. "I forgive you."

A cough made them both jump. A siren was bobbing in the water. "I am sorry to break up such a beautiful moment," she said, her eyes sparkling with amusement. "But I have been looking for you, Captain Stone."

Captain Stone approached the shoreline, his heart racing. Prince Edward joined him. He recognized the siren. It was the same one he had freed before he went to the pirates' meeting. "I remember you. Your name is Ava, right?"

The siren sighed contentedly, flipping her hair back. "It says a lot when a man can remember a woman's name." She said it like a purr. Her gaze landed on Prince Edward. "You must be Serena's new husband. I've heard everything about you."

Then she tapped her chin with her fingers. "Or should I say, I heard Serena. I do not believe I have ever heard a siren scream so loud. My sisters and I had to stuff our ears with our hair until it stopped."

Captain Stone snorted and clapped his stunned brother on the back. "Good man." Prince Edward's face grew red.

The siren giggled and played with her hair. Captain Stone turned back to her. "Why are you looking for me? Do you know where Georgette is?"

Ava's smile faded and she stopped bouncing in the water for a moment. "Yes."

Captain Stone's heart leaped. "Is she alive? Where is she?"

Ava crossed her arms. "She has gone to Atlantis."

"So, it exists?" Captain Stone whispered to himself. Prince Edward stepped forward. "What is she doing, going there?" he asked.

Ava spun around in the water, her blonde hair swirling around her.

"I can take you to her, if you wish," she fluttered her lashes with a sweet smile. Captain Stone began to move forward, but Prince Edward held out an arm to stop him. "Trust me, you don't want to be going down there."

Ava frowned.

"Perhaps she is trying to persuade Poseidon to fight for us," Prince Edward said, rubbing his jaw.

Ava shrugged. "It is a possibility. And maybe she will succeed. From what I see, Georgette is very charming toward men. Do you not think?"

Prince Edward and Captain Stone exchanged looks.

"What do you want from me?" Captain Stone said, resting his hands on his hips. Ava walked out of the ocean on a pair of slender legs, and the water cascaded down her body like a waterfall until she was fully nude before the two men.

"Oops," she said, with a light giggle. She waved her hand over herself, and a shimmering yellow dress formed over her nakedness. "Does this make you both more comfortable?"

Captain Stone leaned to mutter in his brother's ear. "Are all sirens exhibitionists?" he asked.

Prince Edward nodded. "It appears so."

"You know, Georgette would destroy you if she knew

you were behaving this way," Captain Stone said, lifting a brow at Ava.

The siren stared at him blankly before she gave him a bashful grin. "Well, she does not know. Besides, she sent me to protect you. I am here to cater to your *every* need."

If Captain Stone's brows could rise any higher, they would have been sitting on top of his skull. "Well, there *is* something I need you to do for me," he said, leaning in.

Ava's glittering smile widened with anticipation. "Yes?"

Captain Stone pointed at the sea. "I know that Isis has commanded all her sirens to gather at Port Harbor and destroy every human man they come in contact with."

Ava sucked in a breath with a hiss. She stepped back but did not argue.

Captain Stone lowered his head to give her an intense stare. "Tell them that Isis has changed her instruction. They are to follow us, instead."

"And where are we going?" Prince Edward asked, frowning. "The pirates will still be coming for Port Harbor."

Captain Stone squeezed his brother's shoulder.

"Don't worry about the pirates. I have an important task for them. Something that will keep them out of trouble, and finally put an end to this war."

SERENA

Serena stood on the balcony of her room with her eyes closed, listening to the seagulls honking in the sky and enjoying the soft breeze coming from the sea.

Her body ached in ways she had never known. Prince Edward was rough with her, but at the time it had been a welcome release of all the pent-up tension.

Now though, she was more tense than ever. Her husband was out on open water, facing all kinds of danger. She had to stay in the palace and pretend not to be sick to her stomach with dread.

She kept a wide birth from King George, who seemed disinterested in her now that she was married to his son. But whenever she found herself in the same room with him, she averted her gaze and dug her fingernails into her palms. Only relaxing again when he was gone.

Queen Charlotte, however, took great interest in Serena. She insisted on taking her out each evening to walk laps around the walled gardens. She talked about menial things, like sewing, and gossip from other royal families across the seas.

On the third night, Serena looked out the window, restless. She had not heard anything regarding Prince Edward's travels. In his absence, her heart throbbed.

She was still confused by her emotions. She kept swinging from fury at his betrayal, to a yearning to be with him again.

She looked at the unopened letter on the writer's bureau next to her. She had not been even the slightest bit interested in what he had to say then. She had been too angry.

Now the letter presented itself as her only entry into his mind. She snatched it from the table and settled into a chair beside the window. Then she broke the seal with her thumb before she could change her mind and unfolded the letter.

Dearest Serena,

I am not particularly eloquent with words. My mind comes up with all kinds of whimsical and profound things to say, but they get lost somewhere between my brain and my mouth.

It is difficult to explain to you what is going through my mind.

It may help for you to understand a little background. You see, I was a young man when my father told me I was betrothed to marry a maiden who was far too young for me. It was odd to watch this child grow into a woman, knowing that someday we would be wed. We became friends and I cared for her as deeply as a friend.

We started our courtship after her twenty-first birthday, and suddenly, the thought of marrying Georgette did not seem so strange. Our friendship became something more. Or so I believed.

When she was snatched from me, I set my mind on a mission to bring her home at all costs. You know the rest of that story.

But what you don't know is that I believed I was in love. Upon reflection, I know in my heart that the way I love Georgette is not the same way I love you.

Yes, I still care for her. I think part of me always will. But I do believe it is a platonic, brotherly love.

Now, allow me a moment to share my feelings with you.

You see, while I was on my quest to rescue Georgette, I met a most enchanting, fascinating creature.

My men had her tied up in a net, and though they taunted her with their weapons, her gaze was unnerved, strong, and powerful.

I remember the first moment you made me blush. You sat on the edge of my ship, tossing back your fiery hair to reveal your breasts. I confess I did not know where to look.

Ever since, you have been a constant presence in my life. Then you took over my mind. You became the first thought to wake me and the final thought to kiss me goodnight.

When we were captured by those pirates and they surrounded you like wolves, I felt that my chest would burst. I knew then that you had not only invaded my mind, but also claimed my heart.

I am entirely, completely, and utterly yours.

If you will not forgive my grave error, I shall spend the rest of my days in penance—making it up to you for all of eternity. You deserve nothing but happiness and safety. I wish to provide you with both, whatever it takes.

Please know, that despite our schemes and make-believe, when we exchange our vows, I will be speaking from my heart. My feelings for you are true.

I made a terrible, awful, unforgivable mistake. And there are not enough words in the world to convey how deeply sorry I am for hurting you.

But if you will still have me, I vow to be your devoted husband and bow the knee to you, my dearest Serena. You are the true love of my life. I will do anything for you.

Always yours,

Edward.

Serena grumbled as she folded up the letter and set it on her lap. The prince could pen a humble note. But his words only filled her with more annoyance. How could he be so sweet and perfect, but utterly foolish at the same time?

Serena's heart went back to hating Georgette for ruining such a good man. He was damaged in a way Serena thought might never be truly healed.

She sat in the dusty, vacant bedroom, watching the sun set over the horizon, and her heart throbbed again.

In truth, regardless of the hurt and anger, she missed him.

Unable to stand the silence anymore, she walked to the dressing table and picked up the small, ornate hand mirror. She waved her hand across the glass, and it transformed into a bubble.

It wobbled before her while she pictured Prince Edward in her mind. "Show me, my Prince," she whispered.

The bubble swirled and fell flat across the mirror-like glass again, but this time she could see a picture. Amidst stormy seas was a fisherman's boat, its mast split in two, crashing into the water. As Serena squinted, the picture shifted, revealing Prince Edward. He bobbed in the water, surrounded by numerous sirens. They bared their pointed teeth and hissed, ears elongated and nails like claws as they turned to him.

Furious, Serena gripped the handle of the mirror and trembled. Then she pulled up her skirts, held the mirror between her teeth, and scaled the tall vines outside her balcony. She dropped and hurried down the garden to climb up the compound wall, heading for the sea.

"If anyone is going to kill Prince Edward, it will be me," she said with a scowl as she ventured off to rescue him.

GEORGETTE

Georgette swam to Atlantis with her heart racing with anticipation. Somehow, she instinctively knew the way. She swam straight down, until a soft blue glow illuminated the darkness. Then she followed the light until it grew so bright, she had to squint.

Finally, she pushed through a bubble-like texture—a force of some kind surrounding the city—and fell to her knees within.

She transformed back into human form in an instant and patted herself down as much as she could. She cursed when she looked down at her naked form, wishing she had learned how to conjure up clothes like Ava and Isis could.

She took a deep breath and waved her hand over

herself, picturing a red gown on her body, but nothing happened. As always. She tried again. And again.

Clearly, she was missing something.

Frustrated and feeling exposed, she looked around and found a small stone house. She tried the door and her heart jolted when it swung open freely. She rooted through the drawers but could only find men's garments.

She reasoned it was better than nothing. So, she pulled on an oversized gray shirt that came to her knees and picked up a length of rope from a hook beside the door.

With the rope, she made a makeshift belt around her waist that made the shirt look like a dress, then slipped on a pair of sandals she found by the door. They were too big, but they would at least offer her feet some protection on the long walk ahead.

Georgette set out, making her way through the winding, narrow, cobblestone streets of the vast city. As she approached the gleaming gates of Atlantis, she passed several strong men dressed in shining armor and wielding spears. They stared at Georgette with piercing eyes that seemed to question her every move, but she held her head high and walked with purposeful strides.

When she reached the guards at the gate, one of them crossed his arms and began to speak in a strange language. Georgette stared at him blankly, wondering what to say. Then he asked in a gruff voice "Who are you?"

Georgette squared her shoulders and mentally rehearsed the words she had so carefully planned.

"My name is Georgette, daughter of Poseidon and Isis," she said, not once breaking eye contact with the guard who had spoken. "I am here to seek an audience with my father."

The guard looked her up and down, taking in her makeshift outfit, then nodded. "Very well," he finally said, motioning for her to pass through the gates.

Georgette walked forward with a sense of awe at the grandeur that surrounded her. Marble buildings stood tall on either side of her as she made her way through the city. She stopped when she reached an impressively large palace at the city center.

The doors opened and a towering figure emerged. Broad shoulders, a fine mane of hair, and piercing eyes looked down on her. When Georgette first set her eyes on the man, she knew this formidable being was Poseidon, King of the Sea… And her birth father.

It took all of her willpower not to collapse to the ground.

The steps trembled as he descended them. When he reached her, he took her face in one broad hand, and a tear leaked out of Georgette's eye. "My dear Georgette, you have come home. Finally," he boomed.

The tender moment was short-lived. Georgette staggered backward, shaking her head as though to break from a spell.

"This is not my home," she said, the words cutting the back of her throat. She looked around him to see the vast entrance hall within the palace.

Was her sister somewhere in the palace?

Poseidon appeared unaffected by Georgette's reaction. He stood firm and calm while Georgette vented to him.

"You welcome me like a long-lost daughter who was taken from you against your will, yet we both know that it was you who kept me from my real family. Why did you do it? Why separate me from my sister? And how can you stand there and welcome me back like you did not have a hand in all of this ugliness?"

Poseidon's smile fell and he crossed his arms. Georgette stopped, taken aback by his bulging muscles. His brute strength and the severity of his gaze reminded her who she was talking to.

A god.

He was not just a mere absentee father, but a formidable god of the sea, who could easily take her life with his bare hands, should he be so inclined.

She swallowed, trying to think of the words to scale back the tension. Poseidon broke the ice first.

"Come, my child. Follow me."

Georgette exhaled in relief at the softness in his voice. She had worried that her words overstepped a mark. Poseidon turned and led her into the palace.

They walked the halls, their footsteps echoing in the vaulted ceilings. It was cool and crisp, and the air smelled like salt and strangely sweet.

When they ended up in a library with rows upon rows of bookshelves, Georgette stood in awe, looking at them all.

"You shall be disappointed to learn that your sister is not here," Poseidon said, thumbing through the pages of a nearby book. He returned it to the shelf and picked out another one.

"I sense courage in you. You are headstrong and you know your mind."

He paused to look at her over his book. "In many ways, you are so alike."

Georgette held her breath. After growing up as an only child, she dreamed of spending long days with a playmate. In her mission, she never stopped to chew on the revelation Isis gave her.

She was a twin.

"Where did she go? There is a war going on, you know? Sirens are not safe."

Poseidon gave her a look of mild amusement. "And yet, here you are. Swimming around without a care in the world about your safety."

"I am trying to do what I can to help, Father."

Poseidon closed the book with a slam and gave Georgette a piercing look. "Indeed, you are."

Slowly, he reached to a higher shelf and withdrew a final book with a mysterious hum. "This is the one. I'm most certain of it."

"What are you looking for?" Georgette asked, giving in to her curiosity. Poseidon flipped through the delicate pages until he landed on the one he wanted with an "Aha!"

Then he turned the book around and handed it to Georgette.

"You came for the prophecy, didn't you?" he asked.

Georgette was about to ask how Poseidon could know that, but he gave her a meaningful gaze and she decided against it. She looked down instead and read the verses written in faded ink.

Behold, a prophecy of a diverse fellowship bold,
From far-flung lands, their story to unfold,
A prince, a pirate, a fallen god of might,

Twins with locks of red and blonde, and a virgin bride with light.

Their quest for lost love and a curse to break,
To make right what had been long at stake,
But their noble actions, with unintended cost,
Could lead to a danger that humanity may be lost.
So, listen close to this prophecy told,
Of valiant heroes and their destiny to unfold,
What symbol can you see, of their quest and its toll,
As the fate of all rests on their ultimate goal?

"You think this is about me and my twin?" she asked Poseidon.

"Her name is Serena, and yes. When I saw you both as babes, it was clear as day to me that you two have a terrible fate."

Georgette sucked in a sharp breath, taking it all in. "Is it true that Isis has placed a curse on your bloodline?"

Poseidon's smile faded and his eyes darkened with fury. "It appears so. Not one of my sons and daughters has borne a child in more than twenty years. Ever since the day the curse was made."

Georgette clutched her stomach. "I was with child."

Poseidon lifted his brows. "You—"

"I lost it," Georgette cut in, her eyes prickling at the memory. "I lost it because of the curse, is that what you're telling me?"

Poseidon nodded. "I am afraid so."

Georgette read the verses over and over, then shut the book with a sound of frustration. "I am terrible at deciphering riddles. Twins of red and blonde is clear enough. It mentions breaking a curse... So, it is possible?"

She looked up at Poseidon with pleading eyes, silently demanding he speak the truth. He gave her a small, sad smile, one that did not fill her with much hope. Then she looked down again, recounting more of the prophecy.

"But should we break the curse, it will put everyone in grave danger."

She gritted her teeth and shut her eyes. The thought of the curse made her sick to her stomach and she hated the fact that her mother was cruel enough to make everyone suffer in such a way.

"Georgette, now you understand why I had to keep you and Serena apart, at least until you were ready to hear these terrible truths."

Poseidon reached out for Georgette, but she shrugged his hand away. "No, I don't understand. You could have raised us both here in Atlantis. To imagine my sister, alone here in this desolate city—"

"She had nine hundred brothers to keep her company," Poseidon said, lifting a brow.

Georgette touched her cheek as though his words smacked her in the face. "*I* was alone," she whispered.

Then she pointed at Poseidon. "And you were down here. I was raised by a man who I believed to be my father, but it was all lies. Now he's gone, and you're here, but my sister is nowhere to be seen, my own mother has made me barren, and I don't even know if my husband is alive…"

Georgette stumbled under the grief, overwhelmed by it all, and fell into Poseidon's arms. He held her with surprising tenderness and smoothed her hair. "You are strong, Georgette. Do not become discouraged." She pulled away to look into his intense eyes. Upon closer inspection, they looked like two stormy seas, swirling like whirlpools. A strange sense of peace flooded her, and a quiet confidence overcame her, thinking that all was well.

Poseidon nodded. "Your husband is strong too… For a human." He winked at her. But then he cradled her hands. "You will find him when you return to Imerta. There you shall also find Serena."

Georgette frowned. "I just came from Imerta, they weren't…"

But then she stopped at the sight of Poseidon averting his gaze, his eyes glazing over. "Why am I getting the feeling that we are all just pawns in a game of the gods?"

Poseidon looked at her again, smirking. "We all have our roles to play, my child." He squeezed her shoulder. "I know you wish to break this curse, and I see in your eyes that you desire to kill Isis." He sighed. "But you must know… Should Isis die, the curse will never be broken."

Georgette stole a breath, her shoulders sinking with disappointment. Poseidon chuckled. "If it was that easy, I would have borrowed one of my brother's lightning bolts and killed her myself." His hand balled into a tight fist. "You think I wanted my bloodline to be cut off? There is no greater pain."

Georgette dragged her fingers through her hair with a sigh. "You say I am to return to Imerta…but if I am not going back to kill Isis, what would you have me do?"

Poseidon took Georgette's hand and placed it in the crook of his arm. "Come, my child. Walk with me and listen closely."

PRINCE EDWARD

CAPTAIN STONE SECURED THE GAFF MAINSAIL AND SETTLED between two crates.

"I have sent a message out. All we have to do is sail to Imerta and wait." He looked around himself. "It feels good to be on a ship again," he said, patting his thigh. "Even if this one does stink of fish."

Prince Edward resisted the urge to roll his eyes. He picked up a length of rope and practiced a beer knot. "It was the only vessel we had left."

Captain Stone grunted. "So, it is true. The Royal Navy has been destroyed after all."

Prince Edward shrugged. "Father is recruiting more men as we speak. We will regain our strength." There were always men eager to serve King George and even more keen to get away from Port Harbor and sail the seas.

In the absence of the Royal Navy, more men would turn to piracy instead. It was a truly unthinkable thought.

"Tell me, brother." Prince Edward set down the rope and picked up a sheepskin flask instead. "What is it about piracy you love so much? Do you condone the terrible acts that are being committed right now?"

Captain Stone growled, a vein in his temple bulged while he looked down in thought. "I have seen with my own eyes the dead sirens, pinned up like trophies in the sea. It is despicable."

"They line the beaches too," Prince Edward added.

"Nay, but that was done by the Navy. Not pirates."

Prince Edward watched his brother. Then a thought struck him.

"You have no control over the pirates, have you?" he thought aloud.

The words hung in the air as gray clouds shrouded the sunlight, casting an ominous shadow over the ship. A chill rushed down Prince Edward's spine. If Mannington was unable to keep the pirates in check, then all hope was lost of ever regaining peace.

"Recent events will change everything," his brother said confidently. "After all, news travels fast. I tore the head from the formidable Blackbeard. All pirates tremble when they even hear that name. Now they will come to fear me even more."

"So, you plan to rule by fear?" Prince Edward asked his brother, unable to hide the skepticism in his voice.

"I would rather rule by fear than have fear rule over me," his brother grunted back. Captain Stone pulled out a small knife and held it up at eye level. The clouds parted just enough for a small bead of sunlight to illuminate the rusty blade. "I have commanded the pirates to gather as much dynamite as they can fill their ships with and meet us off the shores of Imerta. Once Isis is dead and her tower falls, you will see every single one of them bowing the knee to me."

Prince Edward shrugged. "I hope you are right, brother." He cleared his throat, looking out at the horizon. "Perhaps Poseidon will be able to convince Father to sign a peace treaty," he said. "And then I can persuade Serena to forgive me."

"For calling out another woman's name while making love?" Captain Stone snorted. Irritation rose to the surface as Prince Edward glared at his older brother. "What about Georgette? Where is she anyway?"

The question wiped the smirk off Captain Stone's face, and he hunched over, playing with the knife.

"I am not sure," he mumbled.

Prince Edward jumped to his feet. "What! Mannington, after everything that has happened, how can you have no idea where your wife is? Are you not concerned? What about the child—"

"There is no child," Captain Stone growled. Prince Edward stopped in shock and settled down again to look at his brother. He was taken aback when a tear rolled down his older brother's cheek.

"She lost it," Captain Stone finished.

Edward's heart bled for his brother. "And you don't know where she is?" he repeated, dragging a hand over his face.

Captain Stone looked at him, and the sheer devastation on his face was enough to shut Prince Edward up.

"She blames me for her suffering," Captain Stone said. "In many ways, I *am* responsible. It has been weeks since I last heard from her, Edward. I fear I shall not see her again until it pleases her."

He was about to say more but clenched his jaw instead. Prince Edward placed a hand on his shoulder.

"I guess we're not so different, after all," he said, rising and walking off to the side of the boat. "We both long for the same thing."

Captain Stone joined him with a sigh. "And what is that?"

"Redemption."

Before Captain Stone could respond, the boat lurched suddenly to one side, knocking several fishermen off their feet. Surprised shouts flooded the air. Then a terribly beautiful sound took over.

Siren song.

"Ava has betrayed us," Prince Edward whispered.

Captain Stone's eyes glazed over, and he held a hand over his heart. Meanwhile, several of the fishermen staggered to their feet and tried to scale the high sides of the dogger boat. "What beauty. What peace!" they cried.

To Prince Edward's horror, each man climbed up and willingly threw themselves over the edge.

Prince Edward jabbed Captain Stone in the gut, breaking him from his spell. The captain shook himself. "Rope. Tie me to the mast," he said, realizing what was happening.

Prince Edward did as he was told, and roughly tied Captain Stone to the boat. The siren song was like an ethereal bird singing in the dark. It made Prince Edward warm inside, and Serena's soft face came into his mind's eye.

He silently thanked her for the binding ritual. Once again, it had saved his life. But he could not understand why Ava brought the sirens back to attack them.

He flew to the side of the ship and peered over at the endless sea of women's faces.

Long, flowing hair of all colors and eyes like diamonds glinted in the sunshine as the clouds burned away. Pointed teeth and claw-like nails were on show.

"I am Prince Edward, husband of Princess Serena. There is no need to attack, for no one shall harm you," he called out.

The sirens began to crawl up the sides of the ship, their claws scratching the wood like nails on a chalkboard. Prince Edward winced.

A brunette siren reached him first. She fisted his shirt and slid her tongue from his jaw up to his temple, sending a sick shudder through him.

"Who better to exact our revenge on, than the sons of the wicked King who orders the mutilation of our sisters?"

She yanked and Prince Edward tumbled over the edge, into the siren-infested waters.

"Serena," he whispered, just before his body crashed into the water.

The pressure of the water around him felt different. And his hearing remained impressively clear even though it should have been muted in the sea.

Whispers surrounded him as the sirens closed in. "Serena will be unhappy if we kill her lover."

"We are forbidden to have lovers, and Serena is not one of us."

"But I heard she did a binding ritual."

Prince Edward floated, suspended in the water, and watched as the sirens conversed with each other. He realized none of them were moving their lips.

They were conversing in mind speak, and he could hear every word.

"I am your brother now," he thought, lifting his left hand to show them his wedding band.

The sirens hissed, turning to look at him with surprise.

"You are no brother of ours!"

Several minutes ticked by. The sirens watched him. They seemed to be waiting for something. It took some time for Prince Edward to understand.

They were waiting for him to drown.

He opened his mouth and followed instinct, gulping in a rush of water. He expected it to burn in his chest. But it flooded him with strength and warmth instead.

Alarmed, the sirens backed off as he curled his fingers and formed two fists.

He felt powerful. Invincible.

He looked around at the shocked faces.

"I am not my father. I am sickened by the acts that both pirates and my father's people have committed toward sirens."

The sirens began to turn back into beautiful women once more. Soon there was not a single claw in sight.

"My brother and I have made our vows. Our allegiance is with the sirens, and we have a plan to end this wretched war."

The sirens hissed. "A plan to kill our mother. She has done nothing to harm the humans."

"She has manipulated and controlled you all. Enslaving you."

"We are not slaves!" Hissing surrounded him, but Prince Edward remained firm. "If we are to end this war, we must first face the facts. My father and your mother are two sides of the same coin. One manipulates and enslaves with fear and suppression. The other controls and attacks because of fear and suppression."

He took another gulp of water, empowered with every drop.

"Do you not wish for a time where humans and sirens can co-exist in peace? Do you not value the freedom to live your own lives and not succumb to the wishes of your mother?"

The sirens fell silent. Several of them exchanged looks.

"I do not want any more bloodshed. Perhaps there is a way to end this war without having to kill Isis. You must allow us to at least try and speak with her."

One of the sirens scoffed. "She will tear you limb from limb before you utter a word."

Prince Edward inclined his head. "If that is so, allow me and my brother to sail to Imerta. If I am wrong, Isis shall destroy us, and you will get your revenge."

He pointed up toward the surface of the water. "Regardless, there are scores of pirate ships on their way to Imerta right now. They have enough explosives to destroy the entire island. You have left your goddess unprotected."

The siren's eyes flashed dangerously. "If what you say is true, we must protect our mother at all costs. We shall go."

Prince Edward nodded, his body releasing tension now that the imminent threat was over. He jabbed his thumb toward the underbelly of the dogger floating above their heads.

"You have seen with your own eyes what I have become, and I have told you which side I am on. Now, let me show you the strength of my convictions, by destroying every last pirate there is."

The sirens' eyes grew wide, but grins washed over them all. Pirates had been their enemy far longer than mere humans. Prince Edward swam back up to the ship and watched the sirens disappear as they swam on.

"Come, we must make haste," he said, freeing his

brother from his binds. Captain Stone frowned and grabbed Prince Edward's arm to stop him from running off. "I thought you were dead. What did you say to them that made them let you go?"

Prince Edward shrugged with a cocky grin. "I made them an offer they couldn't refuse."

SERENA

Serena plunged into the water, the salty waves crashing against her skin. An overwhelming sense of being home flooded her as she soared through the ocean.

She held the mirror in one hand and propelled herself forward with powerful strokes of her tail, clinging to a hope that she could reach Prince Edward before the sirens did him any harm. The mirror in her hand glowed blue, showing her which way to take. Serena followed its directions, desperate to reach her prince.

She swam for what seemed like hours, dodging sea creatures of all shapes and sizes. Suddenly, something wrapped itself around her tail, encircling it tightly in its grip and yanking her out of the water. Serena screamed as she was pulled up from the depths of the ocean. She broke through the surface and found herself surrounded by a group of pirates. They gawked at her in disbelief as they inspected their catch—a siren with wild eyes and a glowing mirror in hand.

"What do we have here, gents? Looks like we caught ourselves a siren," one of the pot-bellied pirates said. Serena saw the handle of his sword sticking out of his leather belt.

Her heart pounded as once again; leering pirates loomed over her. Many of them withdrew their weapons. Her eyes narrowed on their gleaming swords, knowing that if she did not fight for her freedom now, she would be doomed to something worse than captivity.

She was not as fearful of the steel blades, not since the confrontation with King George. The memory fueled her with hope.

Adrenaline and determination surged through her. Twisting and turning in an acrobatic display while trapped in the net, Serena used her small size to her advantage and evaded the pirates' every move as they stuck their swords into the net.

After several failed attempts to gut her, a disgruntled pirate slashed the rope holding the net and she fell to the deck in a crumpled heap with a thud.

Tangled in the mass of rope, Serena lay helpless while the pirates took their weapons and prepared to slash her body, just as she had seen them do to countless other sirens.

Something remarkable happened then. The first man jabbed at her, and his blade shattered. Shocked, he paused and stared at his blade. Another shoved him out of the way and attempted to pierce her belly with his own blade. Just as the first, his blade broke on impact.

The other pirates examined their weapons and hesitated, unwilling to lose theirs the same way. After a moment of consideration, they all stepped back. "What is this witchcraft?" one of them asked in a hollow voice.

Serena seized the moment to wrestle free from the net. Once free, she hissed at them, rage turning her body into its most threatening form.

The shock of her impenetrable skin had worn off at this point, and seeing that she was about to escape, they scrambled to contain her. It was too late. Serena was free, and they found that she was far stronger than any of them. A savage attack ensued as Serena tore through the pirate crew like a tornado.

She snapped pirate bones like twigs in an uncontainable wrath. Screams of terror echoed.

The pirates who had not yet fallen to her teeth and claws fell to their knees as one, raising their palms and crying out for mercy.

Serena was disgusted by the sight of them. "Did you

show my sisters mercy when you brutally attacked them?" she spat.

The oldest pirate limped forward, the last to land on his knees.

"Our captain forbade us from harming sirens. Please, forgive us for our trespasses. We are on a sacred mission to put a stop to this war for good."

Serena paused and looked at the man. He held a scroll in his hand and was offering it to her. "What is that?" she asked, her curiosity piqued.

Prince Edward needed her, but so much time had been wasted already. She glanced at the hand mirror on the deck. In all the commotion, the glass had shattered.

The pirate coughed, drawing her attention back to him. "A raven came to us with instructions to gather as much dynamite as possible and meet Captain Stone on the shores of Imerta."

Serena blinked several times as she digested the words. "Imerta? What do you mean to do with dynamite at Imerta?"

The mature pirate removed his hat. "Captain Stone has joined Prince Edward. They plan to destroy Isis and form an alliance with the sirens. Then they will overthrow King George of England."

Serena hitched a breath. "Prince Edward? They are

together?" she asked in a breathy voice. "When did you get this news?"

The pirate mumbled something inaudible as Serena's ears rang. She looked out at the horizon and her heart pounded with anxiety.

Without the mirror to show her where Prince Edward was, she could only hope the sirens had taken him prisoner. They knew who he was to her. Isis would use him as leverage against King George, not knowing how cruel and heartless the King was. She was certain that if Isis threatened Prince Edward, King George would sacrifice his own son if it meant winning the war.

She jumped off the edge of the ship. She only hoped she could reach Imerta before it was too late.

GEORGETTE

Georgette's heart sank as she arrived on Imerta—the once prosperous city was now engulfed in chaos and destruction. The air was thick with a sorrowful fog, which seemed to permeate her very soul. Everywhere she looked there were scenes of death and ruin, the despair almost palpable.

Cautiously, she made her way through the twisted wreckage of Imerta's dockside, overwhelmed by the violence that filled the air. Everywhere she looked there were scenes of devastation—ships and buildings smashed and broken in a tangled mess of wood, metal, and debris.

The sound of battle echoed as waves of pirates clashed with sirens in a chaotic frenzy, armed with cutlasses, guns, and grenades. Georgette could see the faces of some of the combatants—young men who had been reduced to savagery after weeks of battle on the seas. It was clear the war had reached new levels of brutality as sirens and pirates cut through each other.

Georgette shook as adrenaline coursed through her veins. She took out a bundle of clothes from the satchel Poseidon had given her, and hid behind an oak tree, preparing for battle.

Poseidon's final parting words rang in her mind. "The fate of all mankind is resting on your shoulders. You must lead them, or the destruction will continue from all sides until there is nothing left."

Georgette pulled on a pair of scratchy brown trousers and yanked on a pair of leather boots. When she stuffed her oversized cotton shirt into the waistband, she tied on a black leather corset. Her hair dried in the sunshine as she dressed and fell freely in waves. Finally, she wore a three-point hat made of the softest brown leather.

Poseidon's voice entered her mind once more. "You are a Pirate Queen. It is time you behave as one."

She pulled out one last item in the satchel—a small, silver blade with a stone handle. The outline of the city of Atlantis was etched into it, reminding Georgette where she was truly from.

She clutched the handle and gritted her teeth, ready to face her uncertain future. Suddenly, she was startled by a loud, booming voice that seemed to come from everywhere at once. It was a deep, menacing voice that filled the air with raw power and terror. She recognized it in an instant.

Isis.

"This is the harbinger of doom," Isis said. "Flee or face certain death, *pirates*!"

Georgette froze as an ear-shattering boom flooded the air. One of the pirate ships had exploded into a million splinters of wood. Drops of blood and gore rained down as everything and everyone on the ship was obliterated.

Georgette froze in terror, unable to comprehend what she had seen. The dockside was in a state of uproar, with the bloodthirsty screams of pirates intermingling with the screech of sirens. The air was thick with the unmistakable odor of gunpowder and the acrid stench of smoke.

Canons blasted. Sirens screeched.

Georgette stumbled forward in a daze. The clamor of pirates and sirens grew into an unearthly din that seemed to swallow every sound on the island.

Suddenly, one shot rang out and everything stopped. Georgette spun around to see a figure standing on one of the burning ships, a shotgun in his hand and a blank expression on his face.

The pirates and sirens alike seemed to recognize him,

and the atmosphere changed abruptly, as if the fear of death had been replaced by a fear of this man.

A rush of joy and relief took hold as she recognized the form.

"Gentlemen!" Captain Stone bellowed. The howling wind carried his shout throughout the entire beach. He had brought momentary calm to the chaos. All faces turned toward him.

Georgette rushed to the ship, tears falling freely as she climbed up the side of it. Smoke clung to the back of her throat and her eyes stung, but she didn't care.

It did not matter that they were in the throes of war and that the bloodthirsty attack could continue at any moment. It had been too long since she had held his hand in hers. Too long since she stood by his side. If he was going to go down with his burning ship, she was determined to stay with him.

Captain Stone's severe look softened when she found him, and his resolve cracked enough for him to give her a wink.

But he quickly returned his attention to the onlookers.

"Gents, our fight is not with sirens."

Georgette stepped forward. "Sirens, the pirates are not our enemy."

She turned and took Captain Stone's hand. "Listen to me. The true enemy is—"

"Isis!" Captain Stone roared. The pirates cheered, raising their weapons to the sky. Georgette dropped his hand.

"No! It's not... Listen... LISTEN to me!" She screeched and shouted, but the pirates were storming the beach, carrying crates of explosives. Others went back to fighting the sirens determined to defend their mother.

Her eyes prickled as she watched her sisters, dressed in gladiator-style clothing, fighting with the men. Their movements were strong, and they put unrelenting force into stopping the pirates from their terrible mission.

But behind their tough exteriors, Georgette saw something else.

Desperation and utter exhaustion.

She turned to Captain Stone. "What are you doing?" she asked in anguish.

His smirk faded. "I know she is your mother, but this is something I have to do."

He tried to cup her face, but Georgette stepped back. "If Isis dies now, the curse will be permanent."

"What curse?" Captain Stone asked, his face twisting with confusion.

"Serena!"

Georgette swiveled around to see Prince Edward,

wounded, and leaning over the side of the ship, looking out to sea.

"Edward…" she mumbled, confused. She looked at Captain Stone for an explanation, but he merely shrugged. "It seems we have some catching up to do," he said.

Georgette coughed as the burning ship groaned beneath their feet and the smoke grew more intense. "Perhaps we can finish this on the beach?" she suggested.

Captain Stone nodded and picked up his brother gruffly. Prince Edward grunted, crimson blood drenching his white shirt. His face was as white as marble, but his expression was of pure bliss as he looked out to the sea.

"Serena," he said again.

"What happened to him?" Georgette asked, as she took Prince Edward's other arm and the two of them helped him down from the ship. Captain Stone looked grim as they worked together. "He made a foolish deal with the sirens and got into a fight with a pirate."

"Why would he make a deal with sirens?" Georgette asked, aghast. But it was Prince Edward who replied.

"Because I'm in love with one."

When they set him down, another explosion went off. They all ducked as flying debris shot over their heads. More screams.

Prince Edward gasped suddenly. Georgette followed

his line of sight and looked out toward the water. A lone siren with bright red hair was swimming toward them.

Georgette's heart flipped. She turned to Prince Edward and grabbed his face to look him in the eye. "Did you say Serena?" she asked.

"Get your grubby hands off my husband!"

Georgette jumped and turned to look at the siren.

She was a force of nature. The wind blew her hair around her, and she stood over them in a skin-tight silver dress that split in the middle, revealing two silver pant legs.

Her eyes were blazing with fury as they bore into Georgette. Georgette observed her calmly.

This was the product of being raised in a city with hundreds of brothers and a god for a father.

A prickle of jealousy nipped at her insides, but that quickly gave way. She spread out her arms and dashed forward to give her a hug.

"Serena, I've been eager to meet you, I'm—"

Smack.

Georgette stopped short and stumbled back. She clutched her cheek, and her ears rang. Before she could throw her arms around her sister, Serena had slapped her across the face.

Captain Stone lurched forward. "What in the blazes—" he roared. He stopped when Georgette raised a palm. "It's all right. I was foolish to think she would be happy to see me."

Serena spat at Georgette's feet; her face full of disgust. "Why would I be happy to see you, after the hell you've dragged my husband through?"

Georgette swallowed as she took in the word husband and turned back to glance at Prince Edward, who lay panting on the beach, clutching his bleeding stomach.

"Move," Serena barked, prompting Georgette to jump aside. Without hesitation, Serena strode over to Prince Edward and lowered herself to his side. His adoring gaze never left hers.

"I am so grateful to see you again, even if it is for one last time," he said between pants. He took a shaky hand and touched the side of Serena's face.

Georgette and Captain Stone looked on, equally dumbfounded by the scene.

Serena's hard expression softened as she lowered her voice. "Shh. My foolish Prince. You will be fine."

Prince Edward pulled his hand away to reveal a gray rib sticking out of his wound. "I do not think so, my love. But I can die happy, seeing you again."

Georgette and Captain Stone exchanged looks. Serena's cold laugh drew their attention back to them. "Lay still," she commanded. Then she waved her hand over the wound. Prince Edward groaned in pain as the bone crunched back into place and new tissue closed up the wound.

After a few tense moments, the prince panted and patted the healed wound, then looked at Serena like she was a vision.

"I thought I was—"

"I would never let that happen."

Prince Edward sat up and cupped Serena's face. "I thought you would never—"

"Just shut up and kiss me," Serena cut in. Without waiting for him to act, she gripped his shirt collar and claimed his lips with hers.

Georgette was too stunned to move as she watched her twin sister kiss her former fiancé. It was not jealousy, just surprise. Never in her wildest dreams could she have foreseen this.

But another bang thrust them all into the severity of the moment. She looked up at Captain Stone. "We have to stop the pirates from killing Isis. Or we are all doomed."

"But I was commanded—" Captain Stone began. He stopped under Georgette's intense stare.

"Right," he said bashfully. "We need to move."

Captain Stone raced ahead, and Georgette was close behind.

Serena and Prince Edward scrambled to follow. The

four of them raced to Isis's tower, where a clanging reverberated in the air like a warning bell. Georgette's heart pounded as she sprinted ahead of the others, desperation lacing her every stride. The pirates had set up explosives nearby, and Georgette knew that time was running out.

Captain Stone raced toward the tower, but the pirates were several steps ahead of him. With a deafening rumble, they detonated explosives that shook the foundation and sent the entire structure crumbling like an avalanche around them. Georgette screamed. She was thrown off her feet and into Captain Stone's arms. He held her tightly against his chest, shielding her against the onslaught of rocks and shattered wood raining down on them.

The force of the blast decimated Isis's tower in a single instant, sending its crumbling remains in all directions.

Pirates cheered in victory and headed back for the beach, while a collective scream from the sirens further down cut through Georgette like a knife to the heart.

She broke from Captain Stone's embrace and tried to make sense of what was happening. She found Serena on her knees.

Serena clawed at her face as tears streamed down her face. "Isis is gone," she said in a horrified whisper.

Georgette sank to the ground, clutching her stomach. "The curse will never be lifted now," she said.

Serena turned sharply and her eyes narrowed on Georgette. "What curse?"

Georgette blinked at her through misty eyes. "Isis placed a curse on us all. We cannot bear children."

Serena's eyes flashed dangerously. Before either Captain Stone or Prince Edward could step between them, she reached out and grabbed Georgette by the neck.

"What are you talking about? You are having a child. The curse is a myth."

Georgette shook her head. "I… I'm no longer…" She couldn't say the words. Not again. Serena let her go and her mouth formed a perfect 'o'.

She rested a hand over her stomach. "You mean—"

"How sweet is this?"

Everyone turned in surprise at the silky-smooth voice of a woman behind them.

Isis stood tall and regal, her long gown flowing gently in the breeze. Not a single hair on her head was out of place. She smiled at them all like old friends.

"I never expected to see so many tears at the news of my demise," she said with a small sound of delight. "Fear not, I am quite well as you can see."

Georgette was stunned. She stared at her mother

with a mixture of surprise and relief. A tiny part of her was disappointed, however. Even if she could not break the curse upon her, at least the war could come to an end with Isis dead.

"I see you have been reunited with your twin sister," Isis said, looking at Georgette with a smile.

Serena's head snapped in her direction. "*Twin?*"

Georgette frowned at the repulsion in Serena's voice. "Hey, I don't know what I've done to deserve such derision from you, but is it so bad to discover that—"

"Yes, it is!" Serena said, rising to her feet. "You are intolerable. I can hardly even look at you."

Georgette looked at Prince Edward, wondering what he'd told her. Serena hissed and darted forward. "Keep your eyes away from him," she warned, her face an inch from Georgette's.

"Girls. Calm down," Isis said, sounding like an ordinary mother talking to two bickering daughters.

Her gaze landed on Georgette once more. "Did you go to Atlantis? Did he give you the prophecy?" she asked, sounding hopeful.

Georgette nodded. Before she could speak, Serena made a noise of frustration. "You went to Atlantis? You saw Poseidon?" Then she blinked. "What prophecy?"

Isis finally looked at Serena.

"My spirited girl," she said, reaching for her cheek.

Serena froze, her eyes widening as Isis touched her. "All of your questions will be answered in time. But now, I must send our visitors off and make some preparations."

"I will order them to leave in peace if you call off the sirens attack," Captain Stone said, stepping forward.

Isis looked at him, her expression hardening. "Will they follow your command?"

Georgette noticed a movement to her side and caught sight of Prince Edward's jaw bulging as he balled his hands into fists. His eyes were narrowed, but Georgette could not guess what was going through his mind. He was barely recognizable from the last time she saw him.

Georgette realized she had missed something when Captain Stone began to follow Isis into the woods. Georgette grabbed his arm and he stopped. "Do not worry, Georgette," Isis said, halting beside a tree. "I will return with your love in one piece, you have my word."

Georgette scowled at her. "Forgive me, Mother, but I do not entirely trust your word."

Isis clasped her hands together and looked around at them. "I have brought all of you here for a special purpose. This—" she gestured to the destruction around them. "Has all been part of a very special plan."

Georgette and Captain Stone exchanged looks, then turned to Prince Edward and Serena. They shrugged back.

They had all come to Imerta for their own reasons. There was no conceivable way the goddess might have engineered any of this. Isis laughed again.

"We all have our roles to play," she said, echoing Poseidon's words in Atlantis. Georgette frowned. Isis pointed to a cluster of small homes nestled in a grove of trees on a hill. "I have taken the liberty of preparing your dwellings. Rest. We shall meet back here at dusk. Then I will reveal everything."

When Georgette hesitated, Captain Stone gave her a reassuring pat on the hand. "Go. I'll find you when I'm done."

Georgette hesitated, hating the idea of ever being apart from Captain Stone again. But she nodded.

Serena and Prince Edward walked arm in arm as they followed the winding path to the row of houses. They were like little cottages, each sporting a steep thatch roof and a small smoking chimney.

"Look," Prince Edward said, pointing at one of the doors. The words Serena and Edward were etched into the wood.

Georgette could not take her eyes off Serena. They were the same height and size, but her hair was almost enchanting. It blazed like an actual fire atop her head. Just before they stepped into their cottage, she shot Georgette a furious look to match.

Georgette walked into the cottage with her and Captain Stone's names above the door. She sighed heavily when she was alone.

She removed her boots, closed her eyes, and just stood on the cool stone floor as she tried to make sense of everything.

Serena, her twin sister, was married to Prince Edward.

Not only that, but she loathed Georgette.

Numerous pirates and sirens were dead. Destruction surrounded them. And as far-fetched as it seemed, Georgette could not stop wondering if Poseidon and Isis were working together somehow.

Perhaps they really were just pawns in an elaborate game of the gods.

There was a steaming bath in the corner of the room. The water was frothy and smelled sweet, like honeysuckle. Georgette undressed and sank into the bath, sighing as the water rose to her chin and enveloped her with heat.

Then the door opened, and Captain Stone entered.

"The pirates are gone. Isis is working her magic to repair the damage," he said, taking off his hat.

Then his gaze met Georgette's and they stared at one another for a while.

The horrors and revelations of the past rose to the

surface. There were new lines on Captain Stone's face, and Georgette knew she must look different to him as well.

So much had transpired, they were both changed forever.

Without a word, Captain Stone undressed, never taking his eyes off Georgette, and climbed into the bath, nestling behind her.

When he wrapped her up in his arms, his stubbled chin resting on her shoulder, Georgette's heart swooned. She leaned back against his hard chest and took his hands, interlocking their fingers as she moved them over her breasts.

They didn't speak. Words became redundant as the two lovers embraced.

Though they were still in a foreign land, facing uncertain dangers ahead, Georgette relaxed. Captain Stone kissed her neck, keeping his touch soft and sensual. He cradled her like she was the most precious thing in all the world, and his actions spoke to her.

His fingertips grazed over her heart, whispering *I've missed you*.

His lips peppered her jawline with kisses, saying *I'm sorry*.

Georgette drew circles over his thighs and took deep breaths as she allowed herself to be enveloped in his love.

His breaths grew ragged, and his body heat made her core ache for him to make her whole. All of the hurt, devastation, and unanswered questions melted away as the two of them rediscovered their bodies.

He lifted her up and positioned her over his hard length, then they reconnected, and he clutched her waist with an agonized moan. The way he bit into her shoulder told her *I'll always be yours*.

After their bath, Captain Stone carried Georgette to the four-poster bed and set her down tenderly. Then he carefully inspected every part of her body. He kissed each scratch and light bruise. He massaged the painful knots out of her legs and turned her over to smooth out the tension in her back.

Georgette sighed, giving in to the moment. The air was still and quiet, and the only sounds were the soft moans from Georgette as Captain Stone worked on her.

When he was done relaxing every last sinew, he flipped her over again and she lay beneath him, her hair splayed out across her shoulders and the pillow.

"I shouldn't have said those things before I left," she whispered to him, emotion constricting her throat. "I shouldn't have left at all. I should have—" Captain Stone silenced her with a rough kiss on the mouth.

When he finally drew away, he hovered near her ear. "You have nothing to apologize for. You have been through more pain and suffering than anyone should ever have to endure, and I know I am responsible for much of it." He paused to suck on her neck, slowly and sensually, prompting a sigh to escape her mouth. She arched her back, pressing herself against him. She never wanted to be apart ever again.

Captain Stone pulled back to look into her eyes. "I vow to do everything in my power to give you nothing but pleasure, from now on."

He kissed her and Georgette smirked. "Pain can be enjoyable too."

Captain Stone matched Georgette's grin as he leaned in to brush his lips over hers. "As you wish."

PRINCE EDWARD

Prince Edward watched Serena pace the room, rubbing the dull ache in his chest. Though he was healed, the memory of his broken ribcage was fresh in his mind.

"The way she just walks around like she owns whatever land she walks on…" Serena continued to rant. The second the door shut behind them, she had begun to vent about Georgette.

Prince Edward listened for as long as he could, but the conversation ran in circles. All the while, fury radiated from Serena like fire. He watched her dress bounce with her movements, the gentle curve of her breasts moving in a way that had him entranced.

Eventually, he couldn't take it anymore. He silenced

Serena by grabbing her waist and pulling her to him until her hips bumped his.

"What do you think you're doing?" Serena asked, her eyes wide and indignant.

Prince Edward smoothed her hair away from her face and the stiffness in her body began to melt away. "Allow me to tell you something," he said. "When I thought I was going to die, all I thought about was you."

Serena froze, blinking under his loving gaze. "Not Georgette," he continued. "Not anyone else. You." He held her waist and ran his palms over the curves of her bottom. "You have no need to be jealous, Serena."

He picked up her leg and she yelped. "I am *not* jealous of her. I would never be jealous. Obvious—"

"Good," Prince Edward cut in, squeezing her thigh. "Because I only have eyes for you. And if it pleases you, I shall cut out my own tongue so that I never betray you again."

Serena rolled her eyes, not believing him. So, Prince Edward dropped her leg and fell to his knees. Serena stepped back, her eyes narrowing as he fumbled in his jacket and pulled out a pocketknife. Then he held out his tongue and positioned the knife under it.

"No!" Serena said, rushing forward. She grabbed the knife and tossed it across the room. "I can think of much more pleasurable things you can do with your tongue."

They undressed each other like animals, their movements frantic and awkward. Airs and graces flew out the window when Prince Edward made love to Serena right there on the stone floor.

Her fingertips grazed the scar on his chest as he nudged his manhood inside of her. Her core tightened around him.

A rush of total bliss flooded his senses and Serena's hot breaths misted his cheeks while they made love.

"I will never forgive you," she said between his slow thrusts. Prince Edward's hands slipped over her clammy back and he groaned, lost in the buildup of pleasure rising inside of him. They picked up their pace with a sense of urgency. Serena mewled as Prince Edward fisted her hair and yanked her head back. Then he bit her breast and released.

Out of breath, Serena rolled her hips over his and leaned forward against him. Her hair fell like a curtain between them and the room. "But I shall permit you to try and change my mind," she finished.

Prince Edward took her in his arms and carried her to the bed, where they spent the entire night alternating between lovemaking and cuddling.

Spent, Serena lay nestled in Prince Edward's arms and the two of them slept the next day away. For the first time in months, Prince Edward's dreams were nothing but sweet.

As dusk fell the next day, Prince Edward and Serena followed the narrow path to a soft orange glow, where the tower used to be.

Captain Stone and Georgette were already there, standing hand in hand beside Isis. Serena took Prince Edward's arm and sucked in a nervous breath. Now that they were out of their safe haven, all of her misgivings and unanswered questions came tumbling back.

He knew from the way her eyes narrowed on Georgette and her lips pressed together that her mind was spinning.

Prince Edward gave her hand a squeeze.

"There they are. The newlyweds have finally decided to grace us with their presence," Isis announced with a warm smile as they reached the clearing.

They stood on a circle of old stones, surrounded by rocks with old runes on each one.

Serena could not contain herself any longer.

"What curse have you placed upon us, Mother?" she snapped. "Is it true we cannot bear children?"

Isis nodded. "For what it's worth, my love, I am deeply regretful of my actions."

Serena seethed next to Prince Edward, her nails digging into his arm. He patted her hand to remind her she was not alone.

"Reverse it," she snapped.

Isis laughed. "I thought you of all people would understand blood magic, Serena."

Prince Edward felt Serena's body stiffen next to him. "You said you would reveal everything to us." Serena pointed at Georgette. "If she is my twin sister, why am I only just learning about it? And why was I forced to grow up in Atlantis, away from my sisters?"

Isis waved a hand aside as if to bat her questions away. "My dear Serena, I expected better questions from you."

Serena sucked in a breath and Prince Edward tried to soothe her with a hand on the small of her back, but she shrugged him off and stepped forward. "You can't throw all of this at me and expect me to just take it all as though it is entirely ordinary to find out you have a twin sister, and your own mother cursed you to be barren."

"What must be done to reverse the curse?" Georgette cut in, her voice firm and commanding. Isis looked at her with far more respect. She nodded to Serena.

"*That* is a good question."

She flicked her wrist. "You may come out now."

Everyone looked wildly around them at the sound of rustling leaves. Captain Stone gasped. "You!"

Prince Edward's gaze settled on the blonde-haired siren who stepped into view. She gave them all a sheepish smile, but it did nothing to quash Prince Edward's anger.

"You betrayed us," he said to her.

Before anyone else could speak, Isis lifted a hand. "She was working under my orders. As she always does."

Georgette and Serena looked stunned.

Isis paid them no attention. She rested a hand on the siren's shoulder.

"This is Ava. My oldest daughter and most-trusted ally."

Georgette frowned. "This whole time, you were working for her?" she hissed.

Ava clasped her hands together with a guilty grin. "I implore that you all listen to what Isis has to say. After all, her plan will give us what we are all looking for."

"And what is that?" Captain Stone asked.

Ava shrugged. "A prosperous future."

Isis stepped into the middle of the circle and raised her arms. "Each of you has been hand-picked by the gods to fulfill a sacred prophecy." The group exchanged looks with one another as Isis paused to smile at them.

"Every choice you have made, and every action you have taken has led you right here. To this very moment. And now you are all here, ready to fulfill your destiny."

"How do we do that, exactly?" Prince Edward asked, not fully understanding Isis's words.

She grinned at him. "You want to put an end to the war, and you want to break a curse. You will get both peace and the promise of new life, should you succeed."

Captain Stone pointed to Ava. "What has she got to do with this mission?"

Isis chuckled low and deep. "My dear pirate friend, Ava is the most important part of this mission. She is a gift to the one person who can lead you."

"Who?" Prince Edward and Serena asked in unison.

Isis began to walk around in a circle, breathing low and deep with her hands behind her back.

Her long gown swished as she went past Prince Edward. A waft of a sickly-sweet scent washed over him. "Long ago… Long before I was with Poseidon… I was a Queen of Egypt."

She stopped near Georgette to give her a piercing stare. "And I was *truly* in love."

Everyone held their breath as Isis told her tale.

"His name was Osiris, and he was a powerful, ruthless man. A true king. But he had many enemies."

Her eyes flashed with anger. "He was ripped from me

by jealous men. They tore him limb from limb and hid his body all around the world so that I could not resurrect him."

Isis took in a sharp breath. "You four know the pain of being apart from the one you love," she said, looking around the circle. Prince Edward and Serena looked at each other with a sense of longing.

Captain Stone took Georgette's hand again.

Isis continued.

"I was banished to this forsaken island, and my enemies built a tower on top of this sacred resurrection site. So that I would remain in solitude for all eternity."

She gestured to Ava. "Poseidon found me one day and we struck up a romance. But it was not the same as my love for Osiris. He was unfaithful." She looked at Georgette. "When I gave him a taste of his own medicine, Poseidon took my youngest daughters from me in an act of revenge. Even though you were twins, he split you two up, determined not to let the prophecy be fulfilled."

Everyone was quiet, watching Isis with rapt attention. She stopped walking for a moment. "Ava has the gift of prophecy. She will guide you to the burial places. You will bring the bones of my lover back to this spot. And here, my beloved Osiris shall rise again. Peace will be restored upon the earth, all curses broken."

Georgette hummed. "Why would Poseidon try to stop this from happening?"

Isis's smile faded. "He is a jealous god. He thinks he is the only person worthy of any happiness in this world. Why else would he raise up an army and stay hidden in the sea?"

She shook her head to herself. Then she looked at them. "Will you do it? Will you find the lost bones of Osiris?"

Captain Stone and Prince Edward exchanged looks. "Let us not forget that there are pirates behaving like savages in the towns. If they do not have the iron hand of my brother to keep them in line, I fear for the safety of anyone who crosses their path."

"Then I suggest you waste no time," Isis replied with a shrug. But she lifted a finger. "Before you go looking, there is one place you must go first."

"Where?" Serena asked.

"There is a slight complication to the mission," Ava explained. "Guarding each burial site is a terrible monster. We shall need to work with a warrior who is skilled in battling such beasts if we are to have any hope of surviving our quest."

Prince Edward rolled his shoulders back and nodded to Captain Stone. "I am sure we can handle whatever—"

"This is not a negotiation," Isis cut in sharply. "First,

you shall sail to a remote island off the coast of Greece. There you will find the most formidable warrior of all time."

"My future husband," Ava added, delighted. She clasped her hands together. "I shall be an offering to persuade him to lead us."

The group took a collective breath. Prince Edward looked around at everyone. He thought he had left his pioneering days behind him. What he truly wanted was to go home and plot the eradication of piracy for good.

Serena looked at him with a sense of longing. If they did not do as Isis wished, she would never be able to carry a child. It was something he knew she had wanted for a long time.

"If this is the only way to break the curse, I will do it," Georgette said, determined.

"So will I," Captain Stone said.

"I have no intention of leaving my fate up to anyone else. I will join the quest," Serena added.

All eyes fell on Prince Edward. His insides twisted as he pondered the situation. Was this another one of Isis's sick traps? His breath quickened as he glanced toward Serena. Her wide eyes pleaded with him to act. Heaving a deep sigh, Prince Edward declared his agreement. "Very well, then. Who is this fearsome warrior?"

A wicked grin spread across Isis's face, and she urged Ava forward to tell them. Her cheeks blushed crimson as they waited with bated breath.

"His name is Hercules," she said.

THE END

EPILOGUE

AVA

Ava looked out at the horizon as they sailed toward their destination. A mountain on a strip of land grew with every stroke, bathed in the golden rays of the setting sun. She knew this was where she would find her husband.

Ava had spent many years yearning for the comfort of a man in her life. She wanted to be married more than anything in the world, and now she was so close to her heart's desire, she felt she could reach out and hold it in her palm.

Soon, they arrived on the old Greek island and were welcomed by a small fishing village. The locals spoke little English but were friendly enough. Several of them pointed to the abandoned pier across the beach surrounded by jagged rocks. They were warned to avoid sailing too close; apparently, there had been sightings of a beastly man lurking near the shoreline. One who was most unfriendly.

Ava held her breath with anticipation. The fear in their eyes was as clear as day, but it did not stop her from having hope. Soon, she would meet her husband.

A part of her wondered if he might take one glance at her and become dismissive. What if he did not find her pleasing?

She cast the worry aside. She had spent her whole life observing people and found herself most interested in lovers. She watched silently as her crewmates walked hand in hand, oblivious of her presence. She heard the muffled *oohs* and *ahhs* they made at night. And she envied the way the men looked at their wives.

She longed to have that too.

When they eventually reached the shoreline, they saw him—a hulking figure with muscles like tree trunks and eyes that glinted in anger.

When the ship approached the beach, the monstrosity of a man swaggered forward, thick arms swaying, and scowled deeply at them all.

Ava's eyes landed on Hercules for the very first time and her stomach knotted. He was a beast of a man—strong, rippling muscles from head to toe. He wore nothing but a tiny pair of cotton shorts, and his thighs bulged out of them.

His dark eyes landed on her, and she wondered if he might smile. He did not. Their boat slid onto the sand, drawing to a halt. Ava climbed out of the boat and turned to face a man who towered over her, his breaths coming out hot and heavy.

"Who are you to disrupt my peace?" he growled, his hands balling into fists.

Captain Stone and Prince Edward brandished their weapons and made to move forward, but Georgette raised a hand and stepped up to Hercules instead. It was she who eased the tension. She bowed low, gesturing for the others to follow her.

Ava curtsied, smiling shyly at the man, but he did not look in her direction again. Her chest grew tight. "We have been sent by the goddess Isis to beseech your help, great Hercules," Georgette said, straightening slowly. "Are you he?"

The man crossed his arms across his broad chest and smiled for the first time. His skin shone like he was covered from head to toe in olive oil, and his complexion was a beautiful caramel shade as it reflected the sunlight. He threw his head back and laughed. His thick, dark hair shook with the effort. "Isis sent you? Then I hope you brought me the gift she promised all those years ago."

"Indeed," Serena said, gesturing to Ava.

Ava stepped forward. "It is my honor and privilege to be your wife," she said, just as she had rehearsed with Isis so many times before.

Hercules hummed so low the ground vibrated beneath Ava's feet. His penetrating stare moved up and down her body. Then he grumbled something inaudible and walked away.

"Do not follow me if you want to keep your heads," he shouted over his shoulder.

The group watched the demigod walk into a cave. When he was gone, Captain Stone sighed. "Well, that did not go as planned."

Ava hugged herself, the sting of rejection burning at her insides.

Serena nudged her. "Do not worry. Men are fickle beings. Demigods are even more so. I am certain he is just tired. We shall try again when he returns."

"I do not think I please him. Am I not pleasing to look at?" Ava asked, worried.

Captain Stone and Prince Edward started to argue, but both of them promptly went quiet under the furious stares of their wives.

"Let us make camp. Serena, I have a favor to ask of you," Georgette said. Prince Edward and Captain Stone busied themselves collecting wood from the boat to make a fire. Serena and Georgette huddled further down the beach.

Ava pretended not to listen, but she tucked her hair behind her ear so that she might hear their conversation more clearly.

"I know you hate me," Georgette began. Serena scoffed.

"I do not hate you. I simply do not like you," she said.

Georgette sighed. "All right. But we are about to embark on a hazardous journey. We will face unworldly creatures, and I was hoping you could teach me how to use my siren powers."

Ava snorted, and the two women looked at her. She turned away, blushing. After a pause, Serena spoke up. "No. You do not need to know them. Besides, it took me years to conjure a simple handkerchief. From what I have heard, you already mastered the art of healing."

Georgette sucked in a breath. "Please, Serena. I need a way to protect Mannington that does not involve me watching him die every time. My soul cannot bear it."

Serena made a noise to say she was thinking about it.

"How much do you love him?" she asked.

"Is that a sincere question? Is it not obvious how earnest my affections are for him? I would give my life for him."

"Would you give your immortality?" Serena said.

Ava's heart jolted. Before a second thought could change her mind, she ran to the two women.

"Serena, you cannot be thinking—" she started.

Serena shrugged. "Why not?"

Ava dragged her hands through her hair. "It is *forbidden magic*, Serena. With unknown consequences."

Georgette frowned, looking from Serena to Ava like she was following a tennis match.

"What is this forbidden magic you speak of? Is it the same Isis spoke of?"

Ava nodded. "Serena and Prince Edward practiced a binding ritual."

Georgette looked over her shoulder at the two men moving around on the boat, then turned back to meet Ava's pointed look. "What does a binding ritual do?"

Serena held up her palm to show the light scar. "You combine blood. He is part siren, and I am part human."

Georgette made a sound of amazement. "Will you do it for us?"

Before Serena could reply, Ava grabbed Georgette by the shoulders. "Please, do not do this. I shall teach you how to enhance your powers. I am sure you will pick it up quickly."

But Georgette was looking at Serena with eyes wide

and full of hope. "Will you do it, Serena?" she asked again.

"Please! Think about this!" Ava said, shaking Georgette. "You are sacrificing your immortality. One day, you shall die!"

Georgette shrugged. "Last year, I thought I was human and expected to die one day. In any case, I would rather live one full life with my husband than exist for an eternity alone."

Ava let Georgette go. Her words had cut deeper than she could ever know.

"Do what you will," Ava said.

She kept a distance as Serena performed the ritual. Captain Stone and Georgette knelt before her like a bride and a groom.

Ava winced and turned away when they made the cuts. She tried to block out the sounds of their chants as they performed the forbidden ritual.

She focused instead on the mouth of the cave, her heart fluttering faster than the wings of a hummingbird.

When she could no longer bear it, she stood and headed for the cave, knowing that the two pairs of lovers would be too caught up in their sacred activity to notice her absence.

At the entrance, she peered inside the dark cave and

listened for Hercules. All that she could pick up on was the steady inhale and exhale of a person sleeping.

Ava curled her hands into fists at the humiliation of coming all this way, only to be rejected at first glance. Her body trembled with terrible fury, and she boldly strode forward.

When she rounded a corner, the cave opened up. A gust of ice-cold air blasted her, and a candle flickered to her left.

Hercules lay face down, fast asleep on a bed far too small for him.

Angry and disappointed, Ava marched forward and poked his back. He slept on, blissfully unaware of her presence.

Ava pranced around, pretending to be in distress. She shrieked at an imaginary spider. She pretended to trip and twist her ankle.

When Hercules did not stir from his sleep, she let out a scream as though a savage beast had entered the cave.

Still, Hercules slept on.

Frustrated and even more humiliated, Ava turned into her most terrifying form and let out a bloodcurdling scream. She clawed at Hercules's back, screaming at him and unleashing decades of disappointment.

Finally, Hercules jolted awake, his face flushed with color. He sat up, panting.

When his focus rested on her, Ava calmed enough to return to her human form. She placed her hands on her hips, her blood still boiling.

"I have waited over one hundred years to be married. I have never been with a man. Not a kiss or a hand-hold, not even a hug. Isis promised me a husband who would give me great satisfaction. And after waiting so long, you reject me? No, sir. You do not reject me, I reject *you*!"

She summoned her deepest scowl, shook a fist at him, and then swiveled to walk out. But quick as a flash, the candle blew out, thrusting her into darkness. She stopped. Then a heavy hand clutched her waist and she felt hot breath on her neck.

"Ava. It has been more than a century since the last time I felt this alive," Hercules said. His voice was like honey, drenching her senses in sickly-sweet warmth.

"I am sorry to have disappointed you, my lady," he continued. This time, his breath tickled her other ear as he moved around her. A flood of tingles set off a chain reaction in Ava's body as his fingertips grazed her arms.

"You will have to forgive me, for I have been alone for more than two centuries. I did not know my error."

"Then you accept me?" Ava asked.

Hercules growled, dragging Ava's hair away from her neck. She nearly fainted at the touch. Her senses were running wild, and her imagination concocted all kinds of scandalous things she expected Hercules to do next. They were alone in a dark cave, after all. She had admitted she was his virgin bride. What was he going to do about it?

As though he had heard her thoughts, Hercules's hand left her body. Ava shivered at the absence of his warmth. Candlelight filled the cave once more, illuminating Hercules's big intense eyes. He was not looking at her face. His gaze traveled over her body. This time, he looked at her with more care and attention.

"I accept Isis's gift. What ludicrous mission has she got in mind?" he asked.

Ava led Hercules back to the beach, where the others were sat beside a roaring campfire. Everyone jumped to their feet as he approached, and Hercules raised his palms. "Forgive my rudeness earlier. I am not accustomed to having company," he said. Then he wrapped an arm around Ava and squeezed her waist.

"Tell me about this quest."

Ava sucked in a deep breath. "There are nine burial sites. Each one is guarded by a monster. We need to retrieve all of the bones of Osiris and return them to Isis."

"Ah," he said, grubbing his chin in thought.

"So, will you lead us?" Serena asked. Hercules looked at the faces watching him and gave them all a grim look.

"Are you prepared to die for this mission?"

"Yes," everyone replied in unison.

Hercules shrugged. "Then I will lead you."

Excitement and anticipation grew as everyone started to talk in whispers. Hercules walked toward the sea, then waved his broad arms in a circular motion. A portal opened up in thin air.

Georgette looked from the portal to Hercules to the group around her. "We're going now?" she asked, incredulous.

Hercules looked back at her with a smirk.

"Oh, no. Not yet. We need supplies. Weapons. And I will not go anywhere without my golden mace."

Captain Stone frowned. "Where is it?"

Hercules jabbed his thumb toward the blue portal, then grabbed Ava by the hand. "My wife and I need to pay my uncle a visit."

There was a measured silence, then Prince Edward asked the question on all of their minds. "Who is your uncle?"

Hercules saluted them, tugging Ava to the edge of the portal.

"Hades," he said.

Ava's heart lunged as they fell through.

The swash-buckling adventure continues in Sworn to a Demigod by Athena Rose. Read Now.

If you would like to read the SPICY bonus epilogue in Captain Stone's point of view, click here!

If you enjoyed this book, it would mean a lot to me if you would leave a nice review. They really help me find new readers! Thank you so much for coming on this wild journey with me, Captain Stone, Georgette, and their friends. I take reader feedback very seriously, if you would like to have your say in what you want to see in the next book, click here to fill out a short survey.

Printed in Great Britain
by Amazon